RED RATTLE BOOKS

# SLIPPED NOTES

Jack Swift lives in Liverpool. He teaches English
Literature and English Language. This is his fourth novel.
His previous novels *Undead Underneath*, *Cool Blood Walk* and
*Slow Lump Jump* are all published by Red Rattle Books.

red rattle
BOOKS

Slipped Notes

2021

Front and back cover Robin Castle

Cover image © Shutterstock / Philipp Tur

Copyright © Jack Swift and Red Rattle Books

The moral right of the author has been asserted.

A CIP catalogue record for this book
is available from the British Library

ISBN 978-1-909086-30-2

www.redrattlebooks.co.uk

# SLIPPED NOTES

JACK SWIFT

red rattle
BOOKS

# ONE

The three men heard a bang and then another.

'I'll go,' said Owen.

Rhys and Will said nothing.

Owen climbed the stairs. Owen had expected Rhys and Will to protest and argue. Rhys and Will followed Owen up the stairs and remained silent. Owen remembered other times when Hailey had lost her temper, everyone else smiling away inside a party and Hailey and him arguing in another room. Owen arrived upstairs. Hailey was not in any of the four bedrooms. The door to the bathroom was locked. He charged it with his shoulder. Nothing happened.

Rhys and Will arrived at the bathroom.

'We'll have to break the door down,' said Owen.

'That door isn't long on,' said Will.

Owen let his face say what had to be said.

Rhys and Will nodded their heads. The three men charged the door. It still did not move.

'I'll sort this,' said Rhys.

Will and Owen waited by the bathroom door while Rhys went downstairs and returned with a large mallet hammer. Each of the three men took turns to hammer the door. Rhys pointed to the spot where he reckoned the bolt was located on the other side. They hammered and shouted for Hailey to answer. The door flew open, and Owen walked into the bathroom and past the walk-in shower. Hailey was sitting on the tiled bathroom floor. One of her shoulders leaned against the side of the white enamel bath. Her right knee pressed against her left calf, and her left foot touched one of the four short metal legs that supported the deliberately old-fashioned enamel bath. Because of the wrecked look on her face, Owen searched for vomit. There was none. He saw blood on the mirror, bath and floor.

The head of his wife rested on her chest. Some of her shoulder-length hair obscured her face. Under her chin her neck looked crumpled. Her mouth was open. The side of her head rested against the rim of the bath. Owen looked around. Elsewhere in the bath there was blood but not much. On the wall, mirror and inside the sink, which were to the right of the bath and close to the bathroom door, there was more blood. Owen knelt down at the side of Hailey.

His brother Rhys stood in the doorway of the bathroom and leaned against the doorframe. Will stood behind Rhys and outside the bathroom. The chin of Will rested on the shoulder of Rhys. Will bit his lip and peeked in at what was happening. In the doorway the faces of Rhys and Will touched.

'You'd better call the ambulance,' said Owen.

'I'll do that,' said Will.

'Call the police as well.'

'The police?'

'This looks like a crime scene. I think she's dead.'

Will put a finger in his mouth. Rhys and Will were thinking about what had happened inside their bathroom. The chin of Will slipped from the shoulder of Rhys.

'She's definitely dead?' said Will.

'Make the phone calls,' said Rhys.

He turned his head around to look at Will.

'We shouldn't be in here,' said Owen.

'There hasn't been a crime,' said Rhys.

The head of Will leaned forward, and Rhys took a step back. Their two heads passed one another. It looked odd to Owen. He ignored what Rhys had said. There were a couple of spots of blood on the denim jeans of Owen. He adjusted how he knelt, pushed his head forward and pressed his ear close to the mouth of Hailey. Owen moved his head from side to side. The cold tip of the nose of Hailey brushed against his cheek.

'Definitely,' said Owen. 'She's definitely dead.'

'Feel her pulse,' said Will.

'Haven't you gone yet?' said Rhys.

'I couldn't find a pulse to save my life,' said Owen.

No one said anything else. Rhys and Will were thinking about what Owen had just said. Owen looked at the woman he had been married to for twelve years. He hoped remembering the number of years might have an effect on what he saw or discovered. It did not.

'Rhys, you have a look at Hailey,' said Owen.

Rhys was unenthusiastic but walked into the bathroom. Owen stood up and looked at the bloodstains on the mirror and the taps and sink.

'What a mess,' said Owen.

'It's terrible,' said Rhys.

Will remained at the bathroom door.

'Make the phone calls, Will,' said Owen.

Will did not move.

'Someone has to,' said Owen.

'Will, fuck off and make the phone calls,' said Rhys.

Will turned around and walked down the stairs. Rhys knelt down close to the bath and did what Owen had done a minute before.

'I can't feel any breath,' said Rhys.

'There isn't any fucking breath,' said Owen.

He stepped away from the body of his wife. He stared at his face in the bloodstained mirror. There was a coarse bewilderment in his eyes that he did not recognise. Rather than look at himself, Owen stared at the bloodstains on the mirror, sink, bath and bathroom floor. He did not count them but his brain aggregated them into something. He passed the bloodstained sink and mirror. He waited by the bathroom door.

'I'm so sorry' said Rhys.

'She didn't deserve this,' said Owen.

He walked out of the bathroom and waited on the landing. After a few seconds of doing and thinking nothing he sat down on the floor and leaned his back against one of the wooden panels in the bannister on the landing. The voice of Will on the phone could be heard but what was being spoken downstairs was indistinct. Owen stared at the bedroom wall on the other side of the landing. He thought about the other people he knew and having to tell them what had happened. Although he did not smoke he imagined what it might be like to seek relief with a Cuban cigar. He tried to think of what had happened as a tragedy that was causing pain for Hailey. Owen failed because the premature death of his wife had become an event that would no longer affect a woman already dead. He pulled up his legs and rested his elbows on his knees. He took deep breaths. The crumpled shape of Hailey, her splayed legs, the open mouth and distraught expression remained a clear picture inside his head. He had other memories. He remembered the first time they met and then him having to meet her parents. The father of Hailey had taken him outside to look at his Mercedes. Her mother had asked Owen where his parents lived.

Owen could see that inside the bathroom nothing had changed. Rhys stared at Hailey and waited for proof of something but everything was the same. There were no breaths from Hailey. Owen watched Rhys leave the bathroom and walk across the landing and towards him. Rhys leaned against the wall that was opposite Owen.

'Will is making the telephone calls,' said Owen. 'I heard him.'

Rhys said nothing.

'I believe this less than I did five minutes ago,' said Owen.

Rhys shook his head.

'I wish I weren't so drunk,' said Owen.

'I don't feel as drunk as I did,' said Rhys.

The two men strained to listen to what Will might be saying on the phone. What they heard was not even a mumble.

'I always imagined Hailey as having the last word,' said Owen.

'This is terrible,' said Rhys.

Owen said nothing.

'So young,' said Rhys.

Hailey was thirty-six years old and two years younger than

Owen but for a long time he had thought of the two of them as being the same age. Owen tilted his head back against the bannister to listen to what was happening downstairs.

'Will's finished talking,' said Owen.

Rhys and Owen heard Will climb the stairs. Owen turned his head to look. When the head of Will appeared above the bannister he stopped climbing.

'They're on the way,' said Will.

Rhys stared at Will who kept the same position near the top of the stairs. The head of Will was near a painting of an old hillbilly that wore a boiler suit and played a banjo. Owen looked away from Will. Owen remained seated and with his back to Will. Owen stared at nothing in particular.

'The ambulance and the police,' said Will.

Rhys nodded.

'I said we had no idea what happened,' said Will.

'Rhys, I'm going to have to phone Mam,' said Owen.

Will appeared at the top of the stairs. Will was the tallest and the slimmest of the three men. He had lived with Rhys for four years. The joke was that Rhys looked more like Will than he did Owen. Will and Rhys had brown hair, fine features, olive skin, slim faces and strong brown eyes. Apart from his trimmed beard and the rest Rhys looked like his mother. Owen had black hair and a wide pale face like his father. Owen remembered how Hailey had been impressed with Rhys when she met him. More than once Owen wondered what might have happened between Hailey and Rhys if his brother had not been gay.

'We should go downstairs,' said Will.

Rhys smiled at Will.

'I'm not going downstairs,' said Owen. 'I'm not leaving Hailey here all alone.'

'Just as well we've got three toilets,' said Will.

The house had a separate bathroom and toilet in the attic and a third toilet on the ground floor.

'I never use the downstairs loo.'

'Gran once said that getting two toilets put in was the best thing she ever did,' said Rhys.

'Shut up about the toilet,' said Owen.

'My hand was shaking when I phoned,' said Will.

'Why not?' said Rhys.

Owen raised his arm until it was parallel to the floor. His fingers pointed at the bedroom wall. His hand did not shake.

'Maybe I should make a coffee,' said Will.

'I feel sick,' said Owen.

'I don't feel like a coffee,' said Rhys.

'I won't then,' said Will.

'I'll have to ring my mam,' said Owen.

'I can do that,' said Rhys.

'I can if you want,' said Will.

'I don't think so,' said Owen. 'It's my place. My phone is downstairs.'

He looked sideways at the bathroom doorway. The bathroom light was bright, hot enough to warm the dead body of his wife, thought Owen. Will went downstairs and found the phone. He returned to the landing and handed the phone over to Owen. Will smiled and touched the hand of Owen. The two men nodded thanks and shared resignation or something. Will headed down the stairs, and Rhys followed him. Owen dialled the phone number of his mother. He remembered his wife when she used her phone to call friends. Often it had irritated him.

'Mam, there's been an accident,' he said.

'You don't sound right, Owen,' said his mother.

'I've had too much to drink.'

'You're not used to it like Rhys.'

'Rhys likes his expensive wines. He doesn't drink so much.'

'Except when he does.'

'Except when he does. You're right, Mam.'

'Are you alright, Owen?'

'Oh, Mam.'

He felt his throat dry and his voice tr~

'Oh, love,' said his mother.

'Hailey is dead, Mam,' said Owen.

His mother was silent.

Owen listened to her breathe and waited.

'I don't know what happened, Mam,' he said.

His mother said nothing.

'None of us know. I was the one that found her.'

This time he heard his mother sigh.

'We've called the ambulance and the police,' said O~

His eyes continued to drip but the tremble in his voice

tug in his throat had calmed.

'You didn't?' said his mother.

'No, Mam,' said Owen.

'You've always had a temper. Hailey and you, you've both go
tempers.'

'No, Mam. Hailey went upstairs to the loo. We heard a couple
of bangs and a scream. I expected her to come down the stairs with
a few bruises or something. When she didn't we ran upstairs. And
she was there on the floor and dead.'

The tremble in his voice became noisy.

'I'm sorry, Mam,' said Owen.

'Don't be daft,' said his mother.

'I don't know what happened.'

'She's had an accident.'

Owen said nothing.

'Had Hailey been drinking?'

'We all had, Mam.'

Owen heard his mother take a deep sigh.

'We're waiting for the police,' said Owen.

'Oh, my God,' said his mother.

Imagining his mother thinking the worst helped Owen manage
the tremble in his voice and to keep the tears to a minimum. He

way what moisture was left in his eyes.

at about your sleep?' said his mother.

grab a couple of hours on the sofa,' said Owen.

er poor parents.'

haven't thought about them.'

I'll tell them if you want.'

Owen said nothing.

'Owen, let me ring her parents. I'll tell them you're talking to ie police and you wanted them to know as soon as possible. It'll ie easier for you tomorrow when you do talk. You'll have to talk to them at some point, Owen.'

'I know that.'

'God knows what your dad would say if he was here. He never much liked women drinking.'

Owen said nothing.

He thought about when his father had died from cancer and having to deal with similar gloom. The deep breaths that Owen took reassured him.

'Thank Christ, you didn't have kids,' said his mother.

'We did try,' said Owen. 'We tried for a while.'

'It's just as well. Imagine having a kid to look after.'

'I'd have had to cope.'

'Owen, the kid would have been terrified of anything happening to you.'

'Well, we didn't have one. Mam, I don't want to chicken out of anything.'

'Son, you'll have enough on your plate.'

'I'll speak to Hailey's parents tomorrow.'

'Of course.'

His mother and Owen waited for the other to say something. He stared at the open bathroom doorway and the bright light. He imagined what he might feel if Hailey walked out of the bathroom.

'Owen,' said his mother.

'Yes,' he said.

'You must be feeling awful.'

'I don't mind doing these things.'

His mother said nothing.

'I think I should if I can. I don't mind.'

Since the father had died Rhys and Owen had maintained regular visits to their mother but Rhys visited more than Owen. Rhys and Owen had talked about the father dying and him not knowing that his son Rhys was gay. Rhys had an excuse. Their mother had wanted it kept a secret from her husband. Owen remembered. He had told his mother he wasn't taking any responsibility for the decision. Rhys had said nothing.

'Owen,' said his mother. 'I'll make these phone calls. Tomorrow we can sit down, and you can tell me how you're feeling.'

'Mam. The doorbell has just rung. The police are here.'

'Owen, we'll speak tomorrow.'

His mother and Owen ended the phone call, and people walked up the stairs. A uniformed man and woman arrived at the landing. Someone downstairs switched on the hall light. The ambulance man stepped towards Owen.

'Is this the husband?' said the ambulance man.

Behind Owen the ambulance woman smiled. Owen nodded his head and stood up in front of the man and the woman. For an odd reason he wanted to shake their hands. He resisted and put his hands in his pockets.

# TWO

Rhys owned a bigger house than Owen. Hailey had mentioned it often. The house was detached and had the extra toilets in the attic and downstairs, the shower and bathroom where Hailey died, four bedrooms, a decent-sized and square study, a living room that Will called a lounge and, separate from the kitchen, a dining room. The Detective that sat opposite Owen and in the comfortable study was a woman.

'This is a lovely house,' said the Detective. 'I like these old houses.'

Her black raincoat was open, and the bottom corners of the raincoat touched the carpeted floor. She sat in the high swivel chair by the desk that Rhys used for his work. Owen sat in a heavily padded leather armchair. The head of the Detective looked down on him.

Owen forgot the name of the Detective almost immediately. The Detective looked about the same age as Hailey. She had blonde-streaked and not quite shoulder-length hair. The transparent hygienic gloves on her hands were stretched over long elegant fingers. A black Covid mask covered her mouth, chin and nose. The black skirt and black stockings surprised Owen. He imagined detectives in trousers. The Detective rested the notebook on her knees. She swivelled in the chair but not by much. She had large brown eyes and strong eyebrows that were a different colour to the hair on her head. Because of Hailey, he could recognise eyebrows that had gel on them. Owen thought the Detective was pretty but he knew his judgement about women was flawed because his mother had told him so. Behind the Covid mask the words of the Detective were audible.

'I spoke to the others first for a reason,' said the Detective.

'Have you seen the bathroom?' said Owen.

'Not properly.'

'You think there's been a crime?'

'I don't think anything. I left you until after the others because you are the husband and will be the most affected. You know the rules on Covid?'

'You want me to wear a mask?'

'I'll be alright.'

'We're all family, just the four of us. We haven't broken any rules.'

The Detective paused and smiled.

'I can give you some extra minutes,' she said.

'No, I can talk,' said Owen.

The Detective paused but not for breath. Owen felt he was being managed and that the Detective was pacing the interview.

'You asked Will to call the police,' said the Detective. 'Will mentioned an accident but couldn't say what. I left you until after the others because I was curious as to why you wanted to call the police. Most people's first thoughts would have just been the ambulance.'

Owen said nothing.

The chair under the Detective swivelled a little and creaked. The Detective smiled.

'Perhaps you could tell me why you're not most people,' said the Detective.

She smiled and raised one of the gelled eyebrows. She knew she was pretty, thought Owen. He wondered why the woman had joined the police.

'I don't feel like most people right now,' said Owen. 'My father died last year, and now this.'

'Why did you want the police here?' said the Detective.

'I work in insurance.' Owen paused, and the Detective waited. 'At the Royal in town.'

'I see. My next door neighbour works for an insurance broker. Funny bloke. His grandkids are never away. I wouldn't mind his mortgage, though.'

'I used to be a teacher.'

'I see.'

'I did that after University.'

'I used to be a teacher before the police. I didn't like teaching.'

'Me neither.'

'I didn't have the patience with kids that knew it all. The kids ignore your good jokes and laugh at the bad ones.'

The Detective smiled.

His own grin was apologetic.

'I went into insurance,' said Owen. 'Hailey was always going on at me to take advantage of the special rates and buy a bigger house. Hailey was restless after Rhys and Will bought this place.'

'Your brother has a lovely house.'

'He should have. He's an architect.'

As Owen said this, it occurred to him that the occupation of his brother was one of the reasons Owen had delayed buying another house. He knew the house would have been chosen by Rhys and Hailey. There were other reasons. Owen wanted to both maximise his salary and the mortgage and time it right.

'I'm sorry,' said Owen.

'About?' said the Detective.

He shrugged his shoulders.

'It's fine,' said the Detective. 'You like working for the Royal?'

'I suppose. I've had a couple of promotions. Hailey works there as well.'

'You've got a few bob then?'

'We're not loaded but we were thinking of buying a bigger house.'

He stopped to take a breath. The Detective smiled. He was aware that someone other than Rhys and Will was moving around the house and outside the study. Owen decided it was safer not to look.

The Detective opened the black notebook that she held flat on her knees.

'It occurred to me, Owen,' she said, 'that perhaps you called the police because you needed us to prove you're innocent.'

'I understand the importance of evidence,' said Owen.

'I see.'

'I know how it can be misinterpreted. I've had to assess accidents where people can't even get right the cars they were driving.'

'Do you need a cup of tea or anything?'

'I'd throw it up. I'm sorry I'm not sober.'

'You don't sound too drunk.'

'I'm trying not to.'

'Your brother Rhys is cursing himself for opening the extra bottle of wine. Seemed like a good idea at the time, he said.'

'My brother likes his wine,' said Owen.

'You'll have a hangover in the morning,' said the Detective.

'Assuming I get to sleep.'

'You'll have a lot worse than a hangover hurting your head.'

Owen looked at his watch and counted the hours before when he would normally wake.

'Are you sure you don't want a cup of tea?' said the Detective.

'I'd throw it up,' said Owen.

'Some water perhaps. I can ask Will to make you some dry toast. He likes to be helpful.'

'Rhys thinks so.'

'I know what Rhys and Will said, and I think I know what happened but I want you to remember it all for me.'

The Detective smiled.

'I've forgotten your name,' said Owen. 'I'm all over the place.'

'Detective Sergeant Jones,' said the Detective. 'My first name is Holly. You can call me Holly if it helps you relax and remember. I'm not here to entrap or trick you.'

'Holly Jones is a nice name. My wife is Hailey. She hated my surname.'

'Pittman.'

'That's right.'

'There's nothing wrong with Pittman. My granddad was a miner.'

'So was mine. My grandfather was Welsh.'

'And so was mine. My granddad came to Liverpool to get out the pit.'

'My father was called William. He was born in Liverpool but loyal to Wales. He had to go the whole hog with the names for Rhys and me. My father worked as a landscape gardener.'

'I see.'

'Our houses always had to have big gardens. My brother was named after the Welsh grandfather, the miner.'

Detective Sergeant Jones smiled.

'So, what happened?' said Detective Sergeant Jones.

Owen took a breath.

'We were sitting at the table talking and drinking red wine,' he said.

'How many bottles were drunk?' said Detective Sergeant Jones.

'At least four.'

'And Hailey drank as much as anyone?'

'She must have. I'm not sure Will drank as much as the rest of us. We were just talking and drinking, and Hailey stands up and leaves the table. I listened to her climb the stairs. I remember that.'

'Was there a reason why you listened?'

'Who knows?'

'You might.'

Detective Sergeant Jones stared at the notebook on her knees.

'Sometimes your wife does something out of sight,' said Owen, 'and you imagine what she might be doing or look like. I don't imagine her on the loo. You know what I mean?'

'Not really,' said Detective Sergeant Jones, 'but I'm not married. I don't remember thinking that way about my boyfriends.'

Detective Sergeant Jones laughed.

'I don't think I listened for long when Hailey climbed the stairs,' said Owen. 'I might have been thinking the stairs would have been a struggle for her. I can't remember. Sometimes I don't like seeing her drunk but I wasn't thinking like that.'

'You worried about your wife's drinking?' said Detective Sergeant Jones.

'She would have been better off drinking less. She's a bit like me. She doesn't know when to stop when she starts. I remember I stopped listening to her climb the stairs. I was drunk. Someone said something, and it went out of my mind.'

'I see.'

'Oh God, my hand, it's trembling.'

The right hand of Owen was pressed flat on his thigh but he could feel the tingles. He lifted his right hand. The Detective and Owen watched the hand tremble and shake.

'It's just started,' said Owen.

'You want to have a walk around outside?' said Detective Sergeant Jones.

'I don't even want to stand up.'

He slid his trembling hand under his thigh and pressed down hard with his leg. Detective Sergeant Jones stared at Owen and thought about where the hidden hand might be. She smiled and waited.

'I'm sorry,' said Owen.

'It happens,' said Detective Sergeant Jones.

'I haven't thrown up. I'm made up about that.'

'You want a bowl just in case?'

Owen shook his head.

Detective Sergeant Jones sat still and looked around the study and at the book-lined shelves.

'I really do like this house,' she said.

'Rhys works in here,' said Owen. 'He's an architect. Now there's Covid he's working from home. He does okay. Where I live isn't as nice as this. I always fancied living on this side of town. Where I live is a bit boring, full of civil servants.'

'I live in Formby.'

'Same side of town as me. Formby is far out.'

'It is a bit.'

Detective Sergeant Jones smiled.

She had a straight and elegant nose under the mask, reckoned Owen. The mouth he would have to wonder about.

'Are you okay now?' said Detective Sergeant Jones.

Owen pulled his hand out from under his thigh. The hand had stopped trembling.

'Good,' said Detective Sergeant Jones. 'I really think you should have a cup of tea and a slice of toast.'

Will knocked on the door to the study and appeared in the room. He grinned.

'I can sort that,' said Will. 'I heard.'

Will left the room.

'He's been standing outside and listening,' said Owen. 'Ah, well.'

Detective Sergeant Jones smiled and pouted.

'I don't feel as sick as I did,' said Owen.

'I'm pleased,' said Detective Sergeant Jones. 'You can have a go at remembering, then. Was there anything memorable about the conversation tonight?'

'I don't think so.'

'Owen, try and remember.'

He leaned his head backwards and put his hands over his eyes.

'Have you got a headache?' said Detective Sergeant Jones.

Owen took his hands away from his eyes.

'I'm trying to remember,' he said.

Detective Sergeant Jones laughed but it was brief and under the mask it sounded more like a cough. She wrote a few words in the notebook that rested on her knees.

'Rhys and Will remember the conversation,' said Detective Sergeant Jones.

Owen waited.

'Before your wife walked up the stairs, Owen.'

'I didn't say I couldn't remember what we were talking about. I was trying to think of what you might want me to remember.'

'Maybe I can help. Will and Rhys said that there was an argument.'

'An argument?'

'That's what they said. Can you remember, Owen?'

'Before Hailey went up the stairs?'

'That would help.'

Owen paused to think.

'It was more like a discussion,' he said.

'You remember the argument?' said Detective Sergeant Jones.

'I remember everyone disagreeing with me. Is that what you're talking about?'

Detective Sergeant Jones laughed. Like before, it sounded like a cough.

'Tell me what you argued about, Owen. Tell me what you discussed. It would help.'

Owen talked and remembered.

'Will was going on about some TV programme he'd seen and someone on the telly saying that love did not exist and that all there was between a man and woman was kinship, dependency and sympathy.'

'You're remembering now.'

'Yes, I am now.'

Detective Sergeant Jones waited.

'Rhys, Will and Hailey,' said Owen, 'all of them said that what this guy on the TV had come out with was all nonsense. I remember saying that I thought the bloke had a point.'

'You'd seen the TV programme?' said Detective Sergeant Jones.

'No.'

'You always argue about this kind of thing?'

'My family can argue about anything. Rhys and me have argued all our lives. If he weren't gay, I'd give him a belt. I know. That shouldn't make a difference.'

'If it stops you giving him a belt.'

'Before I knew we used to battle all the time.'

Detective Sergeant Jones smiled.

'About?' she said.

'Everything.'

'Because Rhys and you are different?'

'Because he's gay?'

'I didn't mean that.'

'I don't argue with Will so much. Hailey could be argumentative. Rhys is a know-all.'

'I see.'

Owen stared at his hands to make sure they were okay. Nothing trembled.

'Will and Rhys thought the argument upset Hailey,' said Detective Sergeant Jones.

'I was the one being picked on,' said Owen. 'Rhys always sides with Hailey.'

'They were friends?'

'Rhys sides with anyone against me.'

'That must be annoying.'

'I'm used to it. My mother sides with him. My father sided with Rhys. God knows how my dad would have reacted to knowing Rhys was gay. My mother was convinced that one day I would tell my father about Rhys. I didn't. I wasn't even tempted. We were brothers. We argued a lot. That was the way it was.'

Detective Sergeant Jones smiled.

'Rhys felt that Hailey took the argument badly. Was that your impression, Owen?'

'I wouldn't have said so. Everyone was agreeing with her.'

Owen paused to remember a couple of critical looks that Hailey had given him during the argument. He looked around the large square room that Will called a study. In films you see architects sitting behind sloping desks but the desk Rhys used was large, flat and normal. On the desk was a keyboard, mouse, two minicomputer processors, a pair of small speakers and two giant monitors. Owen wondered how the study would look when it stopped being the centre of a police investigation. He thought of motor cars when they had been damaged in an accident and how after repairs they returned to normal.

'Tell me what happened when you arrived at the bathroom,' said Detective Sergeant Jones.

'We arrived at the bathroom,' said Owen.

'We?'

'The three of us.'

'I see. At the same time?'

'I was first but there wasn't much in it, a couple of seconds. I tried to open the door but it was locked. I remember saying that we had to break the door down and Will saying that the bathroom had just been done.'

'What did Will want to do?'

'He didn't say.'

'We all charged the door together but that didn't work and Rhys went and got this big hammer. We gave the door a few thumps and it gave way. I saw Hailey sitting on the floor. I went inside the bathroom and, excuse me.'

'That's okay, Owen. Take a breath. How's the hand?'

He lifted his arm. The hand was level and still.

'Looks okay to me,' said Detective Sergeant Jones.

'I don't know how to take a pulse,' said Owen. 'I just sat down next to her.'

'Hailey?'

'I sat down next to Hailey and tried to hear if she was breathing. I thought she wasn't but I asked Rhys to listen and check. I then went and sat down on the landing and waited.'

'You didn't go down the stairs?'

'I didn't feel right about leaving her. I didn't feel right about leaving Hailey.'

'You could have stayed in the bathroom.'

'I didn't want to complicate it when you arrived.'

Detective Sergeant Jones smiled.

'All those years assessing insurance claims,' she said.

'I suppose I wanted to know what happened,' said Owen,

'and that if I kept out of the way you'd be able to tell me.'

Detective Sergeant Jones and Owen waited for the other to speak. Someone knocked on the door and a uniformed policeman walked into the study. He nodded hello to Owen. Detective Sergeant Jones smiled at the policeman.

'And?' said Detective Sergeant Jones.

'The team reckons they know what happened,' said the policeman.

'I'll come and look.'

Detective Sergeant Jones followed the uniformed policeman upstairs. Will walked into the study. He carried a mug of tea and a plate loaded with two thick slices of toasted brown bread.

'I've just put on a tiny bit of butter,' said Will. 'It'll settle your stomach.'

'How's Rhys?' said Owen.

'His head is banging. He's lying down. I didn't drink so much.'

'You're not as daft as you look.'

Will laughed and handed over the tea and toasted bread.

'How's Inspector Maigret been?' said Will.

'I'll find out when she comes down the stairs,' said Owen.

He drank some water and took a bite of the toast.

'If you need to throw up, there is the downstairs toilet,' said Will. 'I threw up in it once.'

Will walked around the study and looked at a row of books.

'I wanted this room to be the home cinema,' said Will. 'You wouldn't have wanted to listen to that argument. Rhys likes to have his way. You get used to it.'

'Give him a smack once in a while,' said Owen.

Will and Owen laughed. The response inside his body made Owen feel queasy. He sat still and ate the toasted bread. Will stood next to the winged armchair that Will and Rhys had picked before they had moved into the house and before enough money had left their bank accounts to make Rhys and Will gasp. Will wrapped his arm around the shoulders of Owen. Detective Sergeant Jones returned to the room, spotted the draped arm around Owen and nodded for Will to leave.

'Of course,' said Will.

Detective Sergeant Jones sat down on the swivel chair in front of the desk. Will left the living room.

'Will was consoling me,' said Owen.

'You could have a worse brother-in-law,' said Detective Sergeant Jones.

She pointed at the tea and toast.

'Is that helping?' said Detective Sergeant Jones.

'I don't think I'm going to throw up,' said Owen.

'I see. Your hand isn't trembling.'

Owen ate the last of the toasted bread. He put the plate down on the floor next to his chair.

'We have an idea what happened,' said Detective Sergeant Jones.

'Are you pleased?' said Owen.

'Kind of. The team figures the lock on the bathroom door was locked and that it would have taken the three of you to force the door open. That might not be forensic enough for a man with your experience in insurance but it does mean that you or your brother or his partner are not suspects. That is good news.'

Owen sipped his tea and nodded his head.

'But this is a death in suspicious circumstances,' said Detective Jones. 'I will have to prepare a report and make recommendations to the coroner. Because of the Covid restrictions, you'll be excused from attending the hearing but you still need to make a written statement. All that can be done tomorrow. I'm conscious you're bereaved and I'm prepared to visit your home and take the statement there. There is also Covid to think about.'

'It'd help me get out of the house,' said Owen.

He put his cup of tea down on the floor and nodded his head.

'There are two possibilities,' said Detective Sergeant Jones. 'Your wife could have slipped, banged her head against the sink and then stood up all groggy, looked at herself in the mirror, slipped again, hit her head against the mirror and then fallen against the bath with a bang.'

Owen tried to imagine the sequence of events that the Detective had described but struggled.

'If it had been a plastic bath, your wife would have stood more of a chance,' said Detective Sergeant Jones.

When Owen thought about the collisions his brain resisted adding force and impact to what he imagined.

'The bloodstain pattern indicates the head hit the mirror with some force,' said Detective Sergeant Jones.

'Christ, poor Hailey.' said Owen.

'The second and more likely possibility is that your wife went upstairs angry and distraught at what was said in the argument downstairs and in a temper butted her head against the mirror. Because she was drunk, she underestimated the impact of the blow and because she was drunk she was more unsteady after the blow than she should have been. Groggy and semi-conscious she fell against the sink and the bath. They're quite expensive, those old-style enamel baths, but they're lethal if you slip and fall.'

Owen said nothing.

Detective Sergeant Jones waited.

'Tell me what you're thinking,' she said.

'Hailey does have a temper,' said Owen.

'Clearly.'

'Even so.'

'Has she ever banged her head against anything before?'

'She throws things when she gets angry.'

'Maybe if she had been at home it would have been different.'

'I don't understand why she was so upset. They were all arguing against me.'

Detective Sergeant Jones smiled. She closed her notebook and stood up. She rested a hand on the swivel chair.

'I'll ring you tomorrow,' she said. 'I'll let you know the time when I'll visit you for the statement. No, it's best I call. I suspect you're stubborn and a bit of a cold fish, Mr Pittman. The more the argument went on the more she waited for you to say something that you wouldn't.'

Detective Sergeant Jones smiled and put the black notebook in the black raincoat. She fastened the buttons of her raincoat.

'It's throwing it down outside,' she said.

Owen stood up and faced the Detective. He was aware that behind him her people were preparing to leave. Owen looked at his watch. He had stopped drinking the wine over three hours earlier.

'You're fortunate,' said Detective Sergeant Jones. 'I'm a bit of a cold fish myself.'

# THREE

'You look terrible,' said the mother of Owen.

'I've had no sleep,' said Owen. 'Maybe I should apologise.'

His mother turned away from her front door and walked down the hallway and towards the kitchen. Owen stared at the straight back of his mother. Her grey hair was longer than normal because of Covid. The extra hair was tied up at the back of her head in a bun. She wore denim jeans and trainers and a long white shirt that looked like a smock. Owen followed her down the hallway, stared at the bun in her hair and thought about how this woman had begun to look like an ageing artist since Covid and the death of his father. His mother opened the door into the kitchen. Mother and son walked towards the sink. His mother leaned her strong frame over the sink and put water into the kettle.

'I've been waiting for you,' said his mother.

'And here I am,' said Owen.

'I spoke to Hailey's parents.'

Owen found a couple of mugs, dropped tea bags inside the cups and turned around to face his mother. Mother and son stared at the boiling kettle. His mother removed her glasses, used a kitchen paper towel and the steam from the kettle to wipe them clean.

'They're upset?' said Owen.

'Distraught,' said his mother.

'I'm not sure what happened, Mam.'

'As soon as you've had your tea, you'll have to ring them. I promised.'

'I need a biscuit.'

He opened the biscuit tin and took out a couple of shortbreads.

'I don't want any,' said his mother.

Owen ate his biscuits and drank the tea.

'Rhys and Will thought it might help if they were here,' said his mother.

'Why not? You could invite the neighbours in,' said Owen.

'They were trying to be supportive.'

'You didn't say yes?'

'I didn't say anything.'

'I'll get through this without Rhys and Will.'

'You have to ring Hailey's mother and father.'

'I'll do it now.'

'Finish your tea, Owen.'

'No, I'll do it now. Mam, is there a chance of dry toast?'

'I've only white bread.'

'You're best burning it.'

Owen hated white bread. He walked into the hall, picked up the phone and dialled.

'Oh, Owen,' said his father-in-law.

'Derek,' said Owen.

'The police have been on the phone.'

'I did wonder.'

'Your mother rang us last night.'

'I was with the police.'

'Your mother said.'

'I don't know what to say, Derek. I can't believe it. One minute we're sitting at the table and finishing off the wine, and the next we hear a crash.'

'I know, Owen. The police have been on the phone. You don't have to go into the details, Owen.'

'If there's anything I can do to support.'

'I was going to say the same thing, Owen.'

'Do you want me to pop around?'

'You don't have to. If you could just keep us in the picture.'

'I have to talk to the police again. After that I will make all the arrangements.'

'If you could keep us in the picture, Owen.'

'I will do.'

'It's awful.'

'I know. I'd do anything for it to not have happened, Derek.'

'Was there anything?'

'Anything?'

'That you could have done, Owen.'

'We were all sitting there at the table. We never dreamed.'

'I suppose.'

'I can pop round.'

'I don't think that would be best. Sarah is very upset. Phone calls are best for now, Owen. We'll meet at the funeral. We can talk then. I'm hoping Sarah will be more settled then.'

Owen said nothing.

His father-in-law took a couple of breaths.

'I just wish Rhys had bought a cheap plastic bath,' said Owen.

His father-in-law said nothing.

Owen hoped his father-in-law realised that the remark about the bath had not been a joke.

'Those trendy baths weigh a ton,' said Owen.

'Who knows?' said his father-in-law. 'Hailey had bad food poisoning as a child. She nearly died. Her face came up like the Elephant Man. A tin of salmon caused it.'

'I knew Hailey was allergic to salmon. I didn't know she nearly died.'

'Your kid nearly dies and recovers, you think fate is on your side.' The father-in-law paused. 'Clearly not. Not this time, eh.'

The mother of Owen walked into the living room. She carried a plate of buttered toast. Without making a noise she said the words, 'More tea?'

Owen shook his head. His mother smiled and left the living room.

'I'll let you know the arrangements,' said Owen.

'The police said it was an accident but it all has to go to the coroner,' said his father-in-law. 'Who knows what to believe.'

'The police are covering their backs.'

'You think, Owen?'

'They don't want to call it an accident and someone comes along later and says it's death by misadventure.'

'They haven't got the idea in their heads it was suicide?'

'Definitely not.'

The father-in-law of Owen waited and said nothing.

'I suppose they're wondering what kind of accident,' said his father-in-law.

'They just want to record the right details,' said Owen. 'I don't know, Derek.'

At this moment Owen just wanted his father-in-law to go away. Owen wished he had said yes to the offer from his mother for another cup of tea.

'You wonder if something could have been done,' said his father-in-law.

We could have not opened the extra bottle of wine, thought Owen.

He said nothing.

'I always think that after accidents,' said his father-in-law. 'There's always something that if it had happened would have changed everything. You know what I mean, Owen?'

'I suppose I do.'

Owen and his father-in-law remained quiet for a few seconds.

'You'll keep us in the know?' said his father-in-law.

'I'll do my best,' said Owen.

'That's all we ask. I was so proud of her.'

Owen and his father-in-law said goodbye.

Owen ate his toast and thought about what could have happened differently to stop Hailey from dying. He remembered Rhys and Will moving into their big house and buying the fancy bath and making a fuss. Owen thought about Rhys and a birthday that had to be celebrated despite the Covid warnings and Liverpool having a high rate of infection. Hailey had arrived wearing a

T-shirt that said Happy Birthday. His wife had laughed and posed. The memories of Owen dug deeper to the day of his marriage to Hailey and the conversations they had shared before they married. On different occasions Hailey and Owen had expressed doubts about marriage and even each other. What could have happened differently to keep Hailey alive? Everything, thought Owen.

He put down the phone and walked into the kitchen. His mother was somewhere else. He returned to the living room. His mother was sitting on the sofa and staring at a quiet TV screen.

'You think I should keep the curtains closed?' said his mother.

The curtains were not closed.

Owen said nothing.

'I'm not sure what I'm supposed to do with a daughter-in-law dying.'

'Bugger the curtains.'

'I feel for Hailey and I worry about you.'

'I'll be alright.'

'Well, if you're not, you open your mouth. I don't want you going without food.'

'I know how to cook, Mam. It's not as if I was waited-on hand and foot.'

'I know you're not like your dad. Rhys is more like your dad.'

'Just as well he has Will.'

'I'm glad of that.'

The living room was a long rectangle but nothing special. The detached house was modern and not cheap but not much more than a superior version of the council house in which the family had lived when he was a child. Owen walked to the end of the room and stood in front of the window that faced the back garden. He watched a small white dog run around the garden. In his mouth the dog carried an old stick that was once a branch on a tree. Owen knocked on the window. The dog ran to the window, put his front paws on the windowsill and wagged his tail. Owen nodded for the dog to come inside. The Westie dog was bought after the father of

Owen had died. The dog was called Pops. Owen left the window.

His mother was sitting on the sofa that was under the living room window at the front of the house. Owen sat on a sofa that was pressed against one of the long adjacent walls. He faced an unlit gas fire. The door into the living room slammed back against the wall, and Pops ran inside. Owen ruffled the white fur and scratched the neck of Pops. A stick fell out of the mouth of the dog. The mouth of Pops dropped open, and he took heavy breaths. The dog plonked himself down on the mat in front of the never used gas fire. Steam left his tongue.

'Look what he brings in,' said the mother of Owen.

'He's doing no harm,' said Owen.

'He'd be company for you.'

'He's company for you.'

'Until you settle, Owen.'

'I'll be alright. I've got work. I can take it seriously.'

'I thought you did.'

'More seriously.'

His mother shrugged her shoulders. The expression on her face was sad.

His mother said nothing.

Although his mother was tall enough to see out of the window while sitting on the sofa she raised her head to stare at what might be outside. Owen imagined her staring over the rooftops of the neighbours and searching for grief- free households. His mother put a finger in her mouth. Pops walked over to the sofa and sat down at the feet of the mother of Owen. Typical, thought Owen. The dog thinks my mother is suffering more than me.

'I'll make another cup of tea,' said the mother of Owen.

'In a minute,' said Owen.

'You like those shortbreads.'

'In a minute. I'll make the tea.'

His mother sighed and prepared herself for something.

'Rhys said there was an argument,' said his mother.

'There was a discussion,' said Owen.

'Rhys said an argument.'

'Did he now.'

'You have a tongue on you, Owen. You don't realise.'

Owen said nothing.

'You must have realised Hailey was upset.'

'The three of them were arguing against me.'

'That doesn't give you licence, Owen.'

'We were talking about a TV programme. I don't have to like what everyone else likes.'

'That wasn't what you were arguing about, Owen, and you know it.'

'There were three of them all saying the same thing. I hate conversations at the dinner table anyway. It always feels like a pose. I wanted to sit down in an armchair and relax. With Rhys and his wine you never get to a pub these days.'

'Then you should have told your wife what she wanted to hear.'

'Like you did with Dad?'

The mother of Owen picked at some fluff that had stuck to the knee of her jeans.

'You sure you don't want Pop's's company for a few weeks?' said his mother.

'I'll be alright,' said Owen.

'Until you settle.'

'I don't think so.'

'The dog would be company.'

'We'd only argue.'

# FOUR

Detective Sergeant Jones smiled. Owen remembered that her first name was Holly. The different mask over her face had a paisley pattern. Her tinted blonde hair looked clean. Owen wore a plain black mask. They both wore thin transparent gloves. The Chromebook resting on the lap of the Detective was open. Owen stared at the letter G on the open lid. The small living room had a long sofa and a wide armchair. The Detective sat in the armchair, and Owen sat on the sofa. The TV was switched off.

'I would have come to the police station,' said Owen.

'We're trying to keep people out of the station,' said Detective Sergeant Jones.

'Were you born at Christmas?' Owen paused. 'Your name Holly.'

The Detective laughed.

'My dad picked it,' she said. 'You remembered my name. That's a first.'

'I thought it might be because of Christmas. And it sounds like Hailey.'

'Just as well I've done you a favour, Owen.'

He waited.

'I've spoken to the coroner. In view of Covid she's prepared to settle for a signed statement. You won't have to go to the hearing.'

'Unless something comes out and I'm arrested.'

'I don't think so. I did think about one of you staying in the bathroom and the other two breaking down the door.'

Owen waited. Not knowing why he grinned.

'The forensics had it all mapped out. There was no struggle. We have all kinds of footprints, where you and Rhys walked after she was dead. The forensics folk save people like me a lot of work.'

'They'll be downgrading your pay.'

'Is that the kind of thing you do in work?'

'I try not to. Hailey's father asked me if someone might say it was suicide.'

Detective Sergeant Jones glanced at the screen of her Chromebook. Something that she saw changed the expression on her face. She returned to being pleasant and normal.

'We don't believe that,' said Detective Sergeant Jones. 'I saw Rhys at his home this morning. Will gave me a statement the night of the accident. I thought it would be okay for him to sign one right away. They said much the same as you, Owen.'

Detective Sergeant Jones closed the lid of the Chromebook.

'I've sorted the funeral and the death certificate,' said Owen. 'I haven't phoned her friends. I'll have to go through her emails.'

'They won't expect a phone call from the husband. Send them an email. I've spoken to Hailey's mother and father. Her mother sat on the edge of the sofa and held her breath. I felt sorry for her.'

'I rang Hailey's father yesterday.'

'He'll keep himself busy, I reckon.'

'Can't blame him for that.'

'No, Owen, you can't.'

Detective Sergeant Jones wore black trousers, a navy blue crew neck pullover and a white shirt. The clothes reminded Owen of the girls he had known at school and their school uniforms. Something about Detective Sergeant Jones made him feel protective but he also felt threatened by whatever she might be suspecting.

'My boss has told people at work,' said Owen. 'If there hadn't been Covid, the funeral would have record numbers.'

'Hailey was popular?' said Detective Sergeant Jones.

'Work always gives a good turnout. There are the people she works with and the people that work with me. They would have had to close the place down. I can't be doing with it. Most turn up for the time off.'

'The police also like to make a fuss at funerals.'

'This will be better. Hailey is being cremated.'

'I see.'

'I'm not keeping the ashes. She wanted them scattered in the Lake District. Swinside Stone Circle, you know it?'

The Detective had a black bag that had short handles and was also meant to be a briefcase. She slipped the Chromebook inside her bag.

'Swinside is a smaller version of Stonehenge,' said Owen, 'a lot smaller. Hailey and I went there before we were married. It's just inside the Lake District, five thousand years old. The drive won't be so much.'

Detective Sergeant Jones grinned.

'Hailey felt something different when she went there,' said Owen. 'She got the idea in her head of having her ashes scattered there. Why not, I thought.'

The notion of her ashes being scattered at Swinside had been discussed by Hailey and Owen on the drive home to Liverpool. In the car, Hailey had told Owen that in the middle of the stone circle she had experienced without warning and out of sequence a powerful rush of menstrual blood. Hailey had thought it had meant something. Owen had thought she was being whimsical and fanciful but he had said nothing. Premature death now gives my wife extra entitlement, thought Owen.

He smiled at Detective Sergeant Jones.

'Long as you can scatter the ashes up there,' said Detective Sergeant Jones.

'It's on private ground,' said Owen. 'You can see the stones from the footpath. I'll throw the ashes over the wall. They won't be that near the stones but you can't have everything. You think it's a bit weird?'

'If that's what she wanted. If that's how you feel, Owen. I keep meaning to go to the Lake District.'

'You've never been?'

'When I was a kid.'

'Hailey and me used to climb the mountains. I've been all over the Lakes.'

'I see. Owen, I expect the verdict from the coroner to be accidental, death by misadventure at a push. It's such a shame. Your wife being healthy and able to climb mountains and having to die like this. Are you coping all right with this?'

'I'm keeping busy. I park all the other stuff.'

'It's a blessing being able to switch off. I thought you might.'

Detective Sergeant Holly Jones smiled at Owen, and he returned the smile. The Covid masks that they wore kept the moment formal.

# FIVE

Rhys was working at home and in his large square study. At his desk the screens of his two Dell 28 inch monitors were filled with alternative architectural plans.

'Looks impressive switched on,' said Owen.

'A Job Centre refurbishment,' said Rhys.

'Looks complicated.'

'If only. It pays the rent.'

'And more, I bet. The funeral is next Monday. I'm taking the ashes up to the Lakes on Tuesday. I go back to work Wednesday. All I need is my mother to stay healthy and cook my Sunday dinner.'

'You can always come here for a meal.'

'I was joking. Mam will live till she's 90. She's thrived since Dad died.'

'If you need cash, you'll shout.'

'I'll be alright.'

'Is Mother making a fuss?'

The way Rhys in University had switched from calling his mother Mam to Mother had annoyed Owen but there were other arguments to worry about.

'She wants the dog to come and stay with me,' said Owen.

'Pops won't mind that,' said Rhys. 'You can walk him to death.'

'I can manage without company.'

'The nights will drag, Owen, after being used to someone.'

'I want to be able to cope.'

'You don't have to relish the challenge, Owen. You are allowed to remember Hailey.'

'I'm not going to forget.'

'I didn't say you were.'

'I didn't know Will made a statement the night Hailey died,' said Owen.

Rhys said nothing.

'You must have known, Rhys.'

The screens on the Dell monitors turned black and the architectural drawings disappeared. Rhys pressed a key and the drawings reappeared.

'He doesn't need my permission, Owen,' said Rhys. 'You were eating dry toast and holding your stomach at the time. The Detective was at the house this morning. She's a handsome woman, Owen.'

'She wears a mask all the time,' said Owen.

'You can still tell. I think she likes you. It's the way she talks about you.'

'How's that?'

'I don't know. She was curious about you.'

'Maybe I'm still a suspect.'

'That wasn't the way she was curious, more like she just wanted to know about you.' Rhys paused. 'I told her there had been an argument. I had to, Owen. Will had said so.'

'As long as Will comes out of this alright.'

'I didn't want her to think we were telling lies. Owen, this is going to a coroner.'

'I know that, Rhys. I'd be lying if I said I remembered the conversation as an argument.'

'We were arguing about whether love existed.'

'We?'

'You.'

'I remember you all picking on me.'

'I was trying to be the peacemaker.'

'You wouldn't know how to make the peace in any argument.'

'I am limited. Why couldn't you just say yes, Owen?'

'Everybody else was saying yes.'

'And we can't have that, can we?'

With his eyes Owen traced some of the architectural lines in the diagram on one of the monitors. Rhys waited. Because they were brothers, neither of them wore a Covid mask although Owen had no idea what the latest rules for social distancing were supposed to be. In the weeks since the Covid lockdown he had visited the office once a week. The plain black mask that he used was in his jacket pocket.

'If love existed, we'd have had an accepted definition by now,' said Owen.

'You're not still arguing?' said Rhys. 'It's a feeling, Owen. Thank Christ, you're not gay.'

'You put me off.'

The two men grinned.

'Owen, it's not against the rules to be sensitive.'

'And gays are more sensitive?'

'They're more sensitive than you. You wouldn't want to be like the gays that aren't, Owen, although with a bit of imagination I could picture you.'

'You've had some bad nights then.'

Rhys and Owen laughed but Owen was being formal. The expression on the face of Owen hardened, or at least he thought so.

'I've had times with Hailey when I wished I weren't there,' said Owen.

'Those feelings are often mutual,' said Rhys.

'I asked Hailey if she wanted to leave me.'

Rhys waited.

'Hailey said I was difficult but not boring.'

'Jason said the same to me before he left. Hailey liked an argument. You'd always have had something to talk about.'

'She wasn't settled, Rhys. I know that. She'd have liked me to have been more sociable. The same woman didn't want to leave me.'

'You should have socialised with her friends more.'

'Every time we linked up with another couple there was always one that annoyed me.'

'Two likeable people out of two is ambitious, I suppose. It is for you, Owen.'

The two men grinned. With his eyes Owen traced the lines of one of the architectural drawings. One of the monitors had an aerial view of the plan of the Job Centre, and the other had the side and front views.

'I wasn't arguing,' said Owen.

'No?' said Rhys.

'I was discussing an opinion.'

'No one is blaming you, Owen. Arguments happen. But.'

'But?'

'She was upset. Couldn't you have just said?'

'In front of you and Will?'

'Why not?'

'Love should be private.'

'You do have feelings then?'

'Everyone has feelings, Rhys. But I still stand by what I said. If love exists, it's no more than a point on an axis.'

'Have your cake and eat it, Owen.' Rhys paused. 'Will knew the two of you were having problems.'

Owen and Rhys thought about what they should say next. Owen remembered that Hailey had collapsed against the expensive bath.

'Will was anxious about the meal and what would happen,' said Rhys. 'Will liked Hailey and he liked you.'

Owen remembered that he had dreaded the meal as soon as he saw the T-shirt that Hailey had decided to wear. An argument felt like a decent antidote to the enthusiasm of Hailey and Will.

'If it gets bad between a couple, people argue for the sake of it,' said Rhys. 'You soon noticed what it was like with Jason and me.'

'I didn't dislike Jason,' said Owen.

'He's found someone else. He said he's very happy.'

'He deserves it. Jason is an honest water carrier. But then so is Will. You collect them, Rhys. Hailey and me weren't water carriers. Hailey liked a lot of attention.'

'A lot or some?'

'Fuck knows.'

'Perhaps Jason did deserve better than me.'

'I didn't say that. Jason wasn't a twat. Hailey had been restless. I shouldn't have put off buying a bigger house. Jesus, I've no idea what the cops have told Hailey's parents.'

'No one is going to say anything at the funeral.'

'There's no reception afterwards. Her parents are happy with it, Covid and everything.'

'And after the funeral you don't have to see them.'

'Hailey once threw the kitchen knife at me.'

'We all have arguments, Owen.'

'She never ever backed down. You're the same, Rhys. And she'd keep coming back to the same arguments, you know, weeks later.'

Rhys pouted and shrugged his shoulders.

'I don't dislike Will,' said Owen, 'but he always brought out the giggles in Hailey.'

'Will is easy enough,' said Rhys. 'You just tell him not to be daft.'

'There was something Hailey said I didn't like.'

'We noticed.'

'We?'

'Will and me.'

'There was a moment she talked about me as if I was a specimen.'

'Will noticed that. Owen, we're never going to know what was going through her head. Maybe you should have said yes to moving house.'

'I was trying to play the market.'

'Since when have you been interested in money?'

'I don't want to pay over the odds for a house.'

'You just didn't want to move, all cosy in your small house.'

'Hailey would buy stuff and send it back all the time. I don't like buying things and sending them back. Once I buy something I feel loyal to it.'

'That's crazy.'

'It's a quirk.'

Owen sighed, and Rhys swivelled his chair. Owen stood but leaned back against the small table at the side of the desk.

'No one makes much sense after a bottle of wine, I suppose,' said Owen.

'Do me a favour,' said Rhys, 'don't beat yourself up about something you said or didn't.'

'No?'

'Christ, no. The last thing you need to do is waste your life remembering one conversation when everyone talked soft.'

Owen waited. The two computer screens became dark again. Rhys pressed a key on the keyboard. Owen looked at the architectural lines on the two monitors.

'If I hadn't married Hailey,' he said, 'she'd be alive now. You know what that feels like, Rhys?'

'I know you can beat yourself up when you have the mind,' said Rhys.

'I lay awake last night thinking about all this, accidents, what makes them happen and why. One minute I feel responsible, and the next pathetic.'

Both Rhys and Owen stared at the architectural lines on the two monitors.

'If you're pathetic, Owen, then we all are,' said Rhys. 'I've bought this red. One glass each won't do us any harm.'

Rhys switched off his PC and the two monitors. The architectural drawings disappeared. Owen said no to the glass of red wine.

# SIX

His mother and mother-in-law both wore black trousers. His mother wore an open-necked white shirt and dark trainers which fortunately were of leather. They looked like shoes or almost. Owen was pleased that for once she was not wearing glasses. His mother-in-law wore a heavy black woollen and ribbed pullover. Owen reckoned that she had bought it for the funeral. The pullover added bulk to her slight frame. Rhys, Will, Owen, and his father-in-law, all the men, wore suits and dark ties.

'Will's removed his earring,' said Rhys.

'I hadn't noticed,' said Owen.

'You think it makes him look older?'

Will tilted his head so that Owen could look at his reformed ear. The missing earring had left a tiny spot. Owen smiled at Will.

'It's his face that makes him look older,' said Owen.

Will stuck his tongue out.

The father of Hailey smiled but said nothing. He stood with his legs apart, and his hands were clasped in front of his stomach. His stance looked like a pose from a gymnasium. He had wide shoulders that had been developed through weightlifting. The father of Hailey had a handsome face and strong wavy hair. When they were both sharing doubts about getting married Hailey had told Owen that her father was a womaniser. The father of Hailey had been seen in a nightclub by one of her girlfriends.

'That's the risk you take,' Owen had said to Hailey.

'What does that mean?' Hailey had said.

'It was a joke.'

'You're joking about my father betraying my mother?'

The argument had continued until Hailey and Owen had gone to bed. A year in which that particular argument had not been referred to and remembered by Hailey was exceptional.

It occurred to Owen that he could have passed the whole funeral remembering that argument. The father of Hailey looked at Owen and thought about something. Owen reckoned both of them needed an alternative to memories.

'We sailed through from Southport,' said the father of Hailey.

'Right,' said Owen.

'No cars on the road or anything.'

Owen nodded and did not encourage his father-in-law.

'Car is running like a dream,' said his father-in-law.

'You're not going to change it then?' said Owen.

'It'll outlast me.'

The mother of Hailey walked over to Owen. She had not aged as well as her husband but then she had been betrayed.

'Oh, Owen,' she said.

The mother of Hailey grabbed the hands of Owen and held them tight. Owen noticed that the woman wore thin gloves. The small face of his mother-in-law was wrinkled. Her lack of weight revealed cheekbones that added force rather than charm to her face. Owen had a specific policy regarding his mother-in-law. He said as little as possible. Any conflict and criticism he had always absorbed with silence. It had meant his spirit taking body blows from the woman but being remote had helped Owen to resist breaking her neck.

'We should stay in touch after this,' said the mother of Hailey.

Owen nodded his head.

Fuck no, he thought.

'Is this it?' said the mother of Hailey.

Six people stood in the annexe to the crematorium chapel. The doors to the chapel were closed.

'It's the Covid,' said Owen.

'But all her friends,' said the mother of Hailey.

'It's best this way. Before Covid there would have been loads from work. I contacted her friends and sent emails to let them know what happened.'

'You've been reading Hailey's emails?'

'Not at all. I just did a search for the email addresses. I've read the replies to me, that's all. I thought I should just in case. The replies were the usual kind words. There's loads of cards in the house. I'll show you later.'

The mother of Hailey patted the hand of Owen. The loose sleeve of the heavy pullover brushed against his wrist. The material felt new. Owen was right, he reckoned.

'I should have spoken before this, Owen,' said the mother of Hailey.

'I understand,' said Owen.

'I've been so upset.'

'I understand.'

'I still can't believe it.'

Owen tilted and nodded his head.

'And how are you, Owen?'

He shrugged his shoulders.

'The last time I saw you in a suit was at the wedding,' said the mother of Hailey. 'You were a handsome couple. I was looking at the wedding photos last night. I said to Hailey before you were married, I'll have beautiful grandchildren.'

Owen was glad not to know that. He felt better about being childless. If Owen had known what his mother-in-law had said and Hailey had become pregnant, he would have felt cursed.

'I'm only saying a few words in the ceremony,' said Owen.

'I'd like to say something,' said the mother of Hailey.

Well, it would not be a funeral if there was not something to make you cringe, thought Owen. Rhys gave Owen a sly wink.

'Of course,' said Owen.

'Did Derek forget to ask?' said the mother of Hailey.

'He probably did ask.'

'I'll try not to cry but I expect I will.'

'Don't worry about it.'

'I wish I were a man like you, Owen. You're not the crying type.'

'I feel numb, I suppose.'

'Hailey always said you weren't the crying type. Derek has shed a few tears. Derek's been very good. He tells me every day that we have to move on. We're not the only people this kind of thing has happened to.'

Owen looked at the heavy black pullover and wondered where his mother-in-law had bought it. Quite trendy for a funeral, thought Owen.

'I'm back in work in a couple of days,' said Owen.

'You can't be looking forward to that, Owen,' said the mother of Hailey.

'I'm working from home a lot of the time. When I stop working from home it will be different. I worry about when I can't work from home.'

'The one good thing about worrying about the future is it stops you brooding about the past. Derek keeps telling me.'

The father of Hailey heard his name being mentioned and looked away from Rhys and Will and over towards his wife. Owen smiled at his father-in-law. The father of Hailey nodded and implied he had an alternative thought to a smile.

'Try and remember the good memories of Hailey,' said the mother of Hailey. 'Don't brood on the bad memories, Owen. I thought the two of you did very well considering the differences.'

Will heard this and looked at Owen. The expression on the face of Will felt to Owen like a challenge for him to do something.

Owen said nothing and waited.

The hostility of Owen to his mother-in-law may have been unspoken but he still knew how to frustrate her plans.

'Hailey was a beautiful girl,' said the mother of Hailey.

She was attractive, thought Owen, but come on. Good wavy black hair and memorable brown eyes but not beautiful.

'There aren't many mothers that are friends with their daughters,' said the mother of Hailey, 'but Hailey and I were very close.'

Hailey would not have married me if you were, thought Owen. Somehow this thought helped him remember an unfair accusation that Hailey had made to Owen in the middle of an argument. Each conversation with him obliged her to listen to at least one lie, Hailey had said. Owen knew that this was not true. Hailey, though, sometimes used arguments with him as rehearsals for the confrontations with her mother. Owen was aware how this had increased his suffering. Unlike Hailey, Owen had never told her mother to fuck off.

Owen remained silent and smiled.

'Because Hailey and I were so close,' said the mother of Hailey, 'it means that I feel I know you very well, Owen. That's why I said you mustn't brood on the bad memories. Of course, a mother always wants her daughter to have happiness.'

The mother of Hailey paused.

Owen imagined the woman refuelling her scorn.

'Whoever she happens to be married to a mother wants her daughter to have happiness.'

Owen held his breath and said nothing.

He remembered the wedding plans and the arguments that had taken place between Hailey and her mother. Those grievances helped him stay calm.

'I'm going to the Lakes tomorrow,' said Owen.

The veins in the scrawny neck of his mother-in-law stiffened.

'You're having a day out?' she said.

'I'm going to scatter Hailey's ashes,' said Owen.

'I know Hailey liked the Lakes.'

'It's just inside the Lakes. I'll just go straight there and back. I'm not sure I'm allowed to visit, what the Covid restrictions are. It's what Hailey wanted.'

'Hailey said?'

'She did once. She wants them scattered around a stone circle.'

'That doesn't sound like Hailey.'

'She didn't mention it to you? I'd have thought she would have.'

Sometimes silence and clipped remarks are not enough, thought Owen. An actual insult offers more. He could not think of one but if there had been one inside his brain, he would have stayed silent. With his mother-in-law in the room Owen felt as if he was in cold storage. Any time spent with his in-laws was wasted minutes, hours, days and months. Will was no longer listening to the conversation of the mother of Hailey and Owen. The father of Hailey was talking to Will and boasting about something. What the hell a man that insisted his life was perfect was going to say about the death of his daughter, Owen had no idea.

The waiting room had walls of polished pine, and the doors were dark something. The lights in the waiting room were lit. There were also toilets.

'I need to go to the loo,' said Owen.

This was the best lie he could manage.

The mothers of Hailey and Owen smiled at one another. The mother of Hailey adjusted her mask. Inside the toilet Owen tried to pee and was half successful. When he stepped out of the toilet a tall bald bloke that wore a black bow tie had opened the doors to the chapel and was explaining the Covid rules that had to be observed during the ceremony. Everyone shuffled forward and walked inside the chapel. The mother of Hailey held the hand of her philandering husband.

'I was in her support bubble,' said the mother of Hailey.

This is news to me, thought Owen.

The tall bald bloke nodded.

The funeral service was very brief. Owen said a few words, the usual stuff he supposed and about how she was loved by her family and respected by all. Owen added that he would miss his wife but said nothing about his sexual fidelity to Hailey although, as far as these people were concerned, that was the nearest he had to convincing evidence about his loyalty. There was a second that he was emotional but then Owen saw the self-satisfied grin on his mother-in-law. He noted the calculating expression on the face of her husband, a man that willingly betrayed his wife and who was already thinking about the timetable for his next steps towards added gratification. The emotion in the throat of Owen soon passed.

After the service the six mourners left the crematorium and walked the few yards to the almost empty car park. The mother of Hailey was too busy crying and being comforted by Will and Rhys to cause trouble. The car park had five cars. Four belonged to the family of Hailey but the fifth, a dark red BMW saloon, Owen had not seen before. The BMW was occupied. The man inside the BMW was about the same age as Owen. He wore glasses and had good brushed back hair. So long into Covid, thought Owen, this had to be regarded as an achievement. The man in the car stared at Owen and no one else. Owen looked and possibly admired the hair of the man inside the BMW. Even when Owen returned the stare the man did not look away. The look on the face of the man was not just curious but anxious, like the moment after a desperate discovery. The man in the car lowered his head and stared at something else. The father of Hailey said something about not staying too long at the house of Owen. The six mourners separated, and Owen walked across the concrete to his Volvo. Owen smiled at the curious man but there was no acknowledgement from inside the dark red BMW. His presence appeared to have offended the man.

# SEVEN

The weather the next day in the Lake District was what English mountains considered routine. Each cloud in the sky had company but below the low grey mass of cloud the day stayed dry. When Owen left the M6 motorway there was a glimpse of distant snow on the odd mountain top. Most of the peaks, though, were covered in cloud. Inside the Volvo it was warm. On the car radio people with nothing better to do were giving advice on how to cope with Covid lockdown. The ashes of Hailey were on the front seat next to Owen. The urn was inside a plain cardboard box. Google Maps told Owen how to follow the road that led to the beginning of the footpath that reached the stone circle. The woman on Google stopped talking, and the phone rang.

'I'm at home,' said his mother. 'Put the phone on Bluetooth.'

'I'm using Bluetooth,' said Owen.

'You sound alright.'

'Voice reproduction or ease of hearing?'

'I'll tell Rhys about you.'

Owen and his mother laughed.

'I always use Bluetooth,' said Owen. 'I don't have a choice. As soon as I sit in the car these things are decided for me. And I drive safely. The Volvo is keeping steady at sixty miles an hour and is on cruise control and using hardly any petrol.'

'Owen, I'll tell Rhys about you not showing me respect.'

'Serves you right for belonging to the modern world, Mam. Whatever happened to old-fashioned parents?'

All the roads to the Lake District from Liverpool had been quiet. This one was only different because it was narrow.

'I just wanted to see if you were alright,' said his mother. 'I won't be long talking.'

'I could do with better weather,' said Owen.

'You looked as if you'd lost a few pounds, Owen. I was looking at you at the funeral. You didn't have much to lose to start with.'

'I'm eating meals, Mam. It's this lockdown. I lost weight soon as it started.'

'Wish I could. I popped round your house. I wanted to make sure you'd locked up.'

'Mam, for Christ sake.'

'It's the day after the funeral, and you have to drive all the way up there. I was worried. The house is all right. You'd remembered to lock it.'

'Just as well you've got a key.'

'I'll give it back if you want.'

'I didn't mean anything. I'm glad you've got a key, Mam.'

'I made myself a cup of tea and read a little,' said his mother.

'Long as you haven't wrecked the telly,' said Owen.

'I can't be doing with that remote. I've borrowed a book.'

'Not the one I'm reading.'

'Of course not. You've had this one for years by the looks of it. I'll bring it back. I picked something I could read.'

'Fair enough.'

'You don't want to take risks living on your own. Rhys is worried about you.'

'I can be doing without that.'

Owen stared ahead. The odd car that passed by on the other side of the road was almost welcome, something to think about.

'I switched on the light to read the book,' his mother said. 'The light switch didn't make a noise.'

'Noise?' said Owen.

'It didn't click.'

Owen tried to remember the last time he had been aware of a light switch clicking.

'None of them clicked,' said his mother.

'You tried them all?' said Owen.

'I wanted to be sure. It's really strange when you don't hear

54

anything. You think you wouldn't notice but you do.'

'You were taking a chance trying them all.'

'I didn't have a shock or anything.'

'The click in the switch has nothing to do with the electricity.'

'I can ring for an electrician, Owen. I can be there when you're not.'

Owen thought about Hailey and him working at home after the lockdown began, her working in a corner of the living room, and him on the bed upstairs and with a laptop on his thighs. The trips to work one day a week were a relief.

'I'll speak to Rhys first,' said Owen.

'Rhys isn't an electrician,' said his mother.

'He's an architect. He'll know someone. I'm curious how it can happen.'

Owen looked sideways at the ashes on the front seat. He imagined Hailey blaming him for the mechanical fault and her complaining about living in a house they should have left years ago.

'Mam, you can always take a book whenever you want,' said Owen. 'You could have taken a couple.'

'I can only read one at once,' said his mother.

'I bet you've never tried.'

'I don't think I have. You all right, Owen?'

'Sort of. This business with the ashes makes me nervous.'

'You could have sprinkled them at the crematorium.'

Owen said nothing.

'If it's what Hailey wanted. You taking photographs, Owen?'

'Doesn't seem right.'

'Maybe of the scenery around the place. You can take a photo of the stone circle.'

'I don't know about that.'

'I won't be long while you're driving. You alright cooking tonight after a long drive?'

'I'll be fine. There's still stuff in the freezer that Hailey cooked. I wonder if I should throw it out.'

'Don't throw good food away.'

'It'll feel weird eating food that she's cooked.'

'Don't do much cooking when you get home,' said his mother, 'not if there's food in the freezer.'

'I suppose,' said Owen.

'Make sure you ask Rhys about the light switches.'

'If I have to.'

'I'll ask him for you.'

'Mam, I'll ask him.'

'Hope it goes okay today.'

'There's not going to be a ceremony. I'll lean over a wall and empty the urn.'

'I hope it goes okay.'

'I might have a couple of sausage rolls when I get home.'

'Don't put them in the microwave, Owen. It ruins them.'

'I told you that.'

'I don't think so.'

'I did. I remember.'

'You know it all, don't you, Owen?'

'I don't know much about light switches.'

'Rhys was talking about what happened Saturday.'

'I suppose he blames me.'

'He isn't going to blame anyone else,' said his mother.

Owen waited.

'He thought your tone with Hailey was a bit cold.'

'Nothing new there, Mam.'

'He didn't blame you, Owen. No one blames you. Hailey had an accident that another girl wouldn't have.'

'I hope you're not blaming Hailey.'

'No, Owen. It's circumstances.' His mother paused. 'It's very unfortunate. I do think Rhys could be more sympathetic.'

'What's he been saying, Mam?'

'Nothing really.'

'Mam, come on.'

'Nothing, honest. I said he should be more supportive, and Rhys said he will.'

'That's something to look forward to.'

Owen and his mother laughed. They said goodbye and more than once they told each other to take care. Owen looked at the cardboard box that had the urn inside and he drove on. He endured what was on Radio 4. Owen was tempted to put on some music but it did not feel the right thing to do, not when the ashes of Hailey were next to him on the front seat. The ashes may have been hidden inside the cardboard box but he had a sense of Hailey being in the car. Owen imagined talking to Hailey about the conversation he had just had with his mother and Hailey sneering. More than once Hailey had accused his mother of being judgemental and disapproving. Owen had said to Hailey that he kept his family at a distance.

Owen spoke to the urn that was on the passenger seat. 'She's only popping round now because you're dead, Hailey.'

Nothing happened but Owen regretted saying what he had.

Owen spoke to the urn. 'I wish you weren't dead, Hailey. I know that.'

Owen remembered Hailey and him sitting in the front of the various cars they had owned and their faces staring at windscreens. Like sharing a bed, it was what married couples do. Owen imagined Rhys and Will doing the same thing. Owen was thinking this nonsense when the car arrived at the beginning of the footpath to Swinside Stone Circle.

# EIGHT

The footpath was on land higher than Owen remembered. The green hills around the footpath were broad round mounds. Too low for the snow that had fallen on the mountains elsewhere, these hills failed to reach the clouds. Scattered on the smooth green slopes of the hills were patches of wet brown bracken and grubby not so brown turf. Owen took the urn out of its cardboard box and put it on the roof of the Volvo. The urn had a plain oblong design and was made of smooth black plastic. The square lid was dark grey. In his study Rhys had bookshelf loudspeakers that looked like this urn, thought Owen. There was no one around but Owen locked the car. He wore a hooded outdoor coat. Owen lifted the urn off the roof of the car and walked. In case a policeman appeared, Owen rehearsed excuses and pleas. The footpath was no more than a mile long and it had a slight slope. The warm wind was behind Owen. The air was damp but fresh, and its weight felt like company to Owen. Even with the urn under his arm he was glad to be there amongst the hills. Owen walked alongside a dry stone wall. There were a few puddles on the gravel path. Tough grass poked out through the cracks between the stones in the wall. Hailey had walked ahead of Owen when they had visited the stone circle. He had been there to keep her happy, as he was now.

The stones were in a wide circle but were of modest size. The tallest were not much more than waist height. The rest were heavy stone lumps lying flat on the ground. Because of Hailey, this stone circle was not the first he had seen. Each time Owen visited a stone circle he felt that the stones looked like they had either been presented for inspection or were waiting for the arrival of the visitors. Owen stopped at the part of the wall which was level with the middle of the stone circle. He felt a few drops of rain on his face. To his left and beyond the edge of the field that had the stone circle there was a farmhouse and a barn. Outside the front door to the house there was a Honda four-wheel drive. The car was stained with mud and an odd dry red dust. The farmhouse had white walls that had grubby edges and corners. White sheep loaded with wool stopped eating the grass and stared. The door to the farmhouse opened, and a man and a Collie dog appeared. The Collie ran ahead of the man and towards the sheep but the man then shouted something and the dog steered away from the sheep and towards the wall at the side of the field. Owen remained behind the wall. The farmer walked towards Owen and crossed the field that had the stone circle. The farmer avoided walking near the stones. Owen rested the urn on top of the stone wall and waited.

The farmer stopped opposite Owen and on the other side of the wall. The farmer wore a heavy tweed jacket and a thick woollen pullover that hung over his stomach and inches away from his waist. His trousers were baggy and had huge pockets on the thighs. His clothes were well-worn and stained. The farmer removed his flat cap and adjusted the rolled newspaper that lined the rim of the cap. The farmer had thinning black hair, a sharp nose and a round red face. The Collie continued to sniff the grass by the stone wall.

'Not much of a day,' said the farmer.

'I've seen better,' said Owen.

'Are you after seeing me?'

'No.'

'I didn't think you were.'

Owen looked down at the urn. The farmer did the same.

'I'm not out walking,' said Owen.

'You're not supposed to be,' said the farmer. 'The stones are on private land.'

'I know that.'

The man nodded his head. He looked down at the urn.

'It's an urn,' said Owen.

'This is private land,' said the farmer.

'No harm in throwing ashes over the wall.'

'Not seen that happen before.'

'It was what my wife wanted.'

'You'd be best going to Castlerigg.'

'That'd be too convenient.'

The farmer laughed.

'She couldn't have been too old,' he said.

'Two years younger than me,' said Owen.

The farmer waited and studied the face of Owen for clues about the age of the dead woman. The Collie ran towards the stone circle. The farmer shouted, and the dog returned to the wall. The Collie used the wall to help him stand on two legs and face Owen. His front paws rested against the wall. Owen stroked the top of the head of the Collie.

'I'm thirty-eight,' said Owen.

'Bloody hell,' said the farmer.

'An accident. She slipped and fell and banged her head against the bath. The inquest is next week.'

'You never know what's round the corner.'

'No. I'm not going to take my time about this. I was going to empty the ashes, watch the wind blow them away and bugger off.'

'Take your time about it, lad.'

The farmer walked along the wall to a gate that had metal bars. The gate led to his drive and the field. The farmer opened the gate. Owen lifted the urn off the stone wall and followed the farmer.

'You won't do too much harm on your own,' said the farmer. 'I had hippies here having picnics and Christ knows what. I had to put a stop to it.'

The two men and the Collie stood in the field. The three of them maintained the required social distance.

'Have you got kids?' said the farmer.

'We left it a bit late,' said Owen.

'It's a blessing. I thought about kids but I reckon I'm better off with the sheep. I'll make you a cup of tea if you want.'

'I'll have to get back to Liverpool.'

The farmer nodded his head up and down and thought.

'I'd shake your hand if I could,' said Owen.

'I don't expect that,' said the farmer. 'I'm not married anymore. My wife had enough of all this. She went down to Preston.'

'The big city and excitement.'

'Not so much. She got fed up of the mud, the oil, the grease and all the shite. She said she never felt clean.'

'Just as well as it doesn't rain much.'

The two men laughed.

'Take your time,' said the farmer. 'If the dog pesters you, give him a kick.'

The Collie barked but followed the farmer to his house. Before he went inside his house the farmer waved a hand.

Owen walked towards the stone circle and stopped by one of the larger stones. He opened the urn and threw the ashes as far as he could. The ashes landed on the ground in the middle of the stones but did not reach the centre of the circle. Owen stared at the small lumps of cinder lying flat on the green grass. The damp wind tickled the back of his neck. He remembered the man that was sitting alone in his red BMW saloon and outside the crematorium. The image of this man was as clear as a photograph. Owen remembered a face that had a wide mouth and a long nose. The eyebrows, he now remembered, were thick and curved. The man had dark brown hair brushed back. The face was fashionable rather than handsome. Even without a smile the man had been confident. To stop thinking about the man Owen had seen at the funeral he stared at the urn. He put the lid back on the urn and sighed.

'Sorry, Hailey,' said Owen.

Sorry for what, he was not sure.

Owen returned to the Volvo. Rain fell on the window, and he turned on the windscreen wipers. The raindrops disappeared from the window. Owen remembered the promises that Hailey and Owen had made to each other when they were young.

# NINE

'You're right,' said Rhys.

'You didn't have to pop over,' said Owen.

'Mother said you wanted to see me.'

'Not quite. I said I might give you a ring.'

'Well, I'm here.'

'I had decided against.'

'You've sorted it?'

'No, just couldn't be bothered seeing you.'

Rhys and Owen were standing alongside a wall in the living room. Beyond the head of Rhys was the small bay window that faced the street. Rhys flicked the light switch. They were close to the door that connected the narrow hall to the living room. The door was opposite the gas fire. Owen leaned his hand on the radiator next to the door.

'There's no noise at all,' said Rhys.

'I know,' said Owen.

'I've got my toolbox in the car.'

'I'm not switching off the electricity.'

'Don't you want me to have a look?'

'I don't want to have to reset all the timers. The electricity works. I'm not going to get a shock.'

'It's a mystery.'

'Not a compelling one.'

'Not yet.'

Owen was not sure why but the playful prediction of Rhys disturbed him.

'It's all the light switches that don't make a noise,' said Owen.

'That doesn't make sense,' said Rhys.

Owen flicked the light switch back and forth. The living room light appeared and disappeared but there was no noise.

'That doesn't make sense,' said Rhys.

'So you've said,' said Owen.

'You're taking a chance, Owen, not looking.'

'It's not an electrical fault.'

'I should look.'

Owen stared at the light switch.

'I'd feel better if I looked at it,' said Rhys.

The two men stared at the light switch.

'I don't want to tell Mother we couldn't be bothered looking at it,' said Rhys.

Owen said nothing.

'She'll have a cob on, Owen.'

Rhys took another look at the light switch.

'Go get your toolbox,' said Owen. 'I'll switch off the electricity.'

What I do for my family, thought Owen.

Rhys opened the living room door and stepped into the hall. Owen followed him and walked towards the fuse box. At the front door Rhys turned his head.

'You haven't asked about Will,' he said.

'What's happened?' said Owen.

'Nothing, he's fine.'

Rhys stepped outside and collected his toolbox from the boot of his Mercedes. Owen was not sure why but Rhys looked inside all the light switches. Without the covers on the light switches the clicks could be heard. Rhys and Owen replaced the covers. The light switches did not make a noise.

'No way does that make sense,' said Rhys.

'I'm not worrying about it,' said Owen.

Rhys scratched his head.

'This will nag me,' he said.

'I don't want you to lose sleep over this,' said Owen.

'I mean if it were just the one it'd be different.'

'Let it go, Rhys.'

'I'll send an electrician.'

'No.'

'This could go on YouTube.'

'I don't think so.'

Rhys took his iPhone out of his trouser pocket.

'I'll Google it,' he said.

'You can have a glass of wine,' said Owen.

'Are you having one?'

'If you are.'

'Can I still Google it?'

'I'll get you the wine. No obligations, Rhys. You don't have to talk to me.'

Because it was Rhys and Owen did not want him sneering with Will about what he bought, Owen opened a decent bottle of wine. The two men sat down and drank wine.

'This is not bad,' said Rhys.

One of his hands held the glass. His other hand held his iPhone. Outside the front window the day was dry and resting. A car entered the cul-de-sac and parked opposite a house that belonged to a neighbour that Owen most of the time ignored.

'There's nothing on Google about light switches that don't make a noise,' said Rhys.

'I didn't think there would be,' said Owen.

'It's got me baffled.'

'Let it go.'

'I'll ask around.'

'If you have to.'

'Mother is going to ask.'

'Tell Mam we fixed it.'

'I wonder if we should get an electrician in, get a health and safety check done.'

Owen grinned.

'I don't know why you think this is funny.'

'Rhys, you're making a fuss.'

'Mother would want a check done.'

'Mam isn't living here. Tell her we fixed it.'

'She'll know we haven't.'

'Tell her it's been checked.'

'I don't like telling her lies.'

'First I've heard of it.'

'Will is going to quiz me about this.'

'He doesn't live here either.'

Rhys sipped his wine. He stared at the wine that was left in his glass and thought about what he was drinking. Owen wondered about how much of his life Rhys spent thinking about the wine that passed through his throat.

'Take the bottle home with you,' said Owen.

'Are you sure?' said Rhys.

'I don't want you going home drunk to Will. We've drunk plenty of the stuff at your house.'

'If the wine reminds you of Hailey.'

'It reminds me of something.'

'Will and me need to cut back on the drinking.'

'Mam said so.'

'I bet you encourage her to think the worst.'

'I don't intend to.'

'I'm not an alcoholic, Owen.'

'I don't think you are. You just like the good things in life.'

'Will wants to have a dry month.'

'That shouldn't be too difficult with lockdown.'

'I'm not so sure.'

Rhys stared at the iPhone in his hand. He sipped his wine and looked around the small living room.

'I still don't understand why you didn't move,' said Rhys.

Owen sipped his wine.

'You and Hailey had the money.'

'I'm glad I didn't now.'

'But the two of you, Owen.'

Rhys sipped some wine.

'Mam and Dad were always moving from one house to another,' said Owen.

'As soon as they had one, Mam wanted another,' said Rhys.

He laughed.

'She survived my dad by gritting her teeth,' said Owen, 'and convincing herself that there was always another house that would solve the problems. It never did. That may have affected me. I'm living in a fashionable suburb and in a quiet cul-de-sac. What is there to want?'

'A bigger house.'

Owen said nothing.

'More space.'

'I don't know, Rhys. Something made me reluctant to buy another house.'

'With the mortgage you could have got.'

'We would have moved at some point. But I didn't look forward to it.'

'I admired Hailey for putting up with it.'

'I know. She had some good points.'

'Dad was proud we had good jobs.'

'He needed us to have good jobs. You should have been straight with Dad.'

'If Mother had said, I would have.'

'I feel sorry for the women you kidded. Bringing them home just to convince Dad.'

'It's complicated growing up. I thought how I was might wear off.'

'If the women hadn't been so gorgeous, Rhys. I never got off with women that looked like that.'

'I wasn't that desperate with girls. I didn't get anxious. The boys weren't as pretty as the girls.'

'Some of them have been.'

The two men laughed.

Owen nodded and poured more wine.

'Why didn't you ask about Will?' said Rhys.

'Hailey has died,' said Owen. 'I scattered her ashes yesterday. I'm not thinking about Will.'

'You could have asked.'

'Is everything alright?'

'I hope so.'

'Hope?'

'Think so. Will is going for a promotion interview. I hope he gets it. I don't want him to feel he's a kept man.'

'Tell him I'll be keeping my fingers crossed for him.'

Rhys sipped more wine. He looked around the living room. There was the usual, a sofa, an armchair and a television. A couple of plants filled out the corners next to the window. A small desk was pushed into a corner on the wall opposite the window. On the desk was a keyboard, a monitor and a remote terminal that was linked to the server at work. The headset that Hailey used before she died rested on the keyboard. Because of his managerial role at the company, Owen was expected to survive through using the laptop.

'Will likes this house,' said Rhys. 'He thinks it's cosy.'

'You know how to keep him happy then,' said Owen.

'I don't think so. You need to go through all Hailey's stuff.'

'Not yet.'

'You'll have to, Owen.'

'I'm aware of that.'

'It'll get creepy if you just leave it around.'

'I know.'

Owen thought about the man that he saw in the car park outside the crematorium. Owen had the Chrome password that Hailey used. I didn't start all this, thought Owen. He told himself that he was entitled to have a peep at what was in her emails.

'This thing with the light switches,' said Rhys. 'That gives me the creeps.'

'I've long given up trying to understand electricity,' said Owen.

'It's odd. Like the switches have been waiting for Hailey to die.'

'What are you trying to say, Rhys?'

'Fuck knows.'

Owen finished the wine in his glass. He put the cork back in the bottle. Rhys and Owen said goodbye. Rhys took the half used bottle of wine. Owen found the Samsung smartphone and Apple laptop that Hailey used and put them on a cushion on the sofa. They were ready to be inspected.

# TEN

In the middle of the black screen on his smartphone the white numbers said it was two in the morning. Owen stared at the ceiling. The room was not as dark as the screen on the phone. Owen touched the top of his left hand with the fingers on his right. His hand was cold, and his knuckles felt sharp. From somewhere there was a noise that sounded like a strong wind. Rather than from outside the noise sounded like it was in the living room downstairs. Owen remained cold but his hearing adjusted to the noise. The noise of the wind was like loud asthmatic breaths that had echoes. He heard something crash. Owen touched the tip of his nose. He was as cold as when he had the flu. Because the duvet on the bed was as cold as his knuckles, he jumped out of the bed. Owen was curious about what was happening downstairs but he did not want to encounter an intruder. He dressed in his clothes from yesterday and remembered the words of the farmer when he complained about the struggle of his wife to stay clean. There was another loud bang from downstairs. The noise of the wind changed into a final sigh and stopped. Dressed but still cold, Owen sat on the edge of the bed. He heard more crashes. He was too restless to stay still. Whatever is happening this is going to cost me a fortune, thought Owen. He walked over to the bedroom window, opened the curtains and looked outside. There was no moon, and the night was dark but warm and still. Owen let the bedroom curtains rest where they were and he switched on the light. The noise of whatever wind he heard had ceased. The bedroom no longer felt quite so cold. There was, though, a strange unpleasant and musty smell, something like bad beer but more powerful. An active brewery would smell like this bedroom, thought Owen. He tried to remember how much wine he had drunk after Rhys had left. He touched his hands and nose. The ice cold feeling had disappeared. Owen had heard no one move around the house or leave. Everything was silent. He looked at the time on the dark screen of the smartphone and counted a couple of minutes. Owen walked downstairs and into the living room. He wished he had a weapon.

The living room was a mess. The sofa and armchair were where they should be but the walls had several scars, and the plaster under the wallpaper was chipped in places. One of the curtains had come loose from the rail. The plants in the corners at the side of the bay window had toppled to the floor. The screen on the television and a pane in the front window were both cracked. The Apple laptop and smartphone that belonged to Hailey and that Owen had left on the sofa ready to inspect in the morning had been thrown against the wall more than once. So it seemed. The force with which the laptop had been thrown against the wall had made a hole in the plaster. A corner of the laptop was buckled. The gash in the wall was an inch deep and the same size as the end of his thumb. Owen ran his finger along the groove. The scratches and dents in the laptop were new. The laptop looked like something that had suffered a sustained attack. He opened the lid of the laptop and tried to make it work but there was nothing but bizarre programming code. Owen threw the laptop onto the sofa and looked at the cracked screen on the television. The TV remote was on the mantelpiece above the gas fire and where he had left it.

Owen switched on the television. Behind the cracked glass of the TV screen the American newsreader looked more distraught than normal. The newsreader was talking about the possible impeachment of President Trump. The message on the bottom of the screen quoted the number of Americans that had died because of Covid. Owen stood in the middle of the wreckage and wasted a couple of minutes watching television. A well-groomed and assured woman talked about something other than what had happened to the living room. Owen felt his hands and face and was glad to be warm. Without switching off the television he inspected the damage to the room. The workstation that had been set up in the corner of the room for Hailey to work at home was untouched. Owen assumed the damage had been caused by the laptop and phone of Hailey being hurled around the room. The headset from work was where it had been left by Hailey. There were a couple of scratches on the monitor. Something had collided with almost everything else in the living room. Owen switched off the television and searched the room.

The mobile phone that belonged to Hailey was lying on the floor, close to the skirting board and a fallen plant and on top of the curtain that was hanging loose from the broken rail. The mobile phone was as battered as the laptop. Nothing else in the room, though, had been moved. Second time around the room Owen noticed that the doors were also scarred like the walls. He sat down on the sofa. His brain acknowledged the damage and what was a mystery but he thought more about the cost of the repairs and having to make a claim from the insurance company. Owen did not think about what might or might not have disappeared. Despite how it sounded the strange wind must have been outside the house. And the cold and smell must have happened because he was tense and nervous. Although Owen was warm he switched on the gas fire. He used the display option that provided no heat. The low flames kept him company. He returned to the bedroom to collect his mobile phone. He remembered that Detective Sergeant Jones had left him a contact card, so he put her telephone number in his mobile. Owen rang the police but not Detective Sergeant Jones. Inside the bedroom he switched on the light. The switch that turned on the light made a familiar click.

# ELEVEN

'I hope you don't mind me poking my nose in,' said Detective Sergeant Jones.

She walked around the room and looked at the damage. Owen showed her the battered laptop and smartphone.

'I wasn't sure if I should,' she said. 'You're on file, and the visit here of PC Richards popped up as a reference. I was curious.'

The mother of Owen was sitting on the edge of the sofa and dressed in her routine outfit, the jeans and a smock shirt that made her look like an ageing artist. Maybe I should buy her some paintbrushes, thought Owen. Detective Sergeant Jones put a finger in one of the gashes in the wall and smiled at his mother. The head of his mother tilted, and her eyebrows rose but the mother of Owen said nothing. She stared through the bay window and looked like someone looking at a foreign land.

'Perhaps we can talk in the kitchen,' said Detective Sergeant Jones, 'leave your mother in peace.'

'I baked the cake on the kitchen table,' said his mother. 'I baked it for Owen but it'll go down better if you have a slice with him.'

Detective Sergeant Jones smiled at the mother of Owen and said thank you.

His mother looked pleased.

Detective Sergeant Jones and Owen walked into the kitchen. Neither of them was wearing a Covid mask. Owen made three cups of coffee. He cut three slices of cake, gave one to Detective Sergeant Jones, cut a thick piece for himself and took coffee and cake to his mother in the living room. Owen switched on the television.

His mother stared at the image behind the cracked TV screen and said, 'Jesus Christ.'

Owen put a finger to his lips. His mother shook her head.

Inside the kitchen Owen stood against the wall that was

opposite where Detective Sergeant Jones stood. The window and the door to the small narrow backyard were in the adjacent wall. He could not hear any noise from the television. He suspected his mother might be talking on the phone to Rhys.

'My mother never baked a thing while my father was alive,' said Owen.

'I'm supposed to be off cakes,' said Detective Sergeant Jones.

'Sling it if you want.'

'I wouldn't do that, Owen.'

He was surprised she had used his name. Owen and Detective Jones were silent. He listened to what might be happening in the living room. He was convinced his mother was speaking to someone. He should have given her the benefit of the doubt but he did not.

'I was going to call you anyway,' said Detective Sergeant Jones. 'The inquest for Hailey is in a couple of days. You needed to know. When I heard about this happening I thought I'd pop round.'

Owen nodded his head in appreciation, and Detective Sergeant Jones smiled. Without the Covid masks on their faces and with them sharing the cake his mother had baked everything felt different. Detective Sergeant Jones was as pretty as he had imagined. Her straight nose, wide mouth and cheekbones were as impressive as her brown eyes. She was taller than he remembered.

'I've ordered a new TV and a bloke is coming round tomorrow to fix the windows,' said Owen. 'I'm going to have a go at the walls and the doors at the weekend.'

'You're handy?' said Detective Sergeant Jones.

'Not at all. A bit of paint on the doors and some Polyfilla on the walls. It'll have to do.'

'I can't see how they got in the house. You like your locked room mysteries, Owen.'

'You think I shouldn't have called the police?'

'I'm glad you did.'

Detective Sergeant Jones smiled. They looked at one another.

Owen was the first to look away. He stared at the dining table and what was left of the ginger cake that his mother had baked.

'You can have some more cake,' said Owen.

'Definitely not,' said Detective Sergeant Jones.

They both smiled.

Owen lowered his voice and said, 'I shouldn't have told my mother what happened. She just has to come and have a look.'

'She cares about you,' said Detective Sergeant Jones. 'I see some right mothers.'

'My dad used to call me a mother's boy.'

'No harm in that.'

'It was a load of nonsense. My dad and me were not the same.'

Detective Sergeant Jones smiled.

She was curious.

'He was more like Rhys,' said Owen, 'which was funny considering how my brother turned out. My father was an enthusiast, and so is Rhys. My mother doted on Rhys, probably because he never stopped grinning.'

Detective Sergeant Jones tilted her head and waited for more information.

'Mam was pleased that she had a son that could keep her husband happy. Someone had to. She wasn't going to do anything to harm that.'

Eating her slice of ginger cake, Detective Sergeant Jones had looked like someone who could break the heart of a man. Even her teeth were impressive, thought Owen.

'If it had been me,' said Owen, 'my mother would not have been so liberal. My father would have given Rhys a belt if he'd known. Dad died a year ago. He had lung cancer, smoked all his life.'

'I'm sorry,' said Detective Sergeant Jones.

'It happens.'

Neither Detective Jones nor Owen were slouched. Their eyes were almost level.

'I don't think the burglars came upstairs,' said Owen.

'They could have woken you up going downstairs,' said Detective Sergeant Jones.

'Nothing downstairs has been pinched. I haven't done a proper search upstairs. I haven't seen anything missing so far.'

Detective Sergeant Jones nodded her head.

'I hope you're lucky,' she said.

Owen waited. There were no smiles this time.

On the other side of the wide kitchen window a seagull flew somewhere.

'I just can't see how they got in,' said Detective Sergeant Jones.

She looked out of the kitchen window and into the narrow backyard. The houses at the back of the house were large and tall and they faced the River Mersey or what was left of it before it became the Irish Sea. A narrow road separated the back of where Owen lived from the houses that faced the sea. None of this was visible from the kitchen window but sometimes the seagulls strayed close to the house.

'I'm not this near the sea,' said Detective Sergeant Jones. 'I live near the village.'

'Formby.'

'That's right. You remembered.'

Owen was tempted to tell her about how cold he had been when he awoke, the strange smell and noise. He was more than tempted. And this was not because he believed that what he remembered had significance. What happened inside his bedroom felt inconsequential a day later.

'If I could help with this I would,' said Detective Sergeant Jones.

'I'll sling the laptop and the phone,' said Owen. 'They're hardly mementos. The house is soon fixed. The worst bit is hanging the curtain. I hate that.'

Detective Sergeant Jones thought this through, and Owen waited.

'I can pop round with the coroner's report,' she said. 'I can see if you've made a decent job of the curtain.'

'My mother will be keen to have it hanged before she sleeps,' said Owen.

Detective Sergeant Jones frowned like someone who had been offended.

'I don't have to pop round with the coroner's report,' said Detective Sergeant Jones.

'I've never seen one,' said Owen. 'It would help. You coming round gives me an excuse to finish this cake.'

Detective Sergeant Jones looked at Owen, smiled and shook her head.

'I'd have liked to have had a forensic team in here to work out just how they got in. But I can't justify that for a burglary where not much has been taken. I'm curious, though.'

'Must have been professionals.'

'That wouldn't make any difference.'

Detective Sergeant Jones put her empty cup down on the dining table. She looked out of the kitchen window.

'I wish I'd bought a house by the coast,' she said.

'If it's a nice day,' said Owen, 'we can walk by the beach and you can tell me what the coroner has said.'

'Why not? That would be nice.'

Neither of them risked a smile. Owen followed Detective Sergeant Jones into the living room. His mother left the sofa and stood. They all stared at the cracked television.

'I'm looking forward to getting a new one,' said Owen.

'If you do have more information,' said Detective Sergeant Jones, 'about things they've stolen or how they got in, you'll have to report it to PC Richards. I'm curious but you'll have to tell her.'

'His brother's an architect,' said his mother. 'He'll know about locks and things. I've asked him to pop round.'

Detective Sergeant Jones smiled at Owen. He reckoned the smile was sympathetic.

# TWELVE

Rhys stood next to the small bay window. His mother was sitting on the sofa and in the same place where she had been when Detective Sergeant Jones had visited. Owen watched Rhys examine the bay window. Thanks to his mother the curtain was back on the rail.

'I haven't a clue how they got in,' said Rhys.

'You're as good with locks as you are light switches,' said Owen.

Rhys shrugged his shoulders and walked away from the bay window.

He knows fuck all, thought Owen.

Rhys tried the light switch.

'You fixed it,' he said. 'How'd you manage that?'

'It's complicated,' said Owen.

He paused and enjoyed the moment.

His mother was disappointed but resigned. Rhys sat down next to his mother. They build statues that look like this, thought Owen.

'Will said his interview went okay,' said Rhys. 'He finds out tomorrow. In case anyone is interested.'

'I hope he gets it,' said his mother.

'I do too,' said Owen.

'Will you put up his rent if he does?' said his mother.

'He's not a lodger, mother,' said Rhys.

'I hope he pays his way.'

'Of course he pays his way.'

His mother had a silly grin on her face. Her body rested on the edge of the sofa. Her body had been in this position most of the afternoon. Her knees were pressed together.

'We had a visitor today, Rhys,' she said. 'Nice looking girl.'

'Oh yes,' said Rhys.

'Detective Jones,' said Owen.

'What's this got to do with her?' said Rhys.

Owen waited but not for long. His mother knocked Rhys with her elbow and grinned.

'Our Owen has got an admirer,' she said.

'It's a police matter,' said Owen.

'She likes Owen,' said his mother.

'I spotted that,' said Rhys.

'She's a police detective,' said Owen. 'I've had a burglary. Leave off.'

'She was poking her nose in,' said his mother. 'You want to see the way she looks at him. Your dad always said you should have been a policeman, Owen.'

'I didn't know that,' said Rhys.

'Well, there's a surprise,' said Owen.

'He said the one thing Owen could always do,' said his mother, 'was upset people.'

His mother and Rhys thought this was hilarious. Rhys leaned back into the sofa and stretched his legs past the knees of his mother.

'Owen doesn't upset this policewoman,' said his mother.

Although his mother and Rhys shared the sofa Owen stayed standing and next to the television. He was not sure why but he felt protective of the damaged creature.

'The detective used to be a schoolteacher,' said Owen.

His mother and Rhys looked at one another and grinned.

'She sees something,' said his mother.

'Some women aren't interested in looks,' said Rhys.

He thought this was funny but his mother did not laugh.

'Owen is not plain,' said his mother. 'I was proud of you both at the funeral. I have two handsome sons.'

Rhys and Owen rested and let the compliment land.

'Owen fixed those light switches,' said Rhys.

Owen knew how the brain of Rhys worked. Rhys was trying to maintain the mood. Hailey had said more than once that Owen, unlike his brother, let compliments fall off a cliff. His dad reckoned

Rhys had enthusiasm. This was true but Rhys was also calculating, thought Owen. His father believed Rhys was someone who could get things done. His father, though, worried about Owen. His mother told Owen that his father resented having to worry.

'I didn't do anything,' said Owen, 'the switches came back on.'

His mother and Rhys looked up at Owen as if he had something to say. He was not going to mention what happened in his bedroom. The chaos that wrecked the living room would be sufficient.

'The new television arrives tomorrow,' said Owen.

'Get it set up and you can invite the Detective round,' said Rhys. His mother chuckled.

'It's a bit soon after Hailey but I won't say anything,' said Rhys.

The expression on the face of his mother hardened.

'Let's show some respect,' she said.

'You're right, Mam,' said Owen. 'It is too soon.'

There was something in the remark that caused Rhys to ponder. Owen assumed that Rhys was thinking about the friction that had existed between Hailey and Owen.

'I like setting up new televisions,' said Owen.

'You hardly watch them,' said Rhys.

'That's not the point. I like having one. I just don't like soap operas and football.'

'It might have been different if you had,' said his mother.

'Hailey didn't like football either,' said Owen.

'You know what I'm talking about.'

'Rhys was good at football. That kept Dad happy. Mam, he wouldn't have believed Rhys if he had told him he was gay. He'd have been looking for girlfriends for Rhys.'

Owen grinned, and his mother pouted.

'I was glad it wasn't you that was gay,' said his mother.

'She doesn't think I'm pretty enough,' said Owen.

'See, Rhys, how Owen has to twist it. Rhys, you got round your dad by not saying anything. If it had been Owen, he'd have stormed out the house as soon as he'd found out.'

'Found out?' said Rhys.

'You know what I mean, Rhys. We'd never have seen Owen again.'

Owen left the television to look after itself and sat down in the armchair. Behind him the cul-de-sac was quiet like normal. He considered how he might have reacted to his father if the circumstances had been different, if Owen and not Rhys had been the gay son. Owen reckoned that his father would have soon told him to sod off. The first time his father met Hailey, and after a couple of pints in the local pub, he told her that he didn't know what she saw in Owen. In the early days his father thought Hailey was wonderful. Later he was not so impressed. In an odd way that helped him be less critical of Owen.

'I've ordered a TV with a bigger screen,' said Owen. 'If I only watch the odd movie, why not?'

'In this living room,' said his mother.

'What the hell. The more company the better.'

# THIRTEEN

The new TV arrived the next day, and Owen was able, thanks to his mother, to close the curtains when he needed to watch it. He took a final look at the new and more expensive television before he started lunch. Owen made French onion soup and cut a thick slice from a loaf of sourdough bread. He put on a plate what was left of the ginger cake that his mother had baked. While the soup was simmering the phone rang. His boss mentioned a Zoom meeting the next day. Owen told her how he had intended to resume work the day before but because of the burglary he now wanted to leave it until tomorrow. They talked about Covid and how the usual suspects were calling in sick. They talked about other things. There were moments when Owen wondered if his boss might be missing him. She mentioned that social distancing in the canteen had been the most difficult aspect of the new Covid working arrangements. Canteens and people eating made Owen think of the soup burning to nothing in the pan. After saying goodbye to his boss he dashed into the kitchen.

The soup had not evaporated to nothing, and the saucepan was not burnt. He lifted the saucepan. The gas ring was not lit. The knobs on the cooker were switched off. There was neither a flame nor a smell of gas. He lit the ring and heated the soup. Owen made a cup of tea and sat down at the table. In an odd way this confusion affected him more than what had happened before the crashes and the damage the night before last. He was convinced that he had lit the gas ring. The slice of bread that he had cut was next to what remained of the cake. The bread and the ginger cake that he had put out to eat were now covered by a tea towel. Before he was married it was not the habit of Owen to cover food with the tea towel. The truth was that before he met Hailey he had never thought about food going stale. His casual attitude to food had annoyed Hailey.

Owen was convinced that he had put the bread and cake on a plate and left it uncovered in the middle of the table. He was confused and, despite not wanting to, he dwelled on the confusion that had happened before he had heard the crashes in the living room. Whatever was happening, and something odd had happened, Owen was glad that the soup and pan were not burnt. The food he ate steadied him but he worried about working from home, whether he would be able to concentrate and have purpose. He thought about what had happened and perhaps was happening but, because he was curious, Owen had no sense of panic. Or so he told himself. Owen picked up the phone to ring his boss and tell her that he would like to resume work tomorrow by going into the office. Owen dialled the number but when he saw it on the LCD screen he cancelled the call. In the living room he closed the curtains and switched on the new television. He watched a film that had lots of mountains, forests and lakes. There was also the occasional decapitation but you cannot have everything, thought Owen. He was halfway through the movie when the phone on the landline rang.

'You don't know me,' said the voice on the phone.

'I'm sorry,' said Owen.

'You saw me at Hailey's funeral.'

'Oh yes.'

'I work in insurance just like you.'

Owen waited.

'I'm based in Manchester. Hailey and I met in Peterborough. My name is Robert Briggs.'

Owen remembered Hailey spending a week in Peterborough on some training course that was supposed to give extra background to her work. Hailey had phoned him every night. She had enjoyed the theory and extra context but said all the people on the course were creeps. Owen had bristled at Hailey using the word context.

'We should meet,' said Briggs.

'Who said?' said Owen.

'After we met on the course I used to see Hailey.'

'Oh yes.'

Hailey came home late from the course in Peterborough. Owen remembered sitting at home and waiting. Hailey had said her car had broken down. She had arrived home flustered. Owen remembered his doubts that had appeared and disappeared.

'We kept in touch,' said Briggs.

Owen recalled the movie and the decapitations that interrupted the views of mountains and lakes. He wondered if Robert Briggs was called Bobby by his mates.

'We used to meet halfway between Liverpool and Manchester,' said Bobby Briggs.

Owen would not have wanted to be called Bobby Briggs. But then I'm not from Manchester, thought Owen.

'Thank Christ she didn't have to go to Manchester,' said Owen.

'There was a hotel in Warrington we used,' said Briggs.

'To meet?'

'More than meet.'

The news was a surprise and, although there had been moments when Owen had wondered and been suspicious, somehow the revelation shocked Owen. 79% of married couples were unfaithful, he once read. Owen remembered thinking that the high percentage quoted made infidelity feel like nothing more than the next step on the treadmill. Not the kind they used in gymnasiums, of course.

'Sounds like fun,' said Owen.

'I loved Hailey,' said Briggs.

There was silence on the telephone line. Hailey would have to find someone that loved her, thought Owen. The silence gave him time to think about Hailey acting and being inspirational to a new friend, all her characteristics that had annoyed Owen vanishing like magic. While he was thinking and picturing Hailey giving a performance he deduced Bobby Briggs was not a man of many words.

In the argument that happened the night Hailey died she had told Rhys and Will that Owen was taken in by people that said nothing and just let him talk. The remark had come from nowhere. Even Rhys and Will had looked at Hailey as if she were talking nonsense. Owen listened to the silence on the phone and realised that Hailey had been talking about herself. He imagined this bloke Briggs feeding off Hailey and her being desperate and daft enough to let him.

'You were in the car outside the crematorium?' said Owen.

'I felt I should be there,' said Briggs.

'A red BMW.'

'I didn't want to upset people.'

'You upset me.'

'I stayed in the car.'

'You don't have any choice with Covid.'

'I could have sneaked into the funeral if I'd wanted. I recognised you as soon as I saw you. Hailey would never show me photographs but I knew as soon as I saw you. She used to say you looked like a policeman.'

Owen said nothing.

'Hailey said you were handsome but not as handsome as your brother.'

It occurred to Owen that next time round he had to take a proper look in the mirror. He remembered Hailey, and his mind groped for past conversations with her that, because of Briggs, might have altered meanings. Owen remembered the final argument at the home of Rhys and Will and the look of distaste for her husband that Hailey had been willing to share with them. Owen also recalled other occasions, those moments of impatience from Hailey when he had asked where she might be going with her girlfriends.

'Hailey used to say she was meeting Alex,' said Bobby Briggs.

'I know Alex,' said Owen. 'I never liked her.'

Alex, the lying cow, thought Owen. Alex was a dope that had

a great body and lots of blonde hair. She had married well and wore a white Range Rover as jewellery. It would have been so easy to expose the lies if I had known, thought Owen, but it always is when you know the truth. He learnt that on a management training course. He wasn't banging anyone, of course. He was being loyal to Hailey. Alex and her husband came round for dinner once. It did not happen again. Bobby Briggs was quiet.

'Did you ever meet Alex?' said Owen.

'I bought her a box of chocolates a few times,' said Bobby Briggs. 'A token of appreciation for helping Hailey and I.'

Owen was aware he could not be trusted for an objective opinion but this guy on the phone sounded to him like a right drip. Before this phone call Owen had intended to give the clothes of Hailey to the local charity shop but the idea of organising her clothes into bundles that suited the charity people had made him feel queasy and he had deferred the task. His stomach turned over at the thought of having to go through her clothes and wonder what she had worn for this Bobby Briggs or even maybe had bought to impress him. Sod that and the charity shop, thought Owen. The clothes would be dumped in the bin. The poor would have to go around in rags.

'Would you like to keep Hailey's clothes?' said Owen.

Bobby Briggs was silent.

'You'll have memories.'

'I'm not sure that me having the clothes is right.'

'Banging Hailey in a hotel is what's not right.'

Owen sounded angry but there was a smile on his face. He was not sure why.

'I can take the clothes off you,' said Bobby.

'I don't think so,' said Owen.

'You've just said.'

'I was joking.'

'Funny thing to joke about.'

'You have to have a sense of humour.'

'Hailey said you could be witty when you wanted. Most of the time you were a misery, she said.'

'I can live with that. You making this phone call is funny, strange, in fact. Are you married, Mr Briggs?'

'I didn't get round to it.'

What was that supposed to mean, thought Owen.

'Hailey being dead is doing my head in,' said Briggs. 'I have to talk to someone.'

'Wanking doesn't help then,' said Owen.

'Are you being funny again?'

'I'm not being sympathetic, Mr Briggs.'

'I wasn't sympathetic when Hailey talked about you.'

'How often did you meet?'

'Once a month.'

'You wouldn't have had much chance to talk.'

'This isn't the way to talk now,' said Bobby Briggs.

Owen said nothing.

The battered laptop and smartphone that Hailey owned were still in the living room and under the new television where Owen had left them. They were wrecked but he had the passwords to her Google accounts. The cow was not going to get away with this, thought Owen.

'I'm coming to see you,' said Bobby Briggs.

'I don't think so,' said Owen.

'I know where you live.'

'I'd rather you didn't.'

Owen stared at the silenced laptop and smartphone.

'I have to, Owen,' said Briggs.

Owen did not like being called Owen. He hoped that Briggs did not want to become friends.

'Don't call me Owen,' said Owen. 'You've been watching the wrong kind of movies.'

'I'm coming to see you,' said Briggs. 'I know your house.'

'I see.'

Not just Hailey had been away on training courses. Owen had been on a few himself. He imagined this bloke sitting in the living room and listening to Hailey talking on the phone to her husband.

'There's things I need to know,' said Bobby Briggs. 'This is driving me crazy.'

'How tall are you?' said Owen.

'I don't see why that's important.'

'It is if I give you a smack in the gob.'

Owen pressed the end button on the telephone. His stomach turned over. The phone rang again. Owen ignored it and put the phone back on its handle. Let it ring and let him come.

# FOURTEEN

After the phone call from Bobby Briggs had ended Owen was too unsettled to read a book or to watch anything on the television. He attempted to listen to some music but his mind wandered, and he returned to the new television. Owen played around with the settings and compared alternative colours, tints, contrasts and the rest. This could only be done so many times. Owen lifted the phone from its handle and dialled a number.

'Will,' said Owen.

Will had said nothing but Owen knew it was not Rhys.

'Any news about the job?' said Owen.

'I got it,' said Will.

'I'm really pleased, really.'

The truth is that Owen was pleased. Will was his brother-in-law, well kind of, and, after the strange phone call from before, hearing the news felt like progress. Having someone succeed in the family helped him feel resilient. Owen let Will talk about his new job and what it meant. Owen did not listen to the details but the optimistic words of Will sounded like music to Owen, the kind of thing that people sing underneath flags. Owen knew he was being fanciful but this was a day when some whimsy might help.

'I'm really pleased, Will,' said Owen. 'We should celebrate.'

'Somehow,' said Will. 'Johnson has been on the telly. The Covid deaths have increased. They're going to tighten the restrictions.'

'We'll celebrate your success tomorrow. Is Rhys there?'

Owen offered another congratulation, and Will walked away to find Rhys. The time between Owen talking to friendly Bobby Briggs and phoning Rhys had not been long but sufficient for Owen to decide against digging around Google for dirt on Hailey. He would not honour her with memory or discovery. Some people you begrudged posterity. Hailey was top of that list.

I must be a bitter man, thought Owen.

'Owen, are you there?' said Rhys.

'Sorry, I was thinking,' said Owen.

'Good news about Will.'

'I'm pleased.'

'I'm really pleased.'

It occurred to Owen that his idiot brother would think the promotion would have significance for his relationship with Will. Owen hoped it did not mean loads of training courses for Will, the civil servant partner. 79% of married couples committed adultery, and people celebrated promotions and improved opportunities. Oh dear, thought Owen. He was definitely not going to search around Google for details of what his wife had been doing with a bloke called Bobby Briggs. Hailey and I, had said Briggs. Hailey and I indeed.

'We should celebrate Will being promoted,' said Owen.

'If we get the chance,' said Rhys.

'We can do it tomorrow.'

Owen was not sure why but the idea of celebrating the promotion of Will and the prospect of having more Covid lockdown rules made him anxious. He was relieved that he had cancelled his call and then abandoned the idea of going into the office.

'I've had a weird phone call,' said Owen.

Rhys waited.

'Some bloke has been on saying he was knocking off Hailey.'

Rhys said nothing.

'He said he's coming round to the house.'

'You want Will and me to pop round?'

'No. You and Will enjoy the good news.'

'We can pop round. Might be the last chance we get.'

'No, I'll pop round your house tomorrow. I'll bring a bottle of wine.'

'Are you all right, Owen?'

'I thought she'd have more respect for me than that.'

'We'll come round.'

'I'm all right. I'm pleased Will has got the promotion. Rhys, I'd never have left Hailey. I thought about it but I wouldn't have. I'll be fine.'

This was true. He wouldn't have walked out. Owen had been more than amenable, though, to the idea of her leaving. Owen remembered how much.

'Come round tomorrow, Owen. These things can hit you later. Don't bring any wine. I've got plenty. I don't like the idea of this bloke turning up at your house.'

'The chap sounds distraught. The woman he loved has died.'

'Fuck him, Owen. What a mess. He knows where you live?'

'He's shagged Hailey here.'

'That's not right, Owen.'

'He's from Manchester.'

'He's not from Manchester?'

'I'm afraid so. Hailey has scraped the barrel with this one.'

The two men laughed.

'I wouldn't let him in the house,' said Rhys.

'I don't want some bloke from Manchester on the doorstep screaming obscenities,' said Owen.

The two men laughed.

'Aren't you worried?' said Rhys.

'He works in an office and is not very big,' said Owen. 'He's not going to throw his weight about. He was at the funeral, waiting in his car.'

'I saw that bloke.'

'There you go.'

'I wouldn't say he was small, Owen.'

'I'm not worried. If he does anything, I'll tell Detective Jones.'

Owen and Rhys laughed. Owen imagined Will half listening and thinking that Rhys and Owen were in a good mood because they were talking about the promotion of Will.

'Rhys,' said Owen, 'Hailey was having an affair.'

Rhys said nothing.

'Was I the last to know?'

'She didn't tell me she was. Hailey wondered about you.'

'That I was having an affair?'

'Hailey asked if I thought you loved her. I told her that you were mad about her. You don't think someone asking that is up to something. She said her marriage was really important to her. She said all that not so long ago.'

Owen remembered discovering the gas ring being switched off and the bread and ginger cake covered by the tea towel.

'This bloke is called Bobby Briggs.'

'Sounds like a Northern comedian.'

Owen imagined Briggs in a flat cap and telling jokes in a broad Lancashire accent.

'Rhys, I'd better let you go,' said Owen. 'Will and you have stuff to celebrate.'

'He'll understand. Owen, are you sure you're alright?'

Owen did not say what was obvious, that discovering the betrayal by Hailey would have been a lot more difficult to take if she was alive.

'I'm worried about this bloke coming round,' said Rhys.

'I'll be fine,' said Owen. 'He's a bloke that works in an office.'

'You work in an office.'

'I'll put him in his place.'

'I've no doubt you'll find the right words.'

Owen and Rhys laughed.

'I'll see you tomorrow,' said Owen. 'Don't tell Will about Hailey. I won't mention it tomorrow. We'll celebrate his promotion. I'm really pleased for Will.'

'He'll be pleased you're pleased.'

Owen put the phone down. After the phone call he was wounded in a way that he had not been before, like someone that has just had the bandages applied to a wound and realises the extent of his injuries.

Owen phoned his mother.

'I've been on the phone to Rhys,' he said. 'Good news about Will being promoted.'

'I'm pleased,' said his mother. 'Are you pleased?'

'Of course I'm pleased.'

Owen was more pleased than his mother would realise.

'Mam,' said Owen, 'Hailey was having an affair'

'Oh dear,' said his mother.

'A bloke from Manchester.'

'Not Manchester?'

'Manchester.'

'I'm not surprised. You didn't, did you, Owen?'

'No, Mam.'

He realised he was shaking his head.

'You should have said, Owen,' said his mother.

'I've only just found out,' he said. 'The bloke has been on the phone.'

'These dirty buggers don't have any shame.'

'The death of Hailey has upset him.'

'I hope you told him where to go.'

Owen decided not to mention the pending visit.

'Why did you suspect, Mam?' said Owen.

'I just thought she was someone planning her own life,' said his mother. 'The way she talked about buying houses. She didn't say a word about you. Your father worried about her.'

'About Hailey talking about houses?'

After Hailey had visited the estate agent she had brought home leaflets which she had shown to the parents of Owen.

'Your father knew what men are like,' said his mother. 'Men will say anything to get what they want. He thought Hailey might have her head turned. He knew she wouldn't get much flattery off you. Your dad didn't like Hailey going off on training courses.'

'I went on training courses.'

'Your dad didn't worry about women telling lies to get what

they wanted. You didn't, did you, Owen?'

'I didn't get the chance.'

'Your dad was right then. Owen, are you coping with this?'

Owen said to his mother what he had found impossible to share with Rhys, 'I feel a lot better than I would have done if she was alive. If Hailey were here, I'd want to get even.'

'Well, we can't call it a blessing,' said his mother.

'If I'd found out before she died, we'd have knocked lumps out of each other, the arguments we'd have had.'

'Thank Christ you didn't. You're bound to hurt, son.'

'It hurts but because she's dead it doesn't.'

'It will hurt from time to time, bound to, but you'll get over it. You should phone that Detective. She likes you, Owen. She sees something in you.'

'I don't think so.'

'I don't see why not.'

'You suspected Hailey. Maybe you should have said.'

'There are things you don't think about. I didn't think about you and Hailey in bed. I'm not going to think about her messing around with someone else.'

'I reckon she hated me in the end.'

'She was restless, Owen,' said his mother. 'She wanted you but to be different.'

'The bloke is called Bobby Briggs,' said Owen.

'Sounds like one of those comedians off the telly.'

'He isn't married, never has been.'

'Don't lose your temper with him, Owen?'

'No, I'll keep my mouth shut.'

'Thank Christ you and Hailey never had kids. I sometimes wish you'd never married and just lived over the brush.'

This remark from his mother shocked Owen. It qualified as a revelation.

# FIFTEEN

Owen was still not sure if he had the settings on the television as they should have been but Jason Bourne was coping well enough. On the TV a building somewhere in the Middle East exploded, and at the front of a house in a much more quiet cul-de-sac the doorbell rang. Bobby Briggs, thought Owen.

Because the living room had a bay window, Owen could see it was the man that had been waiting outside the crematorium. He was not short and he was not tall. The man was not quite as tall as Owen. The quiet cul-de-sac was crowded because of the parked cars. This man on the doorstep looked nothing like Matt Damon. He had the thick brushed back black hair Owen remembered but his hairline was receding. The face was round but the features were somehow craggy. Put a tan on his face, thought Owen, and he could have stepped out of the house that Jason Bourne had just seen explode.

Bobby Briggs was wearing an expensive full length Crombie overcoat over black slacks and a red pullover. The late autumn evening was not cold. Owen reckoned the Crombie was meant to impress him. Bobby Briggs would have stood on this doorstep more than once. And no doubt he would have worn the Crombie then. Bobby Briggs noticed Owen staring through the window. Without thinking, Owen smiled and indicated that he would open the door. Owen was wearing slacks and a shirt. There were socks on his feet but no shoes. As he stared at the Crombie overcoat, Owen felt shivers. He smelled bad beer, the same smell that had been in the bedroom while downstairs was being wrecked. Owen realised that the chill around his shoulders was not because he was staring at an expensive Crombie. He was embarrassed by the smell and he worried about what the cold promised. But he had to open the front door. Owen glanced back at the new television. He hoped that the man on the doorstep was a gentle spirit.

Owen walked into the narrow hall. The gap between the front door and the stairs to the two bedrooms was no more than a couple of steps. The hall was as cold as the living room, and the smell of bad beer reached his throat. There are better circumstances in which to meet the bloke that has been banging your missus, thought Owen. Bobby Briggs had an overcoat to keep him warm. Owen was shivering.

He opened the front door. He pulled the door right back and hoped that the air from outside would mitigate the chill and the smell inside the house. Briggs stood in the middle of the doorstep. All the cars of the neighbours appeared to be at home and parked. Outside, everything was normal.

Owen smiled at Briggs. The two men nodded their heads.

'You manage to park okay?' said Owen.

His smile was the required minimum but nothing more. The expression on the face of Bobby Briggs was grim. Jason Bourne fights with people that have friendlier faces, thought Owen. He pulled back the front door a final inch so that it touched one of the walls in the hall. He let go of the door and thought about what he might do with his hands. Owen had spent a working life saying hello and shaking hands. This made Owen think of Covid and that perhaps Bobby Briggs should have been wearing a mask.

'Are you going to invite me in?' said Bobby Briggs.

Owen folded his arms across his chest and stepped back. His cold knuckles were pressed inside his armpits. The smell of yeast was beyond that of a bad pint. He half turned to step into the living room. At some point he would have to explain, thought Owen. Behind him the front door slammed shut. Owen stopped and turned his head around. Bobby Briggs, the cul-de-sac and the parked cars had all disappeared from view. The wind and fresh air were on the other side of the closed door. Owen stepped into the hall and moved to open the front door. The lock twisted okay but when he pulled the door it stayed where it was. Owen put his right foot against the narrow strip of wall at the side of the door and pulled on the lock with both hands. The door was jammed solid in the frame. Owen tried again. Nothing happened except that Owen heard Briggs shout something. Owen walked into the living room and banged on the bay window. Briggs appeared at the window. Owen opened his arms. His knuckles were as cold as they were the night of the wreckage, and the smell inside the house was as strong as what must happen inside a brewery. Owen used his hands to indicate that he had done nothing and he was as confused as Briggs must have been. Owen mouthed the words 'go round the back'. With his hand Owen showed Briggs that he had to turn to the left and then walk around to the back of the house. The instructions were not clear but it was not difficult to walk around a row of houses. This was the man that found his way in between the legs of Hailey. Owen pointed his thumb to the right and then walked towards the kitchen. Inside the kitchen he stood by the window and waited.

The kitchen was an extension that was designed by Rhys, approved by Hailey and paid for by Owen. His memories were becoming catty which had probably something to do with meeting the lover of his wife. The kitchen was fine. It took up most of the back yard and left a narrow gap between its window and the back entry wall that was shared with the next door neighbour. The outside door to the kitchen also faced the back entry. Owen opened the door and waited. The air outside the house was much warmer than inside the kitchen and nor was there a smell of yeast. Owen stood at the top of the narrow gap in the yard and waited. The gate into the yard, like the brick wall on the right, was a couple of inches above head height. The gate opened, and Briggs walked through.

Owen smiled but there was no nod of the head from Bobby Briggs. Perhaps if Briggs had made a gesture it would have been different. Perhaps if Briggs had acted half human Owen would have waited outside to greet him. But Briggs did not, and Owen stepped back into the kitchen and stood in its doorway and next to the open kitchen door. Briggs appeared opposite the doorway and stood facing Owen. The gap in the yard was narrow, and their two heads were no more than a couple of feet apart.

'This isn't in accordance with Covid lockdown,' said Owen.

'No?' said Bobby Briggs.

'I don't think so.'

'Who knows.'

Owen turned and stepped inside the house. The kitchen door slammed forward and hit the side of his arm with enough force to push Owen to the side. The door slammed shut. The arm of Owen throbbed, and the foul smell of bad beer made him feel sick. Owen stood up straight, stepped back, rubbed his arm and imagined the bruises. He heard Briggs knocking on the door.

Owen was not sure why but the sight of the closed kitchen door made him giggle. He remembered when Hailey and Rhys had spread the architectural plan for the kitchen over the floor in the front room. Whatever is happening inside this house has nothing to do with me, thought Owen. He was a pure victim, well, almost pure.

Owen rubbed his arm and groaned a couple of times. As he attempted to clear his throat of the remains of the foul air, Owen walked to the kitchen window. Bobby Briggs stood on the other side of the window and waited.

He shook his head from side to side and disapproved.

The kitchen window had three tall panes that filled the space between the bottom and the top of the window. The pane in the middle was twice as wide as the other two. Owen leaned over the kitchen sink and tried and failed to open the side windows. Something was resisting his efforts. Owen had ideas about what might be happening but he was also determined to open the window. The ideas appeared and disappeared.

On the other side of the large window Bobby Briggs shook his head. In the expensive Crombie and standing in a narrow backyard he looked like a figure of authority that Owen had disappointed.

Bobby Briggs frowned.

'Can you hear me?' said Owen.

Bobby Briggs put a hand to his ear.

Owen rubbed his arm as he talked. His voice was louder than normal. 'I can't open the doors or windows.'

The pain in his arm had not subsided. The foul smell and cold remained but it bothered him less than his aching arm. On the other side of the kitchen window Bobby Briggs appeared to have abandoned any attempt at thought. He looked like someone that might be window shopping.

Owen had no idea what to do next. He stared at the face of Bobby Briggs and thought about the future and being out of the house. A week in a luxury hotel would not make that much difference to my savings, Owen reckoned. After that there were the spare rooms that Rhys and his mother had and which he could use when the house was put up for sale. This idea turned gloomy. Owen imagined showing a prospective buyer around the modest rooms and the smell appearing.

'Open the door,' said Bobby Briggs.

He was either shouting or making no noise and twisting his mouth so Owen could read the words. The two hands of Briggs waved around and added emphasis.

Owen shook his head.

There was a large clipboard in the kitchen that Hailey had used to note things to do. Attached to the clipboard was a ballpoint pen. Owen walked away from the window and found the clipboard and pen. He wrote something simple in large block letters. DOORS AND WINDOWS WILL NOT OPEN.

Owen placed the clipboard against the kitchen window. Bobby Briggs leaned his head forward, read the message and frowned. Owen pulled the clipboard away from the window and added more words. I WILL RING YOU.

The expression on the face of Bobby Briggs mixed confusion and resentment. Join the club, thought Owen.

There was more than one piece of paper attached to the clipboard. Owen tore away the used sheet of paper and threw it over the dishes that were drying at the side of the sink. On the next clean sheet of paper on the clipboard Owen wrote, WILL SEE YOU IN MANCHESTER TOMORROW NIGHT.

Bobby Briggs was not the quickest of readers but it was clear to Owen that this message had given Briggs some hope. Owen believed this was a good thing.

'We can't have you distraught, can we?' said Owen but not loud enough for Briggs to hear.

Owen had a sore arm, a terrible smell trapped inside his nostrils and was now sharing sarcasm with the lover of his deceased wife. Who knows what's waiting round the corner, thought Owen. He held the clipboard close to his chest and breathed.

Owen knew a restaurant in Manchester that was close to the city centre and near the Lowry Centre. Owen pulled the clipboard away from his chest and wrote the name of the restaurant and a time to meet. Owen held up the clipboard but something tried to pull it away from him. Not a pair of hands but a force trapped between the chest of Owen and the clipboard. Owen struggled and cursed but held on to the clipboard. He pressed the clipboard hard against his chest and let the ballpoint pen fall to the worktop.

On the other side of the window Briggs was curious. Owen saw Briggs raise his eyebrows and put his tongue into his cheek. Owen gripped the clipboard. Briggs remained curious but somehow looked indifferent. He looked like a man that was patient and polite.

Owen thought about this as he spun right around and slammed the clipboard against the window and held it there tight with his two hands. The force that had tried to pull the clipboard away from him now felt like a blast. His face and hands were so cold they ached. The crockery and the cutlery in the dish tray rattled. Owen kept the clipboard pressed hard against the window and gritted his teeth. The pain in his arm nagged.

Bobby Briggs read what was written on the clipboard and nodded his head. Owen let go of the clipboard and it spun past his head and slammed against a cupboard that was on the kitchen wall that was opposite the window.

Owen sighed, put two hands on the edge of the kitchen sink and recovered some breath. Bobby Briggs stared at Owen. Sympathetic Briggs was not but it did appear that he had begun to realise that something odd was happening. He mouthed three words, tomorrow and Lowry Centre. The two men stared at one another for a couple of seconds. The smell faded and the air became warmer. None of this bothered Owen because he was recovering his breath and letting his arm ache. And he was beyond worrying about what Bobby Briggs was thinking. Owen watched the lover of his deceased wife turn and walk down the alleyway between the kitchen window and the entry wall.

In a weak voice that no one could hear, Owen said, 'Don't forget to close the gate.'

Bobby Briggs left the gate open but at least he had disappeared. Owen picked up the clipboard and put it back on its hook. He ignored the ballpoint pen that was on the worktop and he walked into the living room. His phone was on the sofa. Owen looked at the phone. He hoped Bobby Briggs was not daft enough to ring. Owen walked towards the sofa, put the phone in his trouser pocket and stood in the middle of the living room. He looked around the room but there was nothing to see. The temperature was normal and the house looked modest and unpretentious as it always did but not innocent. Owen switched on the television. Jason Bourne had left the Middle East and had arrived in Europe. The house of Owen and its walls waited for their owner to say something. He felt obliged.

'If another television gets wrecked,' he said, 'I'll be really annoyed.'

Owen heard muffled but strong noises that sounded like amplified breaths. Owen was not convinced but they might have sounded like a chuckle.

He returned to the kitchen, opened the refrigerator and found a bottle of beer. In the living room Owen drank the beer. He then opened another bottle. The beer was fine and cold.

# SIXTEEN

Owen watched Briggs walk towards him. The restaurants were lined around the square that was opposite The Lowry. Owen stood outside the entrance to the art gallery. The Lowry building had a recognisable entrance but the rest of the building was misshapen lumps of steel. A solid and curved wedge of metal that was the size of a Viking rowboat was perched above the entrance.

'Thought you'd find it,' said Briggs.

'I visit Manchester with work,' said Owen.

The two men looked up at whatever was supposed to be above the entrance.

'They've copied the Guggenheim in Bilbao,' said Briggs.

'Right,' said Owen.

'It's got two theatres as well as the gallery.'

'Really?'

'They opened it in 2000. Cost over a hundred million, just this bit. They must have spent half a billion on the Quays by now.'

'How about that.'

A Pizza Express was to the right of The Lowry and where Briggs and Owen stood. The waitress that stood in front of the Pizza Express wore black slacks, a white shirt and trainers. In between the transparent plastic gloves on her hands she held a long cigarette. She took a drag and smiled at Owen. The plastic transparent Covid shield was pulled back from her face and parallel to the top of her head. She looked like something from an old cheap science fiction B movie but then, thought Owen, so did everything these days. Briggs and Owen walked across the concrete square and towards the Pizza Express.

The waitress lifted her head.

'We'd like a drink,' said Owen.

'Only with meals,' said the waitress. 'The Government insists.'

'It's okay,' said Owen.

'I'm not hungry,' said Briggs.

The waitress smiled.

Briggs was wearing his expensive dark blue Crombie overcoat.

'I haven't eaten,' said Owen. 'I've come from Liverpool.'

'Oh dear,' said the waitress.

She was not so tall and not so young but had friendly eyes.

The waitress smiled.

Whether she would make a suitable alternative for Briggs now that he no longer had a mistress to claim his attention Owen did not know. Although she had a pale complexion the waitress was not English.

'We have to eat,' said Owen.

'I don't want food,' said Briggs.

'I thought you wouldn't have eaten.'

Briggs shrugged his Crombie flattered shoulders. The Crombie overcoat was unbuttoned. The lining of the coat was shiny and impressive.

'I've been here before,' said Owen. 'I had a complicated case and I had to meet these solicitors. It went on for months. Sometimes I used to finish the day by watching a film at the Cornerhouse. Then they closed it.'

Without being interested in what was said the waitress nodded her head.

'I don't go the pictures much,' said Briggs.

Owen was not surprised. With a name like Bobby Briggs he wouldn't have had a chance. The waitress took another drag on her cigarette.

'I heard all about your taste in books and films from Hailey,' said Briggs.

'Was she impressed?' said Owen.

'She was always quoting you.'

'You might feel hungry later,' said the smoking waitress.

'Later I'll be back in Liverpool,' said Owen.

Briggs looked at Owen. Beyond what they wanted to say neither Briggs nor Owen had any intention of extending their meeting. The waitress took a final drag from her cigarette and turned to face Briggs and Owen.

'No?' she said.

'No,' said Owen. 'Thanks.'

The waitress walked inside Pizza Express. Embers from her extinguished cigarette fell on the concrete paving in front of the restaurant. On the other side of the concrete square to the Pizza Express a woman sat on a bench and looked at her smartphone. Most of the tables outside the restaurants were empty but outside Pizza Express a Japanese looking middle-aged couple ate a meal. To the left of The Lowry and outside the concrete square was a wide canal. Tall high rise buildings were on the far side of the canal. Salford and Manchester city centre were also somewhere around but Owen was confused as to what led to where. The two men faced the wide canal.

'We could go for a walk by the canal,' said Owen.

'It's not that far to Media City,' said Briggs.

'Fair enough,' said Owen.

The two men walked by the side of the canal. There were no boats and barges on the water. The sky had a red tint, and there was no wind. The water in the canal was as grey as the concrete in the tall buildings. Owen was not wearing a Crombie overcoat like some but he was not cold.

'I've never been The Lowry,' said Briggs.

'I have,' said Owen.

'If it ever opens again, I'll have a look.'

'You should.'

'It's got two theatres.'

'There you go.'

'There's 12,000 coarse fish in these canals.'

'Well then.'

'They had to clean the water first.'

'I wouldn't have thought.'

'It cost sixty-four million pounds.'

'Cleaning the water?'

'The Lowry. I reckon they've spent half a billion on this place.'

The left hand side of the canal had high rise flats and office blocks. On the right hand side of the canal and in between low apartment buildings there were narrow pedestrian entrances that went deeper into the housing developments. Trees lined the walkway on the right side of the canal, and through the narrow entrances more trees hid the other houses.

'Costs a few bob to live here,' said Briggs.

'No doubt,' said Owen.

'Handy for town.'

'Of course.'

The walking pace of the two men was slow, as if they were stumbling towards conversation. Owen doubted that Briggs was violent but he was pleased that Briggs was nearer to the canal. They passed a metal bridge that had large red girders. The base of the bridge was round and wide and reached by a concrete path. Four teenage lads sat under the bridge and on the wide base. They shouted nonsense and messed around. Briggs and Owen ignored the teenagers.

'Hailey used to worry that I'd cause trouble for you,' said Briggs.

'She would,' said Owen.

Briggs was not as handsome as Owen had first thought. His darkish skin had a rough texture. The black hair and deep brown eyes added coarseness rather than distinction. His own appearance made Owen feel as if he had not yet matured, as if he were something that he had never felt before, not effete perhaps but a smooth decoration.

'I wouldn't cause trouble,' said Briggs. 'I'd be too worried about losing my gun licence.'

'Reassuring, I suppose,' said Owen.

Gun licences indeed, thought Owen.

'There was no one in your house?' said Briggs.

'No,' said Owen.

'No?'

'No there wasn't.'

Briggs stopped walking but Owen continued.

'Hailey said you weren't having an affair,' said Briggs.

'Right,' said Owen.

'I said you must be.'

'I wasn't. Hailey somehow forgot to mention you. I've missed all the details.'

The remark from Owen confused Briggs. This pleased Owen.

'Hailey and I did a syndicate exercise on the training course,' said Briggs. 'Things like that can pull people together.'

'She did mention that,' said Owen. 'I remember her saying someone stood out from the rest. I should have realised.'

Owen did not want to remember the conversation and the enthusiasm of Hailey but he did. Briggs was walking again, and his shoulders were level with those of Owen. Briggs twisted his body so he half-faced Owen. Briggs acted as if he were superior. He stared at Owen as if he were looking at something unimpressive.

'I don't like this,' said Briggs, 'walking and talking like this.'

'There's a price to pay for everything,' said Owen.

Briggs twisted his body back to where it should have been. The two men walked and faced ahead.

'Were you hungry?' said Briggs.

'I am,' said Owen. 'I would have eaten something if I'd known.'

'I wouldn't have eaten anything either way.'

A couple of birds flew across the Ship Canal and up into the sky and past the tall buildings. They had had enough, and so had Owen.

'I've lost my appetite since all this,' said Bobby Briggs.

'Since you started having sex with Hailey?' said Owen.

Briggs stopped walking again but Owen continued. Briggs was by the side of Owen within seconds.

'Since she died,' said Briggs. 'I miss her.'

Owen said nothing.

'I bet you don't.'

'Not so much since I found out about you. I'm hungry now. I'll have a pizza when I get home. Seeing Pizza Express has given me a taste.'

'I won't eat tonight.'

'Well, if you're off your food.'

'You don't care, do you?'

This time Owen stopped walking. Despite all the concrete and the people that must be inside the various buildings everything was silent. The water on the wide canal was still. In the middle of the grey water there was a small pool of bright blue bubbles. Owen pointed at the small patch of clean blue bubbles.

'That might be for the fish,' said Briggs.

'Fuck the fish,' said Owen, 'I've driven forty miles to be here.'

'You wouldn't let me in your house.'

'Mr Briggs, I have no interest in you. I admit I'm curious about what Hailey did with the final days of her life but the truth is I'm not quite ready for the details. I'm not a fan of Lowry or much else that has to do with this city.'

Briggs put his hands inside the pockets of his overcoat. If Owen had known Briggs was going to be dressed up, Owen would have put on his work clothes.

'I'm here for one reason only,' said Owen. 'I couldn't let you in the house and I don't like being rude but as far as I'm concerned you'd no fucking right to be there.'

Briggs said nothing and stared at the grey water on the Ship Canal. Owen read a sign that pointed to different cul-de-sacs within the housing development. The names were invented and meant nothing.

The two men walked again.

'It's best we didn't go inside Pizza Express,' said Briggs. 'We're best walking by the river and talking.'

'It isn't a river,' said Owen. 'You don't have rivers in Manchester.'

'The Mersey starts in Stockport.'

'Stockport isn't in Manchester.'

'The Mersey meets the canal in Irlam. It's not far from here.'

'Inside the pub, by the side of the canal, by the River Mersey or outside my home, I can be doing without this.'

The two men arrived at another canal. The two canals made a right angle. Briggs and Owen faced Media City which was on the other side of the canal that had just appeared. To their left was the Imperial War Museum. This building was in the distance although the sign on the building was large enough to be read. Media City had a tram station, and trams arrived while Briggs and Owen stood at the junction of the canals and stared. The buildings for the BBC and ITV were separated by a large billboard sign that said Media City. A sign on another building said it was The Studio. This building was not as big as the buildings for the BBC and ITV. The other buildings were no bigger than The Studio. Opposite the Imperial War Museum in the distance an old-fashioned brick building had a not so obvious dull grey sign that said Coronation Street. Next to the bridge that led across the canal and arrived at Media City there was a busy restaurant called The Alchemist. Inside the restaurant people drank, ate and almost made a crowd. Owen looked at the plush furnishings, warm light, and people eating. He wanted to rest and feed his stomach.

On concrete posts on the bridge across the second canal there were a couple of notices about Covid and the disruption. Briggs and Owen stood and waited to see another tram arrive. Media City, though, was empty, nothing but concrete and glass waiting for another day. Briggs and Owen turned around and returned along the tree lined walkway. Apart from the odd pool of blue bubbles and the concrete foundations that supported bridges the surface of the canal was nothing but empty grey. Owen felt sorry for the 12,000 fish.

'Don't they have boats in Manchester?' said Owen.

'You get barges sometimes,' said Briggs.

'Maybe they knew we were coming.'

The two men walked and both of them stared at the canal. On the far side someone had made an attempt to make the tall buildings look different, given them jagged and curved shapes.

'Hailey said you wouldn't be playing around,' said Briggs. 'She said you were loyal.'

This was true but Owen knew that he was never truly tested. Women were combative when they met him. Sleeping around when he was married would have been hard work. And, of course, Owen had thought Hailey was being faithful.

'I loved Hailey,' said Briggs.

'Good for you,' said Owen.

'I loved her as soon as I saw her.'

In the sky there were birds. They may have been the same ones from before or new arrivals. Perhaps they were listening, thought Owen.

'You don't even know what love is,' said Briggs,

Owen stared at the grey water in the canal. This was a difficult moment, he thought. Not sure why or how but boats on the canal would have helped. Even a few ducks would not have gone amiss. Briggs stopped walking, and so did Owen. Briggs looked at Owen with distaste. The dark brown eyes of Briggs hardened. Owen looked at the profile of Briggs. This unimpressive dullard at his side was the man that made a favourable impression on the woman for whom Owen had been expected to declare love. The eyes of Briggs were curious but only because he was waiting for Owen to make conversation. Owen remembered what Hailey had said about how some people feed off you and let you do all the talking. Briggs turned his head and saw Owen staring at him.

'What are you smiling about?' said Briggs.

'It was meant to be a smirk,' said Owen. 'It's your sense of grievance and the sincere conviction that astonishes me. I'm not the guilty party.'

'If Hailey had thought you loved her, it would have been different.'

'How different? She'd have stayed faithful? She'd have stayed happily married? I don't think so. She would have still met you, still screwed you. People or men like Bobby Briggs have to flatter, and the flattery, whoever or whomever it came from, would have got her knickers off.'

Briggs turned away from the water and walked. Owen followed him and after a couple of steps he was by his side. This time, though, their shoulders did not touch.

'You don't have anything else to say?' said Owen.

'It's Bob,' he said. 'You keep calling me Bobby.'

'The Bob that did the job on my wife, the sincere lover and the dreadful husband. Where have I heard that before?'

'Hailey wanted to leave you.'

Owen said nothing.

The man was talking and he should be encouraged, thought Owen. It might help with his development and the next syndicate exercise.

'We agreed she'd tell you everything at the weekend,' said Briggs.

'When she died?' said Owen.

'To tell you she was going to leave you.'

'And move in with you?'

'Not right away. We were going to see how it went. Work and travel would have been difficult.'

'But at least you could screw on weekends with a clean conscience.'

'My conscience was always clean.'

'I was thinking more of the woman of your dreams.'

Briggs said nothing.

'I'm still hungry,' said Owen.

They arrived at The Lowry. The two men sat on some concrete steps at the side of the square and not far from where the woman had looked at her smartphone. The middle-aged couple that

Briggs remembered seeing outside Pizza Express and that Owen had thought looked Japanese took photographs of The Lowry. The man and the woman each posed for a photograph that the other took. Briggs sat and watched the Japanese looking couple.

'Wonder if they'll make it home,' said Briggs.

Owen thought about this. He had assumed they were British.

'Wonder if the batteries will last,' said Owen.

'That's racist,' said Briggs,

'I was talking about the phone.'

The Japanese looking couple turned away from the entrance to The Lowry and walked towards Briggs and Owen. The man took off his glasses.

'You want a picture?' said Owen.

The man and the woman smiled. Their wrinkles turned into something fresher.

'He'll take the photo,' said Owen.

He pointed a finger at Briggs. The Japanese looking couple looked at Briggs as if he was a discovery. Without any enthusiasm Briggs stood up.

'Have you got plenty of battery?' said Owen.

The Japanese looking man thought this was a strange question but said nothing. He handed the iPhone over to Briggs.

'See, he trusts you,' said Owen.

Briggs was impressed with the new iPhone and he smiled but said nothing. After showing Briggs where to press on the screen the Japanese looking couple walked backwards towards the Lowry Centre. The middle-aged couple posed and smiled. As they were looking over the shoulder of Briggs, their eyes met those of Owen who also smiled. Briggs returned the iPhone to the couple. He did not sit down on the concrete steps. He remained standing.

'Would you mind if we take a photograph of you two?' said the woman.

Briggs was so uncomfortable that Owen imagined him sweating inside his Crombie overcoat.

'Why not?' said Owen.

Briggs stood next to Owen. Their shoulders almost touched. From the look on the face of Briggs it was obvious that there were words that he would like to have said. Where inside him they were trapped Owen was not quite sure.

'You want Bobby and me to stand in front of the gallery?' said Owen.

'Yes please,' said the woman. 'My grandfather was from Manchester. We planned this trip a couple of years ago but it's not the same since Covid.'

'That might make it more memorable,' said Owen.

'I hope so.'

'Come on, Bobby.'

Owen walked towards the Lowry building and turned around to face the couple. He used the fingers on his right hand to beckon Briggs towards him. Briggs was not pleased but he stepped forward and stood alongside Owen. With his right hand the Japanese looking man held the iPhone in front of his face. His left hand beckoned Briggs and Owen to move closer together. Owen moved to his right.

'Closer,' said the man.

His wife or girlfriend smiled.

The pose and body of Briggs was rigid but Owen moved until his right shoulder touched the left shoulder of Briggs. Worse things happened at school, Owen told himself.

'Cheese,' said Owen.

Briggs said nothing.

'Say cheese,' said Owen.

The two men said cheese although from Briggs it sounded more like a grunt. The Japanese looking man took the photograph. He showed everyone the result.

'You've used the rule of thirds,' said Owen.

'Andy knows what he's doing,' said the woman.

'It's a good one, isn't it, Bobby?' said Owen.

Briggs said nothing.

'I can email it to you,' said Andy.

'Please,' said Owen.

Briggs forced a smile. Owen gave Andy his email address, and Andy typed it into his phone. Owen pointed at Briggs.

'I'll forward Bobby a copy,' said Owen. 'He's funny about emails.'

'Of course,' said the woman. 'We understand. We're from Fulham.'

'Never been,' said Owen. 'I'm not from Manchester. Bobby is.'

'Fulham has become expensive. When we retire we're going to sell our house and move.'

'I like Whitby,' said Andy.

'Good fish and chips,' said Owen.

'Very good fish and chips,' said the woman. 'Lovely castle.'

Andy nodded his head. The few words between them all had made a difference, thought Owen. The couple looked less Japanese.

'I've been to Craven Cottage,' said Bobby, 'by the river. I used to watch United home and away. I was young then.'

'You're still young,' said the woman.

'He's certainly active,' said Owen.

Owen accepted that his remark might not have been a classic quip but it made him smile. Briggs looked away. He put his hands in the pockets of his Crombie overcoat.

The rest was additional pleasantries and farewells. Andy and his wife or girlfriend took more photographs and left the concrete square. They reached another walkway and another canal. As they turned away and headed out of sight, Owen gave the couple from Fulham a final wave. This appeared to please the couple. Briggs and Owen sat down on the same bench where the woman had looked at her smartphone. They faced the entrance into The Lowry. The boat shaped lump of steel above the entrance had no purpose, thought Owen, but he was content to be baffled.

'I didn't think that was funny,' said Briggs.

'Different sense of humour out this way, I suppose,' said Owen.

'You're the one that's different.'

'And you're not?'

'Not as different as you.'

'Then Hailey got what she wanted.'

Owen was tempted to say more but it was clear from the expression on the face of Briggs that he had understood the insult. Owen watched a young couple leave the Pizza Express. The man played with his car keys. The young couple followed the route taken by the Japanese couple.

'This feels a bit chilly to me,' said Owen,

Briggs said nothing and stood up.

Owen did the same. They left the square and followed the canal that faced the entrance to the shopping mall and car park. A passenger boat was parked at the side of the canal. The sign on the boat said SEA CRUISE.

'Told you we had boats,' said Briggs.

'That makes me feel like a tourist,' said Owen.

The two men left the canal and turned into the shopping mall but took the escalator down into the car park. They left the bright lights of the mall and arrived at a lot of empty and almost dark space. Not that Owen had doubted the ambition of the couple from Fulham but there was a motorhome in the nowhere near full car park. He also saw a familiar red BMW saloon. Briggs headed towards his car, and Owen followed. At the BMW saloon the two men stopped walking and stood still.

Briggs shuffled his car keys between his hands and said nothing.

Owen imagined Hailey and Briggs and how they would have behaved, her outlining future plans and this dope sitting there and happy to listen.

'You're the one who wanted to see me,' said Owen.

Briggs took a deep breath.

'I was supposed to see my brother tonight,' said Owen. 'I cancelled so I could be here tonight.'

Briggs said nothing.

'The partner of my brother has just been promoted. We were supposed to celebrate.'

'Is that the brother that is gay?'

Owen nodded his head.

Just how much did this man know about his life and habits, thought Owen. Right now he did not care.

'I need to know,' said Briggs.

Owen waited. He imagined Briggs thinking that Owen wanted to know what he needed to discover. The phrase made no sense but it amused Owen.

'Did Hailey tell you she was going to leave you?' said Briggs.

Owen smiled. His grin was superior but Owen did not feel hostile.

'We were at my brother's,' said Owen. 'We ate, drank, talked and argued.'

'Hailey said that the two of you argued a lot,' said Briggs.

'Everyone was arguing. If Hailey wanted to say anything about you, she was not going to say it before we went to see my brother.'

'She didn't get a chance, did she?'

The Manchester accent of Briggs sounded more distinct than previously.

'Hailey and me had talked about separating,' said Owen. 'More than once.'

'I know you weren't getting on,' said Briggs.

'Nothing to do with you, of course.'

'She promised she'd say something that weekend.'

'And she'd leave me?'

'Hailey was honest with me. She said that if you reacted and told her you loved her she'd stay with you.'

'I'd say I loved her because she was being unfaithful?'

'Because you wouldn't want to lose her.'

'And you were okay with this, one magic word from me and you'd walk away?'

'I needed Hailey to make a decision. I was prepared to take the chance. Why are you grinning?'

'You take the biscuit. They shouldn't let people like you out. You'd bomb Iraq with a clean conscience.'

'I don't know what you mean.'

'I need a drink. I'm going home where I can have a drink.'

Briggs played with his car keys. The red paint on the BMW saloon had an expensive and impressive gloss. No chance of me buying a BMW motor after this, thought Owen.

'I had asked Hailey if she wanted to leave me,' said Owen, 'more than once. The last time happened a fortnight before she died. We'd had more than one conversation about separating but this time it was different.'

'Hailey was different.'

'I was different. I was serious but I wanted her not me to make the decision to leave. Hailey said no. She said she'd seen the men out there and she was better off where she was. I should have said I was going anyway but I didn't. I didn't want to tell my mother that I'd walked out of a marriage.'

Owen had suspected that there might be a trace of homophobia inside him. Because of Rhys there had always been an obligation, a responsibility, to give his mother at least one conventional ending. As far as sons went, he was the only heterosexual option that his mother had.

Briggs moved his car keys to his other hand. Owen enjoyed being able to watch and study Briggs. The man was sad. The Crombie overcoat looked like a burden. Twelve fucks in a year and the man was in love and heartbroken. It occurred to Owen that Hailey and him had done a lot more than that and they had not even liked one another.

'I had to know what Hailey said about me,' said Briggs.

'She didn't get the chance,' said Owen.

'You should have mentioned having to see your brother tonight. I feel bad about that.'

'I'm now seeing him tomorrow night.'

'You shouldn't be celebrating anything.'

'I'm not going to get up and sing. Well, I wasn't.'

Briggs grinned and leaned back against his red BMW. Andy and his wife or girlfriend arrived in the car park. They carried two shopping bags. Owen assumed the couple had wasted time in the mall. The couple headed for the motorhome that Owen had spotted. The two people waved and climbed into the motorhome. Briggs and Owen waved. This pleased the couple. Briggs rubbed his back against his red BMW saloon. He had the doleful look of a rejected lover. God knows what the two men looked like to the couple from Fulham, thought Owen.

'I know about your house,' said Briggs.

'Don't remind me,' said Owen.

'I know what happened when you didn't let me in.'

Owen said nothing.

'I know there was no one else there.'

Owen waited.

Briggs pressed his car key and opened the door to the red BMW saloon. Owen sneaked a look at how the car looked inside. Briggs took off his Crombie overcoat and threw it on to the back seat of his car.

'I didn't slam the door in your face,' said Owen.

'I know that,' said Briggs.

This time Briggs waited. He watched the motorhome of the couple from Fulham leave the car park. The headlights on the motorhome lit up some of the underground car park. The woman was driving. The motorhome left from the other side of the car park but the woman pressed the horn. Briggs and Owen waved their hands.

'Odd things have been happening in your house,' said Briggs.

Owen waited.

'Am I right?'

Owen said nothing.

'I saw how the door slammed in my face.'

Owen said nothing.

'I knew it wasn't you. And I could see there was no one else.'

Briggs was labouring this but at that moment Owen was happy to let Briggs struggle. Owen felt a little queasy. I am hungry of course, thought Owen.

'I didn't have to see the doors close the way they did,' said Briggs. 'I knew as soon as I pressed the bell.'

Owen waited and thought about Hailey and what happened at the stone circle in the Lake District. Owen knew that Briggs was not the only one with intuition.

'I sense things,' said Briggs.

'You didn't know those people were from Fulham,' said Owen.

'No, I didn't know that. But I know your house is haunted.'

'No chance of you buying it, I suppose.'

Briggs and Owen grinned. Briggs switched his car keys between his hands.

'I sense things,' said Briggs.

'Did you sense Hailey was going to screw you?' said Owen.

'We both sensed that. Hailey and me, we both sensed things.'

Owen guessed that Hailey had told Briggs what had happened to her at the stone circle. Owen could have asked Briggs of course. He wondered how many minutes it would take to walk back to the canal and throw Briggs in the water.

'There is a presence in your home,' he said.

Owen said nothing.

'You don't have to say. I know. I knew as soon as I pressed the doorbell.'

Owen said nothing.

Briggs took a small leather wallet out of his trouser pocket.

'I have experience with this kind of thing,' said Briggs. 'It can't be pleasant for you.'

Briggs paused.

Owen waited.

'These experiences are anything but pleasant,' said Briggs.

He took a card out of his wallet. Briggs handed the card to Owen who looked at what was on the card. There were no astral circles or tarot symbols. Owen was a little disappointed.

'This says you're an actuary,' said Owen.

'That's my job,' said Briggs. 'I don't carry around cards for the other stuff. This card has my number. We owe it to ourselves to sort this.'

Owen was not sure if Briggs was being serious. It sounded like a sales pitch. To be fair to Briggs, thought Owen, there had been no mention of money.

'There's one problem,' said Owen.

'You don't want to ever see me again,' said Briggs.

'How are you going to get in the house? Won't the doors slam shut like last time?'

'I have ways of working around that. You're lucky. I have experience. Not as much as some but some. There's a bloke in Hull gets around thirty emails a day about this kind of thing. He has a website, of course. I can't do that type of thing. I've got a job to worry about. Keep the card. You can ring me.'

Owen looked at the business card. His wife had an affair with an actuary that was a part-time medium. In the circumstances that was lucky, supposed Owen.

'I'll think about it,' said Owen.

The small bedside lamp was switched on. Owen was lying in bed and thinking about Hailey and past arguments. He would have a headache in the morning because he always did when he drank a full bottle of wine. Not a terrible headache but something that he would pretend did not exist when he rang his boss. The wine, like the beer the night before, had been to help him not think about what had happened inside the house. Owen liked the idea of having some sleep. He hoped that the lit lamp would encourage restraint in what else might be in the house, the what else that

Briggs referred to as a presence. After the trip to Manchester the evening had been quiet. Owen had watched a long film on the new television and only adjusted the settings twice. There was, though, one incident that might have been sinister. After he had drunk half of the wine the bottle was not where he had expected it to be. He might have misplaced the bottle but Owen was not convinced. When Hailey was alive, there had been a routine where she or Owen would take the bottle away if either thought the other had drunk too much. Inside the bedroom the air was cold. The lit lamp was not helping his pending headache. Owen would tomorrow ask Rhys if he could stay at his house. This was just one night to endure. Worse things happened at school, thought Owen, except they did not. Owen switched off the light and closed his eyes. The alcohol would not let him down, reckoned Owen.

He remembered the famous poem by Robert Burns that he had been taught in school. What was good enough for Tam O'Shanter was good enough for Owen. When Tam was drunk he took on a whole crowd of spirits. Of course, he was also able to beat a retreat on his grey mare Meg. The yeasty smell had not appeared in the bedroom, assuming smells appeared. If they disappeared then they must appear, Owen decided. The drunken nonsense inside his head helped him to relax.

Owen was drifting towards sleep or close enough to it to relax when he felt something like a hand touch his shoulder. He gritted his teeth and took a deep breath but the feel of the hand on his shoulder had not been unpleasant. Owen imagined it was something like how a parent might check if a child was sleeping. Owen remembered when Hailey used to stroke his neck with the tips of her fingers. Hailey would breathe warmth on the side of his face. Hailey used to do this when she thought he was tense, stroke his neck and breathe into his ear. Owen remembered and kept his eyes closed. He was not looking at what might be in the bed behind him. It felt to Owen as if he were alone. There was space around him. Owen was neither tense nor frightened although he was gritting his teeth, more like a child enjoying a daredevil experience than anything. Although this was different the memories of Hailey stroking his neck helped him to relax. Owen thought about affection, pragmatism and responsibility and how a woman could have an affair and yet refuse to leave her marriage when invited. Owen did nothing but keep his eyes closed. He was not sure what his final thoughts were before he drifted to sleep. At some point, though, Owen remembered his conversation with Bobby Briggs.

# SEVENTEEN

Apart from his boss there was hardly anyone in the office. So his boss said. She also told Owen that he was still grieving and that he should continue to work from home. Owen had said to some of the others at work that his boss was the typical sociopathic senior manager favoured by the company. He always added that the same woman was convinced that women managers were more empathetic than men. Whatever her reasons for being sympathetic Owen was now in his living room and, as usual, sitting behind a laptop and working. He had tried to find somewhere to spend some of the day but wandering around the flatlands of Merseyside made him think of decent weather being wasted. He sat behind the laptop and thought about the trip to the stone circle.

The doorbell rang, and Owen opened the door. Detective Sergeant Jones waited on the doorstep. This was not a surprise because in the morning they had already exchanged texts about her visit.

'Are you alright?' said Detective Sergeant Jones.

'I think so,' said Owen.

'You just looked at your front door in an odd way.'

'It's been playing up.'

Detective Sergeant Jones followed Owen through the small hall and into the living room. Owen made some coffee, and they ate the rest of the cake that his mother had made. Owen sat on the sofa. Detective Sergeant Jones sat on an armchair. Her empty plate was next to her two feet. A cup of coffee rested on her knees. Detective Sergeant Jones held the cup with two hands. Her face mask hung down around her neck.

'Are you sure you're alright?' said Detective Sergeant Jones.

'As far as I know,' said Owen. 'My boss wants me to work from home. Because of the lockdown I haven't been out much.'

'You keep looking around, as if there's someone here.'

Detective Sergeant Jones smiled.

'You can look round the house if you want,' said Owen.

'I'm not accusing you,' said Detective Sergeant Jones. 'I just wondered if you were alright.'

'I'm okay.'

Owen said that he was okay but when he looked at the bright brown eyes of Detective Sergeant Jones he realised how reduced he must look. There was a day when Hailey and Owen had completed eighteen miles of walking in the Yorkshire Dales and climbed God knows how many mountains. The two of them had finished the walk convinced of their good health. And then they arrived at the pub and saw how normal and nourished people looked. This was what he felt looking at Detective Sergeant Jones.

'Are you okay?' said Owen. 'You look okay.'

Detective Sergeant Jones smiled.

'I didn't mean, you know, anything,' said Owen.

'As long as you're okay, I'm okay,' said Detective Sergeant Jones. 'We could have done this over the phone, Owen, but I felt, well we have the verdict from the coroner.'

'Have you come to arrest me?'

'Don't be daft. I have news and I didn't want to be abrupt.'

Owen smiled.

Detective Sergeant Jones looked down at her knees. She was wearing brown corduroy trousers and a short sleeved and cowl-necked pullover that was made of something other than wool, the kind of thing that women wear, thought Owen. Indeed it looked like something he had bought for Hailey one Christmas. He had never forgotten the colour of that present, soft oatmeal heather, whatever that meant. Hailey even wore it a couple of times.

'The news from the coroner might disappoint you,' said Detective Sergeant Jones.

'As long as I'm not being arrested,' said Owen.

'No, you won't have to see me again, Owen.'

He picked up the empty cups and took them into the kitchen. The smile on his face could have meant anything. When he returned Detective Sergeant Jones was standing at the bay window and staring outside. Owen did not sit down. He walked towards the bay window. Because her head was tilted away from him, he noticed that she was wearing a small stud earring that consisted of a small black half globe surrounded by a gold rim. Detective Sergeant Jones turned around to face Owen. She leaned back against the window and folded her arms. Owen thought about whether soft oatmeal heather might exist on a hill somewhere.

'You're wearing earrings,' said Owen.

'We're allowed one pair of stud earrings,' said Detective Sergeant Jones. 'Note the haircut, neat and tidy and above the collar of the shirt, cut in a style that allows the cap to be worn. My hair is dyed but not in a colour that is unnatural, no nail polish. I could probably push it a bit more now I'm a detective but, well, following the rules has become a habit.'

'The short hair suits you. It makes your eyes look bigger.'

'That's a good thing?'

Owen shrugged his shoulders, and Detective Sergeant Jones laughed.

'This is nice and quiet,' she said. 'I can see why you don't want to move.'

'Hailey wanted to move,' said Owen.

'A house is only a box.'

'That's what I used to say.'

Detective Sergeant Jones stepped away from the window and unfolded her arms. Owen followed the Detective into the middle of the living room. Detective Sergeant Jones looked at the new television but said nothing.

'There are other reasons I didn't want to move,' said Owen.

'I bet you're a right stick in the mud,' said Detective Sergeant Jones.

'I suppose I am.'

'I am too. I always wanted to be a detective, though. And I still like detective shows. You replaced the television.'

Detective Jones and Owen wasted a few seconds staring at the switched off television.

'I can send you a copy of the report by the coroner if you want,' said Detective Sergeant Jones. 'If you were expecting the coroner to say the death of your wife was an accident, she doesn't.' Detective Sergeant Jones paused. 'The verdict is death by misadventure.'

'Right.'

'People soon forget these things.'

'It's critical of me?'

'Not especially. The coroner doesn't go to town in the report. But it's not the kind of thing you'd want to show your kids.'

'I don't have kids. I'm not worried about people.'

'The coroner can't resist a snide remark about people realising they should listen to one another. That sentence was out of order.'

'What the hell,' said Owen.

'The local press will read the report,' said Detective Sergeant Jones.

Owen waited.

'I can see them sensationalising it. Liverpool woman dies in mysterious circumstances. That kind of thing.'

'The in-laws won't like that.'

'I can tell the in-laws.'

'No, I'll tell them.'

Detective Sergeant Jones turned her head and stared at what was on the other side of the window. Before Covid the cul-de-sac would have been empty of cars in the day. There were plenty.

'My car is the Focus,' said Detective Sergeant Jones.

'Mine is the Volvo,' said Owen.

'I know.'

For some reason this made the two of them giggle. Owen left the middle of the room and walked the few feet from the sofa to the bay window. He thought of what happened when Briggs had visited.

If there was a presence in this house, as Briggs had said, then it was relaxed about Owen being there and talking to an attractive woman. Perhaps the spirit was curious, wanted to see him do something that made it feel vindicated. If the presence belonged to Hailey, it might need to move on. Owen having a quickie with Detective Sergeant Jones might be doing Hailey a favour. Owen imagined what Detective Sergeant Jones might look like without clothes.

'Are you allowed tattoos by the police?' said Owen.

'No but I don't like tattoos,' said Detective Sergeant Jones.

'No skin off your nose then.'

They both laughed.

Detective Sergeant Jones joined Owen at the bay window. They both stared at what was outside. With so many people working at home the houses had become something else, thought Owen, buildings with wider purpose, like dogs that offered comfort when their owners were ill. The sky was not quite blue, and the day was not quite grey. The bay window was small, and Detective Jones and Owen stood close together. He could hear her breathe. The hair on top of her head was clean.

'I've worked a few days at home,' said Detective Sergeant Jones.

Owen stared at her plain Ford Focus. He considered that there might be a neighbour that was imagining him having an affair with this woman that had appeared after Hailey had died. The same neighbour might have spotted Briggs arriving when Owen had been away. This neighbour might have even pictured Hailey screwing Briggs and might now at this moment be imagining Holly and Owen doing the same thing. Owen stared at the back of her head and realised his brain had called her Holly.

'I don't work many days at home,' said Detective Sergeant Jones.

'I do more at home than before,' said Owen.

'I usually manage one day a week. My ambition is two, now there is Covid.'

'Why not?'

'Why not.'

Detective Sergeant Jones sighed. The small bay window felt smaller. She turned around.

'One should take advantage of opportunities, I think,' she said.

Detective Sergeant Jones and Owen faced one another and smiled. It lasted a couple of seconds before he stepped away from the bay window.

# EIGHTEEN

The four people sat around a square dining table. The room was lit by a single standard lamp. The colour of the lampshade made the mother of Rhys and Owen look tanned.

'I reckon it was an invitation,' said their mother.

'Definitely,' said Will.

Rhys was thoughtful.

Owen said nothing.

'You could have brought the Detective along to meet us,' said his mother. 'We're all quite respectable.'

'I don't think so,' said Owen.

'She seemed alright to me,' said Will.

'You could do a lot worse, Owen,' said his mother.

'Not the police, though,' said Rhys.

'There's good and bad,' said his mother.

'You wouldn't have wanted Rhys to have hooked up with a policeman,' said Owen.

'A policewoman is not the same,' said his mother.

'She'll be a bit of a hard case doing that job,' said Rhys.

'She hasn't got tattoos,' said Owen.

His mother, Rhys and Will stopped eating. There were four bottles of wine on the table. Two had been opened. His mother waited and smiled.

'She told me,' said Owen. 'We were talking about what she could wear on duty.'

'I've thought about having a tattoo,' said his mother.

'Mam, no.'

'Why not?'

'They look terrible with varicose veins.'

'I haven't got varicose veins.'

'Well, don't tempt fate with a tattoo.'

The ponytail and ever present jeans and smock were bad enough, thought Owen. Compared to his mother the others looked as if they had dressed for the meal. The three men all wore clean clothes for the occasion. His mother looked like she had been in the jeans and the smock for a week, thought Owen.

'The police do have a reputation,' said Will.

'For what?' said Owen.

'For spreading it around,' said Will. 'They have a high divorce rate.'

'That'll be the men,' said the mother of Owen.

Rhys and Will grinned at Owen.

'What is this we're eating?' said the mother of Owen.

'Chicken and chorizo rice pot,' said Will.

'Very nice.'

The mother of Rhys and Owen put a fork of rice and meat into her mouth. She chewed the food and evaluated something. Rhys poured rosé wine into the four glasses.

'I wonder if our Detective is much of a cook,' said his mother.

Rhys, Will and Owen waited.

The mother of Owen stared at Will and pretended Rhys and Owen had left the room.

'Rhys and Owen are useless in the kitchen,' she said. 'I blame myself. I waited on them hand and foot.'

'I can cook,' said Owen.

'After a fashion.'

'I used to cook the Christmas lunch.'

'More fool Hailey letting you.'

'I can cook,' said Rhys. 'Will prefers to cook and he happens to be better than me.'

The dining table had four equal sides. Each of the four people occupied a side. Rhys and Will sat on opposite sides to each other. Owen sat opposite his mother. She glanced sideways at Will.

'Don't let Rhys take advantage,' she said.

The rest of them waited.

'Will won't have as much time now he's got extra responsibility,' she said.

'If it's longer hours,' said Owen.

'It could be,' said Will. 'That doesn't bother me.'

'Nor me,' said Rhys. 'I'm pleased for Will.'

His mother smiled at Rhys. She turned her head and glanced at Will. Owen ate some chicken and chorizo rice pot. It had a few spices but it was nothing special, thought Owen.

'Don't let Rhys waste the extra money on the plonk,' said his mother.

Will gave Rhys an understanding smile.

His mother looked at Owen. He knew what the look meant. Owen was somehow responsible for any problems that Rhys and Will might encounter.

'We've had a couple of celebrations close together, that's all,' said Owen.

'I don't like to see either of you drunk,' said his mother.

'Are we still in lockdown?' said Will.

'I haven't been paying attention,' said Owen.

'The pubs are open,' said Rhys.

'Sort of,' said Owen.

Owen remembered his visit to Manchester, meeting Briggs at the side of the Ship Canal and having nowhere to go.

'It'll be easier,' said Owen, 'starting a new job when people are working at home.'

'The new work will be more complicated,' said Will. 'My new boss said it's people that create the difficulties whatever the job. Rhys is lucky. Architects don't have to bother with people.'

'Oh no?' said Rhys.

He sipped some wine. His mother watched Rhys drink which was no surprise to Owen because she did this every time that Rhys put a glass to his lips.

'You'll be fine, Will,' said Owen. 'I'm pleased for you. A couple of years you'll be looking to make the next step.'

Rhys and Will smiled at one another. They looked devoted, and Owen had no reason to doubt how they looked. Hailey had once mentioned the shirts on Will always looked cleaner than those of Owen. Ever since then Owen had been aware of the difference.

'Will has a future career,' said Rhys. 'I just have more buildings.'

'At least they get built,' said Owen. 'Detective Sergeant Jones won't put a stop to crime no matter how hard she works.'

'Look, he's feeling sorry for her,' said his mother. 'Hasn't she got a name?'

Rhys and Will grinned.

'Jones,' said Owen.

'A Christian name,' said his mother.

'Holly.'

'Look, he knows her name.'

'She told me the first time we met.'

'It's a nice name,' said Will.

'Owen and Holly,' said the mother of Owen. 'Holly sounds alright. But then I thought Hailey sounded alright. I'm not sure about the name Owen but your dad had to have his own way. I'd give her a ring, Owen. Take her for a meal while you can.'

'I could always cook.'

'Jesus Christ, no.'

'It's too soon after Hailey.'

His mother, Rhys and Will stopped eating and looked at one another. Owen decided this was a serious moment. Everyone was quiet, and Rhys was not drinking.

'If Hailey was having an affair,' said his mother.

'I didn't know, though,' said Owen.

'So?'

'So we never talked about it.'

'I don't understand you, Owen.'

His mother picked up her fork and looked at Rhys and Will.

'Do you understand him?' she said.

'I've never understood him,' said Rhys.

'If it's how he feels,' said Will.

'Detective Sergeant Jones will have to be remembered as the one that got away,' said Owen.

'You've had a few of those, Owen,' said Rhys.

'Including my wife, apparently,' said Owen.

Everyone waited, and moments passed.

'Hailey always thought a lot of herself,' said the mother of Owen.

'Mam, don't,' said Owen.

'Were you playing around?'

'No.'

'Well then.'

'Women don't throw themselves at me. Who knows what I would have done given the chance.'

'You're not a plain man, Owen.'

Rhys and Will stopped eating to listen. Owen watched his mother touch her ponytail. He looked at the white smock and thought about her denim jeans below the table. He imagined his mother in a TV documentary about an artist and her sharing memories of the artist with an interviewer. Owen felt obliged to be interesting.

'Women approve once we've been to bed,' said Owen. 'Either that or they're very polite. It's at the beginning they keep their distance. Women are combative with me.'

'Do you talk this way in front of your mother, Will?' said the mother of Owen.

'I don't talk about women much,' said Will.

Rhys held up his wine glass and pretended to toast Will.

'I was thinking that at my job interview,' said Will.

'I'm sorry,' said Rhys.

'That people who'd approve of me later could disapprove of me now despite not knowing anything.'

'I thought you got the job,' said the mother of Rhys.

'Please, Mother,' said Rhys.

'Why should they approve of me doing a job for the rest of my life,' said Will, 'just because of a few answers to some questions.'

'Well, they did, Will,' said the mother of Rhys. 'And they'll approve of you later. If I hadn't mentioned this Detective being interested, Owen wouldn't have even noticed her.'

'I did notice something today,' said Owen.

'And you did nothing, of course,' said Rhys,

'It's too early after Hailey.'

'She was having an affair,' said the mother of Owen. 'Hailey is the one that should have been in the police. Hailey would have been in her element there.'

Rhys leant forward to pick up the bottle of wine.

'Rhys, leave it for a moment,' said his mother.

'It's a celebration,' said Rhys.

He poured wine into the glasses. The wine in the glass of his mother reached a higher level than in the other glasses. This was deliberate by Rhys. His mother held her breath for a couple of seconds. Owen stared at his mother and whispered the word no.

'I met the bloke Hailey was knocking off,' said Owen.

His mother, Rhys and Will waited.

'He's from Manchester,' said Owen.

'Ah, well,' said his mother.

The others listened.

'I've spoken to him a couple of times,' said Owen. 'He's given me his business card.'

Rhys and Will smiled and glanced at one another. The mother of Owen kept her lips pressed tight. Her back was straight. Owen had not noticed but they had all finished eating.

'He's an actuary or he works with one,' said Owen. 'I'm not sure. He wanted Hailey to leave me.'

'Bastard,' said Rhys.

'I don't think so,' said Owen. 'I felt a bit sorry for him. He was in love with Hailey. He still is. Hailey told him that she loved me.'

'Funny way of showing it,' said his mother. 'She never did support you.'

'She did her best. I don't miss being supported. I can cope. I don't lose sleep over work.'

Talking like this, revealing something, Owen felt the effect of the wine.

'I miss her approval,' said Owen.

'She was having an affair, Owen,' said his mother. 'A weird way of approving.'

'I know she wasn't happy with me but there were moments when I impressed her.'

The others stared at Owen.

'She gave me esteem,' said Owen.

'Esteem?' said Rhys.

'Esteem.'

'Funny way of putting it,' said his mother.

'I'll move the plates,' said Will.

He stood up, picked up the plates and took them into the kitchen.

'Have I embarrassed Will?' said Owen.

'Doubt it,' said Rhys. 'He'll wash the dishes while he's there, though.'

'You shouldn't have let Will cook the meal,' said his mother. 'Not if it's his celebration.'

'Will insisted. He likes cooking.'

'I could have cooked if I'd known.'

Owen listened to all this and thought there was so much that he had been going to tell them. The meeting with Briggs, his need to know what Hailey and Briggs felt for each other, what had happened inside the house after Hailey had died and the offer of Briggs to investigate and, according to him, to help.

'If he likes cooking,' said Rhys.

'If you cooked a bit more, you might drink a bit less,' said his mother.

Fuck them, thought Owen. He swallowed some wine and decided that he would use the card that Briggs left Owen and give the man from Manchester a ring. Owen took another gulp of wine.

'Don't you start,' said his mother.

Will brought in the desserts. His white shirt had a few drops of water that had not dried but it still was as bright as ever.

# NINETEEN

There was rain. The lukewarm sunshine of recent days had disappeared. The in-laws of Owen stood at the doorstep. His skinny mother-in-law held a giant umbrella above her head.

'Is the door alright?' said his father-in-law. 'You were looking at it funny?'

Owen nodded and led his in-laws into the living room.

'I bought a new door for the vestibule last Christmas,' said his father-in-law. 'Sarah keeps clogging the entrance up with shoes. I was pleased with the price. It's guaranteed and everything, double glazing and reinforced PVC but you can't tell. It looks just like wood.'

I bet it doesn't do what my doors do, thought Owen.

He walked into the kitchen and made some tea. He put some ginger biscuits on a plate. The in-laws sat on the sofa, and Owen sat on the armchair.

'Is that a new television?' said his father-in-law.

'I had a burglary,' said Owen.

'When Hailey was alive?' said his mother-in-law.

'Not long after.'

'You poor thing.'

His in-laws looked at one another.

'Have a biscuit,' said Owen.

His father-in-law chomped his way through a ginger biscuit. His mother-in-law shook her head and sighed a couple of times. She wore trousers and a reefer jacket over her thin frame. Owen hated to admit it but the monster looked quite stylish.

'I was going to call round,' said Owen. 'Then I thought you might want to look at Hailey's things and decide if you want to keep anything.'

'Are you keeping anything, Owen?' said his mother-in-law.

'I'll keep the wedding photographs. I've got plenty of photos on the phone. The other stuff, you should have a look first.'

The sight of ginger biscuits had made Owen hungry but he was too self-conscious to eat. His father-in-law stretched out his legs. His thin wife occupied no more than the edge of the sofa.

'I don't think we should look through her things,' said his mother-in-law.

'I don't know what's normal,' said Owen.

'I wouldn't want to do that,' said his father-in-law. 'Kids have secrets from their parents.'

'Hailey was a grown woman,' said his mother-in-law.

'I just want to show some respect,' said Owen.

'We know you do, Owen. If she had a sister, we'd take the clothes and maybe there'd be other stuff.'

Owen said nothing.

What was normal? He wished he knew.

'I'll take the clothes to Oxfam,' said Owen. 'The rest is make-up and jewellery. There's a laptop, a phone. Her books, DVDs, CDs are mixed in with mine.'

'Don't worry about it, Owen,' said his father-in-law.

He took another ginger biscuit and chomped.

'I have my own mementos,' said his mother-in-law.

'Of course,' said Owen.

'We have lots of photographs and even some recent videos. Don't we, Derek?'

'I got a decent camera a few years back,' said his father-in-law. 'Now I just use the iPhone. Not cheap but they gave me a good deal. What did you pay for the TV?'

'I can't remember.'

'Oh.'

'I was in a bit of a state after the burglary.'

'As long as you kept the receipt?'

'I'm not sure I did.'

'You should always keep the receipts.'

'I don't always. I know I should. Hailey used to say.'

There were still ginger biscuits on the plate but not many, and Owen was hungry.

'I'll get some more biscuits,' said Owen. 'I haven't been eating very well. I'm feeling a bit peckish.'

This was a lie about being peckish, about not eating well. The evening before he had eaten too much.

'You look as if you've lost weight,' said his mother-in-law.

'I might have,' said Owen.

This was also not true but let them think, thought Owen.

'I'll make some more tea,' said Owen. 'Do you want to see what the television looks like?'

'I don't mind,' said his father-in-law.

Owen handed the remote to his father-in-law and took the empty cups and the plate of biscuits into the kitchen. While Owen was making tea and finding biscuits he heard noise from the television. Owen watched the kettle boil and listened to his father-in-law change channels. Owen made the tea and returned to the living room. His father-in-law switched off the television. His father-in-law and Owen ate biscuits and drank tea. His mother-in-law took a few sips of tea.

'I had a look at the television,' said his father-in-law.

'I'd intended to keep the other one until it packed in,' said Owen.

'They're changing them all the time. It's worth keeping up to date.'

His mother-in-law paused to have a tearful sigh. She looked at the mug of tea on her lap as if it was a mystical object.

'I'm sorry,' said Owen. 'It's difficult to know what to say.'

He could of course have asked her if she knew her daughter was being banged by a bloke from Manchester. His mother-in-law would have approved of an actuary. Owen reckoned the cow knew.

'No, it's me, Owen,' said my mother-in-law. 'I have these tearful moments.'

'Sarah's done some crying,' said his father-in-law.

'I can imagine,' said Owen. 'I'll get the report from the coroner. I can do some work in the kitchen. I'll give you time to read it.'

This is what they did. The in-laws of Owen read the report while he sat in the kitchen. He stared at the open laptop but without doing any work. He ate a couple of ginger biscuits and then sneaked a look at the prices of iPhones. Owen was not tempted. The kitchen door opened. Owen was eating a ginger biscuit when his father-in-law poked his head around the edge of the door and smiled.

'You were hungry after all,' said his father-in-law.

'I thought I'd better,' said Owen.

'We've read the report.'

'Right.'

Owen followed his father-in-law into the living room. His father-in-law sat down on the sofa and next to his wife, and Owen sat in the armchair. The report was on the lap of his mother-in-law. The empty mugs of tea were on the floor. In her own home his mother-in-law served tea and biscuits on a trolley.

'We were expecting it to say accident,' said his mother-in-law.

'It was an accident,' said his father-in-law.

Owen wondered what judgements Hailey would make if she was here and watching all this. After the meal last night Owen had made an excuse about not wanting to catch a taxi. Rhys and Will had a spare bedroom in the attic. Owen using it had been no hardship. If the others thought it odd Owen had slept there, no one had objected.

'They don't say it was an accident,' said his mother-in-law.

Owen said nothing.

'I'm not sure what death by misadventure means.'

'It means the death of Hailey was more complicated than an accident, murder or suicide,' said Owen.

'She's hedging her bets,' said his father-in-law. 'The coroner, she's sitting on the fence.'

'Hailey wasn't happy but she wouldn't commit suicide,' said his mother-in-law. 'She was a beautiful woman.'

Owen tried to look earnest. Here we go again, he thought.

His mother-in-law looked down at the report.

'It said here that there was a big argument,' said his mother-in-law.

'It was a discussion,' said Owen.

'You were arguing with Hailey?'

'Everyone was arguing with me.'

The lips of his mother-in-law tightened. Her cheekbones sharpened into aspirational claws. His father-in-law stared at the switched off television. He put a hand on the elbow of his wife. Do not encourage the monster, thought Owen.

'Your own mother said you had a terrible tongue,' said his mother-in-law.

'Hailey and Owen argued over stupid things,' said his father-in-law.

Owen waited until these words had settled.

'I suppose the coroner feels that I should bear some responsibility,' said Owen.

'And you, Owen,' said his mother-in-law. 'What do you feel?'

Owen took a breath. He was willing to answer but he hesitated. He thought it was odd how his father-in-law was slouched on the sofa but was still capable of looking down his nose at Owen.

'What do you feel, Owen?' said his mother-in-law.

'I feel responsible,' said Owen. 'I don't need to read the coroner's report for that. I wasn't arguing with Hailey. They were all arguing with me. I thought it was a discussion. Admittedly we'd had too much to drink and people were being short-tempered.'

'Were you being insulting, Owen?'

'No, of course not.'

'You can be insulting, Owen.'

In his whole life he had never insulted this woman that was now sitting on the edge of his sofa. He had, of course, been reticent with the endorsements which was how she knew he resented sharing oxygen with her. But there had never been any insults.

And there had been many times when Owen shared with Hailey his misgivings about the woman. His remark to Hailey about the only difference between her mother and Hitler was that the Führer had drive and determination was probably not thought through. Not that Hailey had disagreed.

'I didn't insult anyone,' said Owen. 'It wasn't that kind of argument.'

'You said it was a discussion,' said his father-in-law.

'It was a heated discussion. It felt like an argument because the three of them were all disagreeing with me.'

'You upset Hailey,' said his mother-in-law. 'You drove her to her death.'

'I don't think so. She slipped in the bathroom.'

'You said you felt responsible.'

'I do feel responsible. Hailey was upset.'

Nobody was saying the obvious, that Hailey in temper had butted the mirror, which was just as well because Owen knew it was that which damned him. He kept this thought to himself. His mother-in-law turned her head to face her husband. He was still slouched on the sofa. To be fair to him he did have long legs and wide shoulders. Owen did not begrudge him comfort. His wife was another matter.

'If Hailey had never met me, she'd be alive,' said Owen. 'But if it had not been Will's birthday, Hailey would be alive. If Will hadn't watched some documentary on the TV, we wouldn't have had an argument. We could go on forever.'

'I wish she'd never met you,' said his mother-in-law.

'I wish she'd never met me.'

'You never loved her. Your own mother thinks you're a cold fish.'

'And maybe if that woman had found a different husband, I wouldn't be. And if Hailey had met someone other than me, she'd be alive. But she didn't.' Owen paused. 'And it hasn't worked out for the best. And I wish it had.'

His mother-in-law scowled, and her cheekbones or claws

became as sharp as daggers. His father-in-law sat up straight. His head climbed up the wall behind the sofa.

'We're taking this further,' said his mother-in-law.

'What is there to take?' said Owen.

He had raised his voice to this woman. This had not happened before.

'The coroner does not think it was a suicide,' said Owen, 'and the police know that she wasn't murdered. For Christ sake what is there to take?'

'I'd prefer you not to raise your voice,' said his mother-in-law. 'I know how you've upset Hailey.'

His father-in-law rubbed the back of his head against the wall. He did the same with his shoulders and some of his back.

'Hailey talked to you about our marriage?' said Owen.

'I know you had problems,' said his mother-in-law.

'We argued. We were argumentative.'

'You argued about daft things,' said his father-in-law.

Owen said nothing.

'You didn't like Hailey having opinions,' said his mother-in-law.

'I wouldn't say that,' said Owen.

'Your trouble, Owen, is you don't like being contradicted.'

Owen stared at his father-in-law. Owen did not expect help. He just wanted this man to be embarrassed, to worry that Owen might have had knowledge of his philandering escapades.

'I didn't think we were right for each other,' said Owen.

'Hailey loved you,' said his mother-in-law. 'That was the only reason she stayed with you.'

'If that was the only reason, it must have been why we argued.'

Owen could have amplified this comment because, as a thought, he reckoned it had potential. But there was nothing sitting on his sofa right then that tempted Owen. He could have said that what two people feel about each other is not enough. Just as important is all the other people out there poking their noses in and demanding feelings and a response. Making a sacrifice and doing without things for someone was not difficult. The problems begin when that particular someone wants you to share her notion of the world. Owen probably could have said more.

'Hailey shouldn't have discussed her marriage with you,' said Owen.

His father-in-law looked across the living room, past the shoulder of Owen and at whatever might have been outside. The mother-in-law of Owen picked up her empty cup and put it back on her lap. Owen assumed the woman was preparing to leave.

'If it makes you feel better to blame me for Hailey's death, feel free,' said Owen.

'We do blame you,' said his mother-in-law.

Her thin face scowled. Owen associated her sharp features with monstrosity but the woman had been attractive. She was still attractive, well, from a distance.

'I take it you've seen the *Echo*,' said his mother-in-law.

Owen said nothing.

'No, you know when to keep quiet if it suits you.'

His father-in-law shook his head. Moral disapproval from a rogue, thought Owen.

'I haven't seen the *Echo*,' said Owen.

This was true.

'It's a damned disgrace,' said his mother-in-law. 'Woman dies in mysterious circumstances after heated argument.'

'It's the papers,' said Owen.

'It's not as if Hailey didn't have options,' said his mother-in-law.

His father-in-law pulled his calves tight against the sofa.

'There's no point in us arguing,' said his father-in-law. 'It's best we go, Sarah. We'll study the report.'

His father-in-law bent forward and picked up his empty cup. These two had a definite aversion to leaving cups on the floor, thought Owen. The mother-in-law took the hand of her husband and as she rose she lifted her husband. Considering how thin she was, there might have been a pulley connecting the two of them, thought Owen. The report from the coroner and the empty cup was in the hand of his mother-in-law and both rested on her bony hip. With her other hand she turned up the collar on her reefer jacket. If his father-in-law had been less tall, Owen might have said nothing and opened the front door like a good son-in-law. But Owen felt that he was being patronised by a man that was a fake loyal husband.

'Did Hailey tell you she was having an affair?' said Owen.

His mother-in-law sighed. Inside the upturned collar on the reefer jacket her head looked tiny.

'I knew she had met someone,' said his mother-in-law.

'Met?'

'Hailey was distraught.'

'Met?'

'Yes, met.'

Owen smiled. The smile was not friendly.

'What exactly did Hailey say about this someone?'

His mother-in-law opened her mouth. Owen heard her take a breath but before she could speak the cup in her hand flew across the room. The cup crashed against the television screen. Owen heard a crack and turned his head. The empty cup bounced back to the middle of the floor and not far from the report from the coroner which had also decided to make the journey across the living room. A small scar appeared in the middle of the TV screen. Fuck, no, thought Owen. Both his in-laws had open mouths. The hand of his mother-in-law that had held the cup was trembling. The air in the room was cold but there was no smell of yeast or mould. The mother-in-law jerked her head and screamed. Not a loud roar but a noise loud enough to be described as a scream. The hair on her head reacted to something and moved around, as if it was being ruffled by a pair of hands. Her body was shaking. The father-in-law put an arm around his wife and held her tight. He looked from side to side, as if there might have been an explanation. In the middle of the living room carpet the empty cup and the report from the coroner were still. Despite the previous interference the hair of the mother-in-law of Owen looked as it had before. There were tears on her face. Her sobs were gentle and pleading.

'Derek,' said his mother-in-law.

'Sarah,' said his father-in-law.

Derek patted the top of the head of his wife Sarah. Her sobs sounded more earnest.

Owen remained in the armchair and where he was immune from accusations.

'There was something on the top of my head,' said his mother-in-law.

'I didn't see,' said his father-in-law.

A sensible remark in the circumstances, thought Owen. Not quite as immune as being sat in an armchair, of course.

'I've only just bought that television,' said Owen.

His in-laws separated. The father-in-law put his empty cup in the corner of the sofa, somewhere snug. His mother-in-law sobbed and shivered.

'I didn't do anything,' said his mother-in-law.

The air in the room was no longer ice cold.

'There was something in my hair,' said his mother-in-law.

Owen could have said something but he was brooding. This was the second television he had seen destroyed in a week and, because of the Covid lockdown, taking the damn things to a refuse tip would be a saga. He was also curious about what it was that this presence did not want him to know. Owen was not terrified but neither was he alone and this was the afternoon. He worried about nightfall and when he would have to switch off the lights. Owen did not even want to think about what had happened to the light switches.

'Like a hand,' said his mother-in-law, 'fingers running through my hair.'

'I've only just bought that television,' said Owen.

'Oh shut up about the damned TV,' said his mother-in-law.

'They're not cheap,' said Owen.

'I'll pay for the TV,' said his father-in-law.

'I'll claim it on the insurance. Sarah can't be the only woman that's wrecked the TV of a difficult son-in-law.'

'Derek, I didn't do anything,' said his mother-in-law.

'It must have been a draught,' said his father-in-law.

'Must have been some draught,' said Owen. 'That cup hit the TV with a hell of a belt.'

The sobs of his mother-in-law had changed to deep breaths. She looked like a sportsman taking exercise before a contest.

'It wasn't a draught,' said his mother-in-law.

'I was sitting here all the time,' said Owen.

This remark was for the record. The eyes of his mother-in-law followed the route from the trainers on her feet to the armchair where Owen sat. The distance and implied geometry defeated her intentions and any excuses. Owen stood up and picked up the empty cup and the report of the coroner. He took the report over to his father-in-law.

'I wish you luck with it all,' said Owen.

'I'll pay for the TV,' said his father-in-law.

'Derek, I didn't do anything,' said his mother-in-law.

'I'll claim it on the insurance okay,' said Owen. 'I hardly claim anything.'

His mother-in-law and father-in-law edged towards the door that led to the hall. They held hands, and the father-in-law made soothing noises. Somehow this made them look older. Both doors in the living room were closed which would give dear Derek something to think about when he was at home. Owen opened the door that was near the bay window and stepped into the hall where he opened the front door. On the other side of the doorstep everything was wet from the rain. Ahead of the in-laws Owen stepped outside and opened the giant umbrella. He handed it to his mother-in-law. Owen smiled and, as has often happened in the past, he felt redeemed by her look of hatred and contempt.

His mother-in-law walked to a blue BMW. His father-in-law paused by the doorstep.

'Owen,' he said. 'I'm sorry about all this.'

'It wasn't a draught, Derek,' said Owen.

His father-in-law nodded his head. His wavy hair was becoming damp from the rain.

'The death of Hailey has hit Sarah hard,' said his father-in-law.

'I understand,' said Owen.

'None of us are perfect.'

'I suppose not.'

'I'll get you a new TV. I'll find a cracker.'

'It's okay.'

'If you're sure.'

'I am.'

'I don't know what happened.'

'I know the feeling,' said Owen.

# TWENTY

He was drunk for the second night in a row or was it the third? His father had once told Owen that it was not possible to get drunk on beer. Well, Owen had proved him wrong on that one a long time ago. Owen smiled at the thought. Owen may have liked to have a beer but he also had an aversion to being drunk. But that was before he lived alone in a creepy house. Being drunk on consecutive days worried him but when it came to seeing his mother-in-law and being drunk he had a tradition to maintain. And there was always what might happen in the house next. Saying that sentence to himself was evidence of how the alcohol was affecting his brain. Owen suspected Hailey might be causing these disturbances but sober he preferred to think about a nameless spirit. The truth was that he would rather not think about any of it. Technology helped. Film 4 was showing a Korean movie called The Look Of Love. Though Owen was more distracted by the film than the crack in the middle of the screen, he accepted that this second TV would have to be replaced. Thinking about the in-laws in their Southport home and them trying to make sense of what happened in the afternoon made him giggle. He imagined his in-laws groping towards an adequate explanation and even perhaps his mother-in-law doubting herself. The woman was so awful, and it was not as if she had murdered anyone. He had once told Hailey that if her mother had the principles of Nelson Mandela he would still find her repellent. Owen understood that the air was for all to breathe and share yet he was not sure if it applied to his mother-in-law. Her hating him was not unimportant.

Right now Owen had a choice. He could watch the rest of the film and make sense of it or have another beer. The damned TV had a cracked screen. Owen decided to have another beer.

He was sitting in the armchair, drinking more beer and,

because the film had assumed less importance, the small crack in the middle of the TV had become more compelling. Owen thought about how much he would have paid on two new televisions in less than a week. The crack, dent or scar was the size and colour of the sixpence coins that people throw in a jar and never get round to taking to the bank. The last time he was given a sixpence was beyond his lockdown memory. In an odd way the markings on the splintered glass related to the engravings on coins. The crack in the television looked more white than silver but what was there was enough for Owen to be fanciful. There was no uniform perfection in this design, no microscopic Giant's Causeway. The physical world had its limits, supposed Owen.

Of course, he did not have a microscope. And he was drunk or loaded or plastered. The alcohol may help him sleep but he would wake up early and no doubt while it was still dark. Tomorrow, Owen would call the estate agent and ask him to put the house on the market. The crack in the TV acted as if it had overheard him. The white centre grew and almost twinkled like a star. More colours appeared, not bright but something other than white and grey. Why not, thought Owen. This was the latest technology 4K colour after all. If the thoughts in his head were flippant, the change in the colour of the crack in the TV screen was worrying. Owen switched off the television. The picture and the movie disappeared but the colours around the crack expanded into something that was the size of a fifty pence coin. Owen was concentrating and drunk. Half of him wondered if he was making an effort to imagine. If so, the efforts were successful. The fifty pence coin became the size of a tennis ball.

The colours around the crack settled and formed an image of the face of his father.

Was Owen seeing what he wanted or was the image there because it needed to make an appearance? Owen knew he was concentrating and that the alcohol was willing him to tease his imagination.

Owen blinked a couple of times, not in surprise because he expected the image to be there when he opened his eyes. The growth in the size of the image was measured and steady. The face of his father was clear and detailed, like something in a photograph but not real. It had the plastic gloss of an artificial image. And there was not the usual critical smile. His father looked as bemused and as curious as Owen felt. On the TV screen the face of his father had grown to the normal size. Everything was in place except there was no body below the neck, but because the face of his father looked like a photograph the image was not gory. His hair looked clean, and, because of his cancer stricken face, his large eyes shone. Owen concentrated and attempted to make the image grow but, like the expression on the face of his father, the size of the face remained the same. Owen picked up the TV remote control and pointed it at the screen. He held the remote as a threatening weapon and hoped it would produce a reaction in the image that was in the centre of the television. The expression on the face of his father settled into nothing more than modest curiosity and reserved expectation. Owen and his father stared at one another for a while. This was not like looking at a photograph. There was recognition in the eyes of his father. Compared to the image on the screen, Owen felt animated. Owen switched on the television but it had stopped working. Only the image of his father was visible. There was a faint trace of a smile. On the remote Owen turned up the volume. He had expected and hoped to hear breaths, perhaps a simple message. There was nothing. On the remote control Owen turned down the volume and pressed standby. Owen left his armchair and walked to the plug on the wall and denied the television electricity. There was no immediate reaction but after seconds or a minute the image of his father shrank at the same rate it had expanded. Owen watched it return to the crack in the screen and disappear. The living room was cold but the heating had been switched off by the timer an hour earlier. What had happened could have all been his imagination, thought Owen. It felt as if he had been willing something to happen but the face of his father on the TV screen had not done anything. The alcohol did not have the effect that it had before he saw the image of his father but Owen felt a lot more tired. Owen went to bed. Before that he used the bathroom. In front of the bathroom mirror Owen cleaned his teeth. Nothing happened but he was terrified because he dreaded his father making an appearance behind his shoulder. His father did not but his absence did nothing to calm Owen. The expression that had been on the face of his father had stayed in the mind of Owen. This time Owen gave the expression some words. 'How about all this?' he imagined his father saying. He remembered when in the past their arguments had run out of words. His father would look the same then. How about all this? What do we do now? Written all over his face. Owen jumped into bed and buried his head into the extra pillow. Owen sought refuge in the pillow of a bed that belonged to a house that was haunting him. It's not the daftest thing I've ever done, thought Owen. He remembered the last time he had slept in this bed. He thought how carefree he had been the night before and in the home of Rhys, everything, even the dark, had been so different over there. Owen expected there to be cold touches on his neck but nothing happened. He was not as terrified as he had been in the bathroom and that helped him to fall asleep. As expected, Owen woke up early because of the alcohol from the night before. The light in the room suggested dawn had arrived. Owen remembered the face of his father. He stayed in bed and remembered. There had been times when Owen had accused Hailey of not being able to end an argument. Owen had believed it was a trait that women had, to be compelled to return to arguments that had been lost. But lying in bed and thinking about the face of his father on the TV screen, Owen realised that his father had been the same.

# TWENTY-ONE

Detective Sergeant Jones was standing on the other side of the front door. Owen had managed a few extra hours of intermittent sleep after daylight. And after that the shower and boiled eggs and toast did what they could to clear the alcohol. Owen hoped he looked okay. Detective Sergeant Jones was wearing a black skirt, black pullover and white shirt, the same as she had worn at their first meeting. Her face mask was black. The reefer jacket that the mother-in-law wore would suit the Detective, thought Owen. He was holding the laptop. The lid was open.

'If you're working, I can call again,' said Detective Sergeant Jones.

'I can take a break,' said Owen.

As Owen stepped inside, Detective Sergeant Jones followed. Owen closed down the task and threw the laptop on to the sofa. Detective Sergeant Jones sat down in the armchair.

'I've met your mother-in-law,' said Detective Sergeant Jones.

'I'll make you a cup of tea,' said Owen.

'I could do with a cuppa.'

'Side with her and you won't get anything to eat. I've got chocolate digestives and ginger biscuits.'

'One of each should see off the mother-in-law. What's happened to the telly?'

'It's upstairs.'

'I don't know what you do with them.'

Owen smiled.

Owen walked into the kitchen. He returned with two mugs of tea and a plate of biscuits. While Owen had been in the kitchen Detective Sergeant Jones had removed her mask.

'You should know what your mother-in-law has been saying,' said Detective Sergeant Jones. 'I also told her I'd come and see you.'

'You should have been a diplomat.'

'I'm more concerned about you.'

Owen said nothing and ate a chocolate digestive. It occurred to him that since Hailey died this was the first chocolate digestive he had eaten and that Detective Sergeant Jones was the first woman to see him eat one. The eyes of Detective Sergeant Jones were the same colour as the chocolate on the digestives. Owen was tempted to say that a superstitious man would have thought it might all qualify as providence.

He said nothing.

'Your mother-in-law came to the station,' said Detective Sergeant Jones. 'She saw my name in the report.'

'I'm sorry,' said Owen.

'Nothing you can do about it, Owen. Her husband was there as well. He didn't say much.'

'He doesn't get the chance.'

'He's been a handsome man.'

'He won't disagree with that.'

'She's been an attractive woman. She's too thin, of course. I recorded her visit and everything but there's nothing more for me to do. That's clear from the inquest.'

Owen said nothing.

'She spoke to my boss. She insisted.'

'Oh dear.'

'My boss backs me.'

'I'm glad about that.'

'He was glad to see the back of her.'

The plate of biscuits was halfway between the Detective and Owen. The plate was perched on the arm at the end of the sofa. Detective Sergeant Jones leaned forward from the armchair and took another biscuit from the plate. Owen sat at the far end of the sofa.

'Two biscuits will be my limit,' said Detective Sergeant Jones. 'I am cursed with a sweet tooth.'

'I like a biscuit,' said Owen.

'You should be told what your mother-in-law said.'

'I drove Hailey to her death.'

Detective Sergeant Jones pouted and took a small bite of her biscuit. Owen chewed the crumbs that were inside his mouth. Detective Sergeant Jones stopped eating her biscuit. Unable to put it back on the plate perched three feet away she kept the biscuit in her hand.

'Maybe I did drive Hailey to her death,' said Owen, 'but if I did, I didn't intend to. And if I did, it happened in a way I couldn't stop.'

'What would have happened,' said Detective Sergeant Jones, 'if you'd prevented it?'

Owen said nothing.

'If you'd heard a bang and found Hailey on the floor and breathing.'

'I'm not sure she'd have told me the truth, what she'd done.'

'You'd have seen the blood on the mirror. You'd have worked it out, Owen.'

'What would have happened? We'd have put on a show for Rhys and Will and then gone home and had a long talk.'

'You'd have told Hailey you loved her?'

'We'd have had a long chat, might have had another argument.'

Detective Sergeant Jones laughed. The grin of Owen was apologetic.

'That is what your mother-in-law thinks,' said Detective Sergeant Jones.

'We shouldn't deny a mother her anguish,' said Owen. 'It won't occur to the cow but she's not the only one suffering. I do understand guilt and responsibility.'

'I know you do, Owen. I don't know what she expects. The coroner pointed a finger at you. Another coroner would have said an accident. I told your mother-in-law, even if we wanted, we couldn't arrest you. She's lucky to get death by misadventure. I didn't say that to her.'

'But you did say you'd come and have a word with me.'

Detective Sergeant Jones smiled.

'It's my job,' she said.

'I know,' said Owen.

'Know?'

'Nothing you can do other than what you have to.'

Owen finished his biscuit, and so did Detective Sergeant Jones.

'We've eaten all the chocolate digestives,' said Owen.

'I only had two,' said Detective Sergeant Jones.

There had been six biscuits on the plate. Owen did not remember eating the rest. I must have done some munching, he thought.

'I just thought you should know,' said Detective Sergeant Jones.

'That she doesn't like me,' said Owen. 'I learnt that a long time ago.'

'Her husband didn't say very much.'

'Derek supports her because he wants a quiet life.'

'He did say you and Hailey weren't right for each other.'

'I don't disagree with that. No doubt Sarah was going on about how Hailey went down in the world.'

'I said you had a decent job, better than Hailey had.'

'They've got a few bob and live in Southport and in this big house painted white. Sarah imagined her daughter being a prisoner here. They hated this house. Half the reason Hailey wanted to move home was to shut her mother up. She was always trying to make the peace.'

'Between her mother and you.'

'Between Hailey and Sarah. I'm the consequence of her beautiful daughter lowering her sights.'

'She was very pretty.'

Detective Sergeant Jones looked around the small living room. Each of the three walls had a large painting. When Hailey had talked about moving Owen had worried about how the paintings would look on bigger walls. The empty plate was still perched on the arm of the sofa. Owen took the cups and plate into the kitchen and returned to the living room.

'Just ginger biscuits next time,' he said. 'Are you sure you only had two?'

They both grinned.

'I bet you thought you'd seen the last of me,' said Detective Sergeant Jones.

'I'm sorry you had to meet the woman.'

'I just thought you should know. I wanted to put your mind at rest. You've been through a bit.'

'Yeah but I'm still here.'

'Accidents happen. I said that to your mother-in-law.'

'I don't like you being put out.'

'That's not a problem, Owen.'

'You've been decent with me.'

'I was on the way home. It's not a problem.'

'You've been decent from the start.'

Owen was wary of staring at Detective Sergeant Jones. He remembered the conversation with Rhys, the moment when he said she would have to be the woman that got away. He looked at the large brown eyes. Because of the circumstances, she was forbidden fruit. This, of course, he realised, did not make Detective Sergeant Jones look less attractive. Owen averted his eyes and stared at the space where the television had been.

'You can't get the television fixed?' said Detective Sergeant Jones.

Owen shook his head. For some reason he pretended this was amusing. The two of them laughed.

'You don't fancy a trip to Currys?' said Owen.

'I can come if you want,' said Detective Sergeant Jones. 'I like spending money, even better when it's not my own.'

Owen looked around the living room and waited for something to happen. Nothing did. Everything was normal or seemed to be. The quiet felt precious. Owen suspected a part of him wanted the Detective to know what had been happening. He had an urge to tell someone.

'I should let you get home,' said Owen.

'Aren't you working?' said Detective Sergeant Jones.

'They're giving me some slack this week. I've done a bit. Next Monday it gets serious.'

Detective Sergeant Jones smiled. Her eyes sprang to life. Her regular features looked friendly and winsome.

'I'm not tired,' she said.

Owen was but not of her. But he should not have been doing this, he thought. He was being unfair to a woman that had died prematurely and whose death was the result of her meeting him and listening to the lies he had shared with her.

'Okay, Detective,' said Owen.

# TWENTY-TWO

The Volvo was parked in the shopping mall car park and opposite the door of Currys PC World. Holly and Owen sat in the front seats of the Volvo. Owen was behind the steering wheel. On the journey to the store he had asked if it was alright to call her Holly. She said of course and giggled. Holly and Owen put on their face masks and gloves. They stared at the huge sign above the shop entrance.

'I call it Currys,' said Holly. 'I bet you call it PC World. I bought my last washer here. I wouldn't trust a man that called it Currys.'

'Don't let Rhys hear you say that,' said Owen.

'I didn't mean anything.'

'I'll stand by you.'

Holly and Owen walked into the store. It was not empty, not quite. There were as many assistants as shoppers. The assistants wore face masks. Owen walked towards the computers but Holly grabbed his elbow and steered him towards the televisions. All were switched on and all had enormous bright unblemished screens. Despite showing programmes and football and rugby matches none of the TVs made a sound. Actors and presenters mouthed silent words. The sportsmen knocked hell out of one another.

A young female assistant walked over and stood next to Holly. She was not as tall as Holly nor as pretty.

'I bought one of these two days ago,' said Owen.

'You're just looking?' said the assistant.

'No, we'll buy a TV.'

The assistant was puzzled and she frowned.

'We can arrange a delivery,' said the assistant. 'Give me a shout when you've decided.'

The young assistant smiled before she walked away. The puzzled frown reappeared on her face.

'That woman is carrying a secret,' said Holly.

'You know?' said Owen.

'I can tell.'

'They don't pay them much.'

'Owen, you do have a heart then.'

'You think so?'

'It's just a little cold.'

'Someone once told me it was solid black.'

'Hailey?'

'Someone else. Hailey worried more about what I was thinking than feeling.'

Holly grinned and pretended she was suffering. Holly and Owen stared at the televisions. Owen wasted time looking at the supersized models that would be too big for his living room. He glanced over his shoulder at the computers, iMacs, smartphones, printers, Bluetooth speakers and everything else.

'I could look at this stuff all day,' said Owen.

'I have left a police vehicle outside your front door,' said Holly.

Owen pulled a face and pretended to be confused.

'If it's pinched,' said Holly, 'I'll say you had to make a visit and I wanted to conclude the interview. I'll think of something. Not that I'd like it to get stolen. My boss has been a right pain since lockdown. He says I have too much pride and not enough ambition. It's not that I'm not pushy. I have to be to get by.'

'The car will be safe but we won't be long. It doesn't look like a cop car.'

As Owen said this, the image from one of the TVs fractured at the corner of his eye and produced pale light that was more a sharp slice than a blob or patch. He turned his head and another slice of pale light appeared at the corner of the other eye. Owen had not been looking at the TVs for a long time. He had spent more time looking at TVs when he had bought the ones that were now parked upstairs at home.

'I'm getting flashing lights,' said Owen.

'My father gets that,' said Holly. 'It doesn't last. You've probably strained your neck. Staring at these TV screens won't help. It sounds like a migraine.'

'I don't get migraines.'

Owen held his head still to avoid the pale flashing lights reappearing.

'I haven't been sleeping well,' he said.

'You could have slept awkwardly,' said Holly. 'You haven't got a headache?'

Owen turned away from the bright glare of the televisions. The pale flashing lights distorted what was at the side of his head.

'My dad closes the curtains,' said Holly. 'He puts the headphones on, has a doze and it usually goes.'

'I've never had it before.'

'It won't be life changing, Owen.'

'It's embarrassing, though.'

'Don't be daft.'

Holly touched the elbow of Owen with her own. He waved to the young female assistant. She walked towards Holly and Owen.

'I'll just get the same Samsung,' he said to the assistant.

Holly and Owen followed the assistant towards the till. He blinked a couple of times to see if it had an effect on the pale flashing lights.

'I'll want the television delivered,' he said.

The assistant nodded with enthusiasm but the expression on her face was soon replaced by another.

Owen typed his credit card pin into the credit card machine. Everything he saw was limited to the tunnel of clear images that existed between the fractured flashing lights that were at both sides of his head. He noticed, though, that the young woman on the till smiled. Holly led the way out of the store.

'The car's insured for any driver,' said Owen.

'I bet you're insured for everything,' said Holly.

Owen and Holly walked towards the Volvo. Holly had the car

keys in her hand. The sunshine had given the flashing lights a sharper edge. Owen turned his head to look at the closed Pizza Hut that was adjacent to Currys PC World. Owen had never eaten in Pizza Hut and although he knew the restaurant would be closed because of lockdown he felt obliged to see it confirmed. The rectangle of light that leaked out of the corner of his eye was bigger than the ones before and it lasted longer than the others. In the centre of the rectangle of light there was a weird and incomplete light grey silhouette of a human figure. The head and torso were complete but the silhouette ended in a point somewhere below the hips. Owen could not distinguish whether the figure was a man or a woman. The figure was in the middle of the square of light that was next to his eye but somehow the silhouetted figure was distant, as if it were hovering somewhere on the edge of the car park around the Pizza Hut. The shape of the silhouette was distorted and unstable. The image rippled and waved like a flag in the wind. The image faded in and out and throughout the face was nothing but blurred features. Owen, though, sensed that the face had an expression. This face was critical rather than accusatory, and it also looked like the figure was desperate about something. Owen felt that he was being warned by someone or something that did not want its pain to be shared. Some of the other flashing lights that had leaked from the corner of his eyes had slight tints of colour around the edges. But there was no colour in this shape of a figure, just shades of black, white and grey. When Holly sat down behind the steering wheel of the Volvo the shape or the figure disappeared. The other pale flashing lights, though, continued.

'You don't look right,' said Holly.

'I've never had this before,' said Owen.

'I can stay for tea, until you settle.'

Holly shrugged her shoulders and her face pleaded.

Owen looked out of the windscreen. At the side of his head the squares of flashing lights persisted but there were no silhouette figures.

'I'll cook the tea,' said Owen. 'I'm not that bad. It's just annoying. I can see what I'm doing.'

'I'll stay with you until it goes dark,' said Holly.

'The time I take to cook, you'll have to.'

They both laughed.

# TWENTY-THREE

Holly and Owen sat at the table in the kitchen. Holly sipped from a glass of red wine. Owen swallowed some spaghetti bolognese. He drank sparkling mineral water. He wore sunglasses.

'The flashing lights have gone?' said Holly.

Owen took the glasses away from his eyes and looked around. He nodded.

Although the evening was not yet dark the venetian blinds on the kitchen window were closed. The light that entered the kitchen came through the window in the kitchen door. In the low light the blonde highlights in the hair of Holly did not look as bright.

'Put the glasses back on,' said Holly.

'I feel like I'm posing,' said Owen.

'I know you're not. They suit you. Migraines don't last long. This low light helps.'

Owen put on his sunglasses.

'Just as well you were there,' said Owen.

'You'd have got home,' said Holly. 'Dad's driven with migraines when he's had to. He prefers not to, of course. I liked driving the Volvo.'

'You like your dad?'

'I don't mind him. He loves me and he's done me no harm. If he's not watching the football, he likes to be kept busy. He's always doing odd jobs around the house. His motor is immaculate. He worked in printing. He used to fix laminating machines. I once had a fella that said my dad spoke the biggest load of shite about football he'd ever heard. That wasn't the reason we split up.'

Owen waited but Holly said nothing. They ate some spaghetti bolognese.

'Your boyfriend?' said Owen.

'All he ever talked about was football,' said Holly. 'All he ever wanted to watch was football. He did know what he was talking about. I don't mind the odd football game. I missed the final in Istanbul, you know, the famous one. I knew it was on the telly but I was seeing a friend that night. He never forgave me. That wasn't the reason we split up.'

'I didn't even like football as a kid. My brother had trials with Everton.'

Holly pretended to be surprised.

'My dad would have liked me to be like your dad,' said Owen. 'Rhys was his favourite.'

'You were your mother's favourite?' said Holly.

'No, everyone liked Rhys. My father went to his grave not knowing Rhys was gay.'

Owen shrugged his shoulders. Shrugs from Owen had appeared in more than one conversation about Rhys.

'I'm curious why you joined the police,' said Owen.

Holly grinned.

'You don't have to tell me.'

'I wouldn't if you didn't have your sunglasses on. When I was really young I wanted to be an archaeologist. I wanted to be Indiana Jones. Maybe it was something to do with the name. I grew up and then started watching crime movies. It was as daft as that. I didn't want to be like my parents. I didn't want to do ordinary jobs. I told myself I might be doing something useful but I'm not sure if I was just kidding myself. Some coppers say they want to help victims of crime. That wasn't me. I suppose there were all kinds of reasons.'

Holly took a breath and a sip of wine.

'I hated teaching and I didn't want to be a civil servant,' said Owen. 'I couldn't think of anything else. My dad was a landscape gardener. He did big gardens, new housing estates. The family did all right. He worked for himself. My dad was made up when Rhys became an architect. I needed something steady. I'm not sure I'd be steady without something steady.'

'The chaos people make gets me down,' said Holly. 'I thought if I were in the police I could sort some of them out. I liked how you phoned the police after your wife died. Most people wouldn't have thought. The coroner should have given you a commendation, not slagged you off.'

Holly smiled and stopped eating. She brushed her fingers against the hand of Owen.

'One of my friends became a policewoman,' said Holly. 'That was another reason I joined the police. It all seems a long time ago now.'

'Hailey stressed over her job,' said Owen. 'She took it so seriously. I tried to explain.'

Owen hesitated and remembered an argument.

'Explain what?' said Holly.

'To do something well,' said Owen, 'it's best if you have contempt for what you're doing.'

Holly put down her fork and banged the table with her fist.

'That's right, Owen,' she said. 'I know what you mean. In the police you're not going to sort anything if you tell yourself you have to. Nobody helps anyone with a good heart. They just burn themselves up. That's what I like in people. The ones who get things done and don't get all emotional.'

Owen waited.

Holly let Owen wait. She picked up her fork.

'Detached decency?' said Owen.

'That's it,' said Holly. 'That's it. That's what I thought when I saw you. You do my job and after a while you know you can't do your job unless you're detached. But it's not just your job with you, is it?'

Owen smiled.

'That's what made me curious, Owen.' Holly paused. 'I also thought you looked alright. That makes a difference.' Holly sipped some wine. 'This bolognese is alright.'

'As good as yours?'

'You'll have to find out, Owen.'

'I'm hoping I can have a glass of wine the next time.'

'A lot of people have the flashing lights. It's not like having heavy migraines. My mother showed me how to cook spaghetti bolognese. I was still at school. She cooked in the kitchens in the same school. I'm not that much of a cook but I can do decent bolognese.'

Owen stopped eating and removed his dark glasses.

'I'm fed up of these,' he said.

He stared at Holly and smiled.

'I also thought you looked alright,' said Owen.

'I didn't think you'd noticed me,' said Holly.

'I was all over the place. I noticed you. I just didn't want to think about it.'

Hailey smiled.

She picked up her glass of wine, put it to her lips but did not drink. She put the glass back down on the table.

'I'd like to see you again,' said Owen.

'Of course,' said Holly. 'You have to try my bolognese.'

'I want to see you again.' Owen paused. 'But.'

'What?'

'This will have to be taken slowly.'

'You have doubts?'

'I have to show some respect.'

'Your wife was having an affair. I hear things, Owen.'

He nodded.

'Still,' he said.

'I understand,' said Holly. 'No sex this month then.'

Owen smiled but said nothing.

'No embargo on goodnight kisses then?'

Owen said nothing.

'And even a couple of hugs.'

Owen said nothing.

'A couple of hugs in a month isn't asking for much.'

'No, Holly, it isn't.'

'Is it windy outside?'

Owen stared through the window in the kitchen door.

'I don't think so,' he said.

'It looks still,' said Holly.

'It is still.'

'Oh, I thought I heard something.'

Owen shook his head and pretended not to worry. Holly and Owen finished the spaghetti bolognese.

'I shouldn't stay and talk,' said Holly. 'Not with the car sitting outside.'

Owen nodded and said nothing. At his front door, and with all the neighbours to see, they kissed and hugged. Owen heard something that sounded like the wind. The evening, though, was warm and still.

# TWENTY-FOUR

Owen was sitting in his living room and reading. The book was called The Welsh Wars Of Independence and was written by a historian called David Moore. The father of Owen had been halfway through the book when he died. Out of loyalty Owen had taken the book from his mother. Until now, though, he had avoided reading it. The light from the standard lamp was not bright. In normal circumstances the room would have been cosy. The flashing lights at the corner of his eyes had disappeared which was just as well, thought Owen, because Henry IV had arrived in Anglesey and was burning monasteries and villages. Thinking about fires and the draught that accompanied flames made Owen remember the noise that Holly had heard outside the kitchen and he had heard on the doorstep when they kissed. The living room was silent and, without the presence of a television, as still as it had ever been. Owen sat on the sofa with his back to the wall and everything else in front of him. He put the book to one side and stared at the gas fire and hearth. His eyes were heavy. The last couple of years Hailey had needed to wear glasses when she read. He remembered Hailey taking him along when she chose a pair and her trying on Owen some of the glasses designed for men. People watching them would have assumed that they liked one another, thought Owen. He saw Hailey no more than a couple of times in her Covid mask. For some reason that felt poignant to Owen.

He picked up the book and, like the people of Anglesey had, he battled on. Owen hoped he would be able to sleep. He hoped nothing would happen except that he knew it would. Owen closed his eyes and imagined Owain Glyndŵr and his men riding over a green Welsh hill and past a stone circle like Swinside. Owen remembered the day he threw the ashes of Hailey on the ground between the standing stones, the conversation with the farmer and the feeling that Owen had made a decision that would have consequences. Or did it? Owen was not sure if he was reimagining history. He looked at the cover of the book. Why not? Everyone else did.

Owen heard something. It sounded like the breath of a powerful loudspeaker or the rumble of a faulty DVD playing through a sound system. It sounded like what Holly had thought was the wind outside.

The noise did not last long, no more than an extended breath from something very large. Owen was thinking about this when mist appeared around the skirting board. The mist was white and silent but he was not alarmed. Owen was weary but curious. The mist filled the corner of the room where the television had been. His mobile phone was on the arm of the sofa. Owen picked up the mobile phone but did nothing. He waited and watched the white mist in the corner of the room. There was more mist than before and it was rising from the floor. The room had turned cold, almost without Owen noticing. He rubbed his hands but the rest of his body had also chilled. Owen rubbed his back against the sofa. The white mist was as high as his knees and had reached the middle of the room. Because the mist was as thick as a blanket and as white as milk, it hid most of the gas fire from view. His body, though, was becoming used to the cold. Instead of rubbing his hands and back he sat still. There was no smell of yeast. The mist did not move towards Owen but it filled the space in the middle of the living room. Owen could see his arms and legs and the cushions on the sofa and the armchair but no more than that. The white mist rose. The painting above the gas fire and hearth disappeared behind white mist. Owen stretched an arm and put a hand into the white mist. More than once he clenched the hand into a fist. The skin on the back of his hand was ice cold. Owen remembered a line from a song. 'You can take my body. You can take my bones. You can take my blood but not my soul.' The mist did not feel like anything. It was no colder than the rest of the room. The hand that was in the mist Owen put on his thigh. The hand was normal but it remained cold. Owen was proud of not being afraid. He stood up and stepped forward so that the white mist surrounded him. The mist and room were cold but there was nothing to feel or hear or smell or see. He had expected the mist to swirl and make shapes in the same way the silhouetted figure had in the pale light that he had seen outside Pizza Hut. But the white mist did nothing other than wait. Standing in the white mist Owen was tempted to speak and to issue a challenge. He did not but being surrounded by white mist that did nothing could not prevent Owen from imagining himself as heroic. Owen was proud of himself. The white mist had probably reached the ceiling of the living room.

Owen thought about the line from the song. Hailey, I took your body to Swinside. I took your bones. I might have even taken some dried blood. I did not, though, take your soul. Owen said these words out loud. His mouth opened and there was white mist on his tongue. It was cold but it did not taste of anything. Owen thought of porridge without sugar.

That was enough heroism for one evening, he thought.

Owen stepped back and sat down on the sofa. He put his legs together and his hands on his thighs. The mist thinned and drifted down towards the floor. The mist slid across the carpet, fractured into separate clouds and shrank into nothing. The room became warmer. There was a final noise similar to what Holly and Owen had heard in the kitchen. His earlier notion that the previous noise had occurred outside felt to Owen now like an idea that would have appealed to an adolescent. He leaned back into the sofa and remembered the white mist. He was not afraid. If Owen did not think of the white mist as friendly, neither did it feel threatening. Owen looked at his hands and remembered them being ice cold. There was a spirit in this house, though, thought Owen, and it could when threatened be violent. The evidence was the two wrecked televisions in the upstairs bedroom. But the white mist was different, calm and supportive and, better than that, curious.

Owen had felt as if he had appeal. Sitting on the sofa, he remembered his marriage and how calm support from Hailey had alternated with hostile antagonism. Appreciation and respect existed but they always had to be punctured at some point by conflict and hatred.

Christ, he felt like a drink.

Because he did not want the flashing lights to return, Owen walked into the kitchen and searched for a biscuit. He ate a couple of digestives. On the table there was a glass of water and a packet of Holland and Barrett magnesium tablets. Owen remembered. Hailey had bought a packet of magnesium tablets because her mother Sarah had a couple of times used the threat of a migraine to win an argument. The threats had not disappeared but, because Sarah hated taking the magnesium tablets, her threats had reduced. Owen picked up the glass of water and the magnesium tablets and took them upstairs. In bed he sent text messages to his brother and Bobby Briggs. Owen put the water and tablets on the bedside cabinet and next to the mobile phone. He did not have a headache nor flashing lights but he took the magnesium tablets that he had forgotten existed.

# TWENTY-FIVE

'Shouldn't you be in work?' said Rhys.

'I've done a bit this week,' said Owen.

'You haven't done much.'

'No, not much. I've done some. My boss is giving me some slack.'

'It could become a habit, Owen.'

Indolence always exists as an alternative for me in the future, thought Owen. I could even become a shabby eccentric. He rejected the idea but it had nothing to do with watching Rhys click the mouse on his computer and peer at complicated drawings.

'I want to get back to work,' said Owen. 'I'm going in next week. They're giving me an office. I'll go in every day.'

'I didn't know you had an office,' said Rhys.

'It was all open plan. Because of Covid, they've gone back to the managers having offices.'

'That'll be alright then.'

'I think so. I don't like sitting in the house all day. Not that house.'

'It is a bit pokey, Owen.'

The two men were sitting in the study that Rhys used. His two desktop monitors were both switched on. Rhys sat at his desk. Owen sat in an armchair. They both drank coffee that Owen had made. Owen was not sure how but he knew his way around the kitchen. Rhys stared at the diagrams that filled both monitors.

'The job centre hasn't half grown,' said Owen.

'This is the new reception for Aintree Hospital,' said Rhys. 'One of them. The revolving door that goes in that space there will cost a few bob.'

Rhys moved his mouse around the task bar at the bottom of the screen and clicked the mouse. A photograph of an all-glass circular and revolving door filled the monitor screen, the kind you see at the front of fancy hotels except bigger, thought Owen.

'You can't begrudge the sick,' he said.

Rhys shrugged his shoulders.

'It could be us one day.'

'I suppose.'

Rhys clicked his mouse and the previous diagrams returned.

'The job centre stuff went off yesterday,' said Rhys. 'I've done a few job centres. It's simple stuff. I can do job centres in my sleep. I was in bed when I got your text.'

'It didn't wake you?'

'I wasn't asleep.'

'You weren't having sex with Will?'

'I can't remember.'

Rhys and Owen laughed.

'I'll tell him what you said,' said Owen.

'Tell him,' said Rhys. 'Will's not like you. He's got a sense of humour.'

Rhys looked at the diagrams on his desktop monitor.

'Hospitals are a pain,' said Rhys. 'There are all kinds of specifications. Miss one and something happens to a patient and we all get sued.'

'They obviously trust you, Rhys.'

'You're joking. My work will be crawled over by all and sundry. We have margins. Since the government sold off the buildings we get away with crazy prices.'

'I read it was competitive tendering?'

'Fuck off, Owen. All it needs is a couple of phone calls.'

'Is everyone corrupt, Rhys?'

'I don't know everyone.'

The two men laughed.

'You can make another cup of coffee while you're here,' said Rhys.

Owen walked to the kitchen and did what he was told. Rhys appeared in the kitchen and sat down at the table. He stared through the large kitchen window and at his back lawn. Rhys pointed at the back garden, and Owen looked. A couple of squirrels ran around the lawn and up and down the three trees that framed the large garden.

'Look,' said Rhys.

'I've seen them before,' said Owen.

Nevertheless, he watched the squirrels.

'Will puts out feed for them,' said Rhys.

'He's a treasure,' said Owen.

'Don't be a twat. Remember, Owen, I'm older than you.'

Owen poured hot water into the two cups and took the cups of coffee over to the table. Rhys and Owen watched the squirrels. They were energetic and had favourite garden spots where they could hide in the foliage. When they disappeared from view it was not for long.

'Will starts his new job in a fortnight,' said Rhys. 'He's already been Zooming on meetings with his new people. He's so excited.'

'No harm in that, Rhys,' said Owen.

'I'm pleased for him.'

Owen drank some coffee.

'You wouldn't have a biscuit?' said Owen.

'We don't eat them,' said Rhys.

'You do look a bit hefty.'

'The doctor said I'm the right weight for my age. I have an Easter egg left over.'

'It'll be alright?'

'Chocolate lasts forever. This one came from Will's boss. It cost a few bob.'

'We can't eat Will's Easter egg.'

'He won't mind. Will's allergic to chocolate. He can eat a little bit if he has to.'

'He eats chocolate to keep the boss happy?'

'If he has to.'

'I hope the pimples are worth it.'

'He hasn't got pimples. He only eats a little bit.'

'I never bought Will a gift for getting promoted.'

'No, you didn't.'

'You think I should have?'

'Will didn't notice. You brought a bottle of wine over for the meal.'

'So I did.'

Owen stared at the trees and bushes in the back garden. He thought about hills and fields and Swinside Stone Circle.

'I'm not sure I should have taken the ashes of Hailey to that stone circle,' said Owen.

'If that was what Hailey wanted,' said Rhys.

'I know but you read stuff about stone circles. I could have been playing with fire.'

'Look, the grey squirrel has found the nut tray. He always gets to it first. The little bugger has some appetite.'

Rhys and Owen watched the grey squirrel eat nuts. The red squirrel was out of sight. Those occasions when the two squirrels were around together they appeared to be friendly. The weather was dry and grey. Rhys stood and searched inside a cupboard. He found the Easter egg and broke it into pieces.

'Aren't there any chocolates inside?' said Owen.

'They were in a separate plastic bag. I ate them,' said Rhys.

He put the pieces of Easter egg on a plate and carried the plate to the table. Rhys and Owen ate pieces of chocolate.

'It's good chocolate,' said Owen.

Rhys swallowed a piece and nodded his head.

'I haven't had an Easter egg for years,' said Owen.

'That's because you're a miserable sod,' said Rhys.

'I'm content enough. I'm just not sociable like you. People are like chocolate. I tire of people quickly.'

'You weren't always anti-social.'

Owen drank some coffee and ate some chocolate.

'I must be getting an appetite,' said Owen. 'Just as well I'm not a squirrel.'

In the garden the red squirrel joined the grey squirrel. They both ate the nuts that Will had left in the garden. Rhys and Owen ate the last two pieces of chocolate.

'You were always going out when you were young,' said Rhys.

Owen said nothing.

The two squirrels separated. They moved at speed which was odd considering that it only took them seconds to cross the garden. Owen thought about the chocolate he had just eaten. He reckoned it was from Belgium. Owen was glad he had visited Rhys.

'Mother remembers you being sociable,' said Rhys.

Owen said nothing.

'Mother said you stopped being sociable as soon as you were too old for boozing, fighting and chasing dirty women. Once being sociable meant gardening clubs and bowls or doing something worthwhile our Owen lost interest. So she said.'

'Bowls?'

Rhys grinned.

'Did you tell Mam about the dirty women?'

'She had you taped, Owen. Dad worried about you when you were young.'

'If he could see me now. I didn't have that many fights. A couple hit me first.'

'Mother said Dad and her were desperate for you to find a nice girl.'

'They certainly made Hailey welcome. Apart from when Dad told her that he couldn't see what she saw in me.'

'He'd had a few drinks. Mother didn't think you'd ever fall in love with anyone. It faded fast, Owen, though, didn't it?'

Owen ignored Rhys and looked out of the kitchen window. The squirrels were not in sight.

'I found that last piece of chocolate sickly,' said Owen.

'You're not going to make it a habit?' said Rhys.

'I don't think so. Who was it said romantic love was selfish? We had to have love in our hearts but it had to be universal.'

'Sounds like Auden.'

'I knew I could rely on you, Rhys.'

'I can't see you loving everyone, Owen.'

'You're not going to miss the deadline on this hospital reception? I'm not holding you up?'

'I've built in margins. Everyone knew Hailey and you had problems.'

Owen said nothing.

'She loved you, Owen. She wanted someone different, and you were.'

Owen said nothing.

In the garden the squirrels had reappeared. They were either arguing or teasing one another. The red squirrel bolted up a tree, and the grey squirrel found a bush by the fence.

'Hailey wanted you to help her engage with the world, and you wanted a retreat,' said Rhys.

'So you've said, often,' said Owen.

The two men stared at the large back garden. The red squirrel climbed down the tree and dashed across the garden and from one corner to the other. On his way he passed the grey squirrel that had come out from the bush by the fence. The grey squirrel headed for the tree that the red squirrel had left.

'Are the two squirrels the same sex?' said Owen.

'We haven't looked,' said Rhys.

'I envy Will and you. You're both sociable.'

'Will more so than me. We've had arguments. Not like Hailey and you. I'm not as bad as you, Owen.'

'Bad?'

'The same.'

'I envy Will and you.'

'You've just said that.'

'Being the same sex. I wanted some space for myself, and my wife thought I was just another selfish male.'

'I can't see you not arguing yourself out of that one.'

'I did, more than once. Hailey wouldn't leave it alone.'

'She wouldn't want you having the last word. You're both like that, Owen.'

'I didn't want the last word. I hate repeating myself. I just wanted some relief.'

'Well, you've got it now,'

'Not that way, Rhys. I didn't wish her dead.'

Rhys picked up the two empty cups and plate and took them over to the kitchen sink.

'You may as well stay for lunch,' said Rhys.

'That chocolate has filled me up,' said Owen.

'By the time I've made it.'

'That detective was around last night.'

'Oh, yes.'

'I cooked a spaghetti bolognese.'

'Not even a lasagne.'

'It was a spur of the moment thing.'

'Oh yes. I hope you don't call her detective.'

'I've started calling her Holly.'

'Wait until Mother finds out.'

'Nothing happened. She left when it turned dark. We just talked. I had a migraine yesterday.'

'Jesus, Owen, what are you doing eating chocolate and drinking coffee?'

'I'm hoping the migraine was a one off.'

'Still.'

'I told Holly I didn't want to rush into anything. I don't want to be disrespectful to Hailey.'

'She had an affair.'

'Hailey is also dead.'

'You keep saying.'

'I'm going to sell the house.'

Rhys said nothing.

'I find it a bit creepy since Hailey has died.'

'You're bound to, Owen. You know my view. Capital assets are important. Look at how our parents prospered.'

'That wasn't why they kept buying and selling houses. Mam was restless.'

'They still prospered.'

'If anything goes wrong with the house, you'd be able to put me up for a few weeks?'

'Of course.'

'Will wouldn't mind.'

'Of course not. You can have the top floor. You'd have your own bathroom up there.'

'It'd be a few weeks at the most.'

'Of course.'

'Between houses. I'm not saying it would happen.'

'I'd make sure you weren't slow about getting another house.'

'Capital assets?'

'Of course.'

On the other side of the kitchen window the two squirrels were moving around the garden. The red squirrel was foraging in the bushes. He appeared and disappeared. The grey squirrel moved between the three trees and climbed them all.

'I'm seeing the bloke that Hailey knew,' said Owen.

'The one that was knocking her off?' said Rhys.

'He's coming round the house tonight.'

'Fuck, Owen.'

'He knows about stone circles.'

'So?'

'It was an interest he and Hailey had.'

'And you're curious about that?'

'I didn't feel right throwing her ashes on the stone circle.'

'If that was what Hailey wanted.'

'It felt creepy.'

'It was her ashes, Owen. He must be weird, popping round the house like that.'

'He's not hostile, Rhys.'

'Good for him. Hasn't he got any fucking shame?'

Owen said nothing.

'This is creepy, Owen, not the stone circle, you seeing him. Tell him to get to fuck.'

'You're shouting, Rhys.'

'I'm annoyed, that's why. What is up with you two? If Hailey were that wonderful, she wouldn't have been shagging you both.'

'I don't think she had much choice.'

'Listen to you, Owen. You just love to beat yourself up. Sell the house and tell this bloke to fuck off. Are you hungry yet?'

Owen said nothing.

'I'm hungry. I'm getting angry, Owen. I always get hungry when I'm angry.'

The eyes of Owen followed the two squirrels around the garden. He blamed them for this talk between Rhys and Owen turning out wrong. Owen had to blame someone. He had wanted to tell Rhys about Briggs and the reason for the planned visit. But every time a sentence formed inside his head it had sounded crazy. The terrible truth was that Briggs was the only person that might understand what was happening. His brother would have thought Owen was crazy, and Holly would have thought Owen was strange and best avoided, and the people in work would have suggested he needed counselling, and not before too long the bosses would have been revising their opinion about their plans for his career. Briggs, the man that had been hanging out of Hailey, was the only man Owen could talk to.

# TWENTY-SIX

Owen returned to his home at two. He worked on the battered laptop until eight o'clock and did what he thought was a solid shift. Not quite a full day but a Zoom meeting and the best output he had achieved since Hailey died. When his boss rang she had told Owen that his own office would be ready for Monday. She stressed how the new office would enable Owen to keep a distance from his colleagues. His boss mentioned the report of the inquest that had been in the local paper.

After Owen had eaten he sat in his bedroom. He sat on the bed and looked through his photographs of Hailey. Owen appeared in some. He imagined old people looking at past photographs and having strange thoughts about how the past had deceived them. Hailey, though, did not look that much different to how she looked the evening she had died. And when Owen appeared in a photo he looked as he had in the mirror that morning. Owen wondered if the strange thoughts of the old might happen to him in the future or whether it would be different because Hailey had died young. Owen realised that Hailey would never be able to look back at her past and wonder. In the photographs she was well-groomed. Owen was as impressed with her clothes as he was with her. In one photograph she wore a grey pencil skirt that made her legs look long even though they were not. The evening light that came in through the bedroom window somehow sanctioned the choices that had been taken by the two people in the photographs. So it felt to Owen. There were more photographs of Hailey wearing T-shirts with slogans that he recalled. Some of the slogans were in French. Hailey looked like a woman that had confidence about the world that was waiting to welcome her. She was a person without doubts and of her time. The confidence in her face implied purpose although in some of the photographs the purpose looked inherited rather than willed. In other photographs, though, the purpose looked wilful, like something that would not be denied.

Briggs had a plan, and Owen had followed it. Part of the plan was Owen looking at the photographs of Hailey. Part was him leaving the front door on the latch. Owen closed Google Photos and Google Chrome and switched off the laptop. While the screen turned black he put his hand on the lid of the laptop. Before Owen could close the lid his hand was holding nothing. The laptop was jerked away by a force or something and thrown off the bed and against the bedroom wall above the headboard. The laptop bounced off the wall and collided with the lamp that was on the bedside cabinet. Both fell to the floor. Owen sucked air and coughed and stumbled. The air in the bedroom was cold and it inhibited the attempt by Owen to recover his breath. There was, though, no smell of yeast. He adjusted to the cold and became calm. The crash of the laptop had left a small dent in the bedroom wall and an odd feeling of pressure inside his ears. Owen heard a loud bang from downstairs. He ignored the bang. The rest would follow now Briggs was inside the house. Owen picked up the laptop and the bedside lamp. This was the second time that the laptop had been hurled at a wall. Two corners of the laptop now had dents. Owen left the laptop on the bed. He walked downstairs.

Briggs was standing inside the hall and facing the open doorway and outside. A solid, grey and large enormous aluminium case was jammed between the front door and the doorframe. Briggs took a deep breath and bent down and dragged the aluminium case into the hall. No one touched the front door but it slammed shut.

'That's temper that is,' said Briggs.

He was wearing a short sleeved red polo shirt and walking trousers that had deep pockets fastened with buttons. The tattoo on his right arm was a small map of the world.

'She's just slung the laptop against the bedroom wall,' said Owen. Briggs grinned.

He picked up his aluminium case and carried it into the living room.

Owen smiled.

'You looked at the photos like I said?' said Briggs.

'And I left the front door on the latch,' said Owen.

'And it worked. I didn't have a lot of time. I hoped you looking at the photographs would be a distraction. Thought it might. The case in the doorway is a trick I've used before. The buggers are good at slamming doors. You looking at the photos of her gave me a chance.'

'Well, you're in now.'

Briggs and Owen walked into the living room. Briggs laid the large aluminium case flat on the floor. He flicked the sturdy locks open and raised the lid.

'I'll make some tea,' said Owen.

In the kitchen Owen made two cups of tea and found some shortbread biscuits which, after some hesitation, he put on a single plate. When Owen walked back into the room the aluminium suitcase was empty and Briggs was attaching a bulky digital camera to a tripod. There was more equipment to assemble but Briggs was more interested in the tea and biscuits. He gulped the tea and ate a couple of shortbreads.

'Have you got more biscuits?' said Briggs.

'I've got a whole tin of them,' said Owen. 'I bought them for when the in-laws came round.'

'Good. We could be drained before we're finished. A bit of sugar will do us no harm. I bought a couple of Mars Bars in case.'

Briggs took a Mars Bar out of each of his deep trouser pockets. The Manchester accent sounded stronger than Owen remembered. Maybe Briggs was just being enthusiastic, thought Owen. It might have had something to do with him not wearing his Crombie overcoat. Briggs stood the tripod and camera in the living room corner where the television should have been.

'Don't you have a TV?' said Briggs.

'Collateral damage,' said Owen.

Briggs grinned and nodded his head.

Briggs finished his tea and ate the last shortbread biscuit. He plugged a cassette player into a wall socket and a long narrow microphone into the cassette player. There was less equipment than Owen expected. Briggs removed the lens cap from the digital camera. On the shelf that was above the gas fire he placed a thermometer, half a dozen cassettes and a torch.

'Best thing I ever bought, that torch,' said Briggs. 'Can light up the sky that thing. Twenty-five quid.'

Owen was not sure what to say.

'This equipment is standard stuff,' said Briggs. 'No point in spending a fortune. Bugger all you can do but record sound, film what can be seen and check the temperature. If there is a shadow or anything, the torch can help. All the other stuff is showbiz.'

'I have a feeling I'm being used,' said Owen.

'Whatever happens it'll be worth a second look.'

Owen said nothing.

'You're sceptical.'

'God knows.'

'This isn't easy for me either.'

'You're here though.'

'I feel obliged. I feel responsible.'

'Not to me.'

'Not quite, I suppose.'

Owen was aware that neither man wanted to use the name of the other. He waited. Owen was tempted to make another cup of tea. He stared at the equipment that was spread around his living room. He would have preferred something mysterious.

'The equipment isn't why it's worth me being here,' said Briggs.

Owen took a breath. He sat down in the armchair. Briggs was sitting on the sofa and in the place where the father-in-law of Owen had sat. On the arm of the sofa Briggs had placed a small notebook and pencil.

'If this gets dodgy, you'll be glad to have company,' said Briggs.

'You want to dig more about Hailey and me,' said Owen, 'and you want something spooky to show your mates.'

'Makes no difference to me not showing anyone else what we record and film. And they're colleagues not mates.'

'You agree to that?'

'No problem.'

'Well, you don't have to.'

'We'll see, eh.'

'If you don't have to, you can.'

Briggs laughed.

He stood, walked over to the gas fire and checked the thermometer on the shelf. Briggs returned to the sofa and recorded the temperature.

'If I don't have to, I can?' said Briggs.

'That's right,' said Owen.

'Hailey said you were odd.'

'She forgot to mention you.'

'I wonder. I bet she left hints.'

'If she was, I wasn't paying attention. If it makes you feel better, imagine that you could have been the love of her life.'

'You don't believe that?'

'I don't think Hailey would have ever settled. My mam didn't with my dad, and the more I see of my mother the more I think she wouldn't have settled with anyone.'

'Hailey is not your mother.'

'No but you wonder.'

'Can we get something straight before we talk about Hailey?'

'I don't want to talk about Hailey.'

'Can we get something straight?'

Rather than sulk Owen pouted.

'I'm not here to catch the spirits of the dead,' said Briggs.

'I feel like another cup of tea,' said Owen. 'We may as well eat the last of the shortbreads.'

Owen refilled the cups, and the two men drank more tea and ate more shortbread. Owen wiped some of the sugar off his biscuits.

'When we die we die,' said Briggs.

'You said,' said Owen.

'I never said I was a medium. I don't believe that stuff. The ghosts that haunt us are not dead.'

'This feels like Hailey to me.'

'It could be Hailey doing all this. It might not be. But if it is Hailey, it will not be the dead Hailey.'

'These biscuits are too sweet for me.'

'You'll be glad of the sugar, believe me. I work on the basis that time is not a day to day business. Moments, past and future, they exist side by side. So if Hailey is haunting this house it will be the Hailey you remember, not some spirit that's left her corpse. But it could be anyone, alive or dead. It could be your father, as he was a few years back. It could be your mother from a couple of years ahead. People who think you need a warning. People who feel threatened by what you might do next. The truth is that we are all around haunting one another. We even haunt ourselves. Most of the time this influence is subtle. We don't notice. But a violent and premature death can disturb the balance. The subtle influences become more profound, and weird things happen. I can recommend a book if you're interested.'

'I get the idea.'

'I've had terrible arguments about this stuff. People swear blind.'

'We don't need to argue.'

'I think you should have the last shortbread. I had the last one the time before.'

'According to you, you're still eating that other shortbread biscuit.'

'In a way I am and in a way I am not.'

Owen sighed.

The evening light outside the window was fading. Briggs stood up, scratched the tattoo of the world that was on his arm and took the torch from the shelf above the gas fire. He had another look at the thermometer. Briggs carried the torch and put it down on the arm of the sofa and next to his notebook and pencil.

'I prefer it to be dark and then switch on the torch when something happens,' said Briggs. 'The temperature isn't budging.'

Owen said nothing.

'My mother says I should write a book on all this but the information I collect is for my benefit. I organise and categorise everything but not so I can put it in a book. I can't see how a book would help with anything. Cross referencing it all is what's important to me. You understand me?'

'You sound like a typical actuary.'

'That would be the next stage, predicting events. That would be something. I'm happy, though, to have the records.'

'And Hailey was interested in all this stuff?'

'I would sometimes bring some notebooks over when we met.'

'Christ, I must have been really dull after all this.'

'She loved you. She said that was the difference between her and me. I had no one to love but she did. Hailey wanted to be loved.'

'And she found you. Well, you have to start somewhere, so why not pick an enthusiast. Nothing like a search, an expedition, to make people feel close.'

'I know she didn't love me. I thought she might down the line.'

'And if she didn't?'

'We were going to take it steady. Imagine if you'd known about Hailey and me while she was alive.'

'She isn't.'

'If she was.'

'I'd have wanted vengeance.'

'And not now?'

'No, not now.'

'What if Hailey and I had talked and convinced one another that we really loved one another and couldn't live without one another?'

'I'd have been upset.'

'I was upset all the time. I am upset. Don't you want to be loved by a woman?'

Owen put a fist to his mouth and sighed. He pulled his fist away and shook his head.

'Don't you?' said Briggs.

'No, I don't want that,' said Owen.

'Everyone wants that.'

'I've never wanted that.'

'You don't want much.'

'I wouldn't say that.'

'Hailey never said what you wanted.'

'Hailey never asked, that's why.'

Owen lifted his arm to put his fist to his mouth but realised what he was doing and stopped. He gripped his knees with his two hands.

'I wanted to be an alternative for Hailey,' said Owen.

'Alternative to what, blokes like me?' said Briggs.

'No, much more than that.'

'An alternative to what then?'

'Everything.'

'Everyone?'

'No, everything.'

Briggs frowned and thought.

Owen watched Briggs ponder and wonder. The two men were silent. Owen imagined Hailey sitting like he was now, her staring at Briggs and wondering what her lover was thinking.

'I assume that was the last of the shortbread biscuits,' said Briggs.

'I've a pack of ginger biscuits,' said Owen.

'I want to save the Mars Bars for afterwards.'

'I wanted Hailey to be an alternative for me.'

'To everything?'

'Everything, but the other person can't be that alternative if they want to be more than your alternative. You understand me?'

'I'm not like that.'

'No, you want something you can put in notebooks.'

'I suppose I do. Hailey was interested in what was in my notebooks.'

'I can imagine.'

'You don't have a hobby like me.'

'I read books. Hailey read a few after I'd finished them.'

'She did say she didn't read as much as you.'

'She didn't read them all, that's true. It wasn't an interest we shared. Maybe if I'd kept notes.'

The remark appeared to baffle Briggs. There was something about Briggs in deep thought that irritated Owen.

'I was joking,' said Owen.

'Right,' said Briggs.

Owen waited.

'We didn't have that much to talk about if I'm honest,' said Briggs. 'Hailey did most of the talking. Hailey liked to talk about how she felt. I told her about my job.'

'And you showed her your notebooks?' said Owen.

'I did. I liked her being curious. Hailey said she hated people with closed minds.'

'Oh, I don't know. Don't knock simple trust.'

'Are you taking the piss?'

'Not really.'

'A lot of what kept Hailey and me together was the physical stuff.'

Owen lifted his head to examine the face of Briggs. Owen had expected to see a superior grin or a sneer but Briggs looked confused and a little lost.

'There was a physical reaction right away,' said Briggs.

Owen looked down at his hands that covered his knees. The knuckles on his hands had a blue tint. Owen sniffed. There was no smell of yeast.

'My hands are freezing,' said Owen.

Briggs nodded his head, stood up and left the sofa. At the gas fire he looked at the thermometer.

'Bloody hell,' he said.

Owen looked around the room but there was nothing to see that was different.

'You sit on the floor,' said Briggs, 'switch on the cassette player and keep hold of it. I'll stand by the camera and try to keep it steady.'

Owen caught the six cassettes that Briggs threw into his lap. Briggs picked up the torch and carried it over to the tripod and camera. He dropped the torch onto the living room floor and put his right foot on top of the torch. Briggs stood behind the camera and tripod and checked the viewfinder.

'Way to go,' he said.

Owen stood up from the sofa and carried the half dozen cassettes over to the wall that faced the bay window and separated the living room from the kitchen. He sat down in the corner of the living room and pushed his back tight against the door that led into the kitchen. Both men faced the bay window. Owen arranged the cassettes at his side and lifted the cassette player onto his lap. On his thighs the metal in the frame of the cassette player felt ice cold and sticky.

'It's definitely cold now,' said Briggs.

Owen said nothing.

'I hope this isn't going to be an anti-climax.'

'There's no smell.'

'That doesn't persist. That's initial manifestation stuff.'

'When do I switch on the cassette player?'

'You haven't switched it on?'

'I was waiting.'

'Bloody hell, switch the thing on.'

Owen put the cassette player on record. He watched the cassette spindles turn. Dusk had arrived outside the bay window.

'We need to shut the curtains?' said Owen.

'I'm not worrying about the neighbours,' said Briggs.

'I should have shut the curtains.'

'Well you haven't. The neighbours won't see much. Hello, I heard something?'

Owen lifted his head and looked at the ceiling. The something was repeated. Owen listened to the knocking on the ceiling.

'That cassette player is definitely on?' said Briggs.

Owen stared at the living room ceiling. The noises became louder, sounded like heavy heels being stamped on the floor.

'The cassette player is definitely on?' said Briggs.

'Yes, yes,' said Owen.

Although the noises came from above the middle of the ceiling the lamp that hung above their heads did not move. The noises from upstairs continued.

'It might be best if you go upstairs,' said Briggs. 'You can leave the cassette player here with me.'

'Like fuck I am,' said Owen.

Briggs scratched his head.

'We're missing stuff, the two of us sat down here,' said Briggs.

'No way,' said Owen.

'We'll just have to be patient then.'

The noises from upstairs changed. They were not as sharp or as precise. Nor did they sound as if they were from the one place above the ceiling. The noises were above the head of Owen but they moved around to different places.

'She's in the back bedroom,' said Owen.

'Sounds like stuff is being thrown around,' said Briggs.

'I keep all my books in there.'

'You've got a study?'

'Not like a study.'

'Like a library?'

'A small library.'

'Are you sure you don't fancy having a look upstairs?'

'Like fuck do I fancy.'

'God knows what we're missing.'

'You go upstairs.'

'I can't leave the camera.'

'Don't fuck around, eh? We stay together.'

The noises changed but were not what they had been. The noises returned to above the middle of the ceiling but this time they boomed and sounded like small explosions.

'We're in the wrong place,' said Briggs. 'Whoever it is wants your attention.'

'You figure, do you?' said Owen.

'Throwing your books around. You're expected to react. If I were you, I'd react.'

'You'd go upstairs?'

'I would.'

'Well, not me.'

The noises continued. They were louder but somehow sounded less like explosions, more like the beats of a giant drum. No more books were being thrown, reckoned Owen. The lamp hanging from the ceiling shook and vibrated. Briggs took photographs. Owen heard the lens click. The noise of the clicks was sharp in his ears and nagged him. Owen checked the tape on the cassette player. The spools continued to turn. The two paintings in the living room slapped against the walls. The painting above the sofa fell off the wall, collided with the arm of the sofa, fell forward and hit Owen on the arm. Owen rubbed his elbow.

'I don't think that was deliberate,' said Briggs. 'We've no real evidence of malevolence.'

'How nice,' said Owen.

The noises upstairs became louder, sounded like something from a busy construction site.

'The neighbours are going to hear all this,' said Owen.

'Don't be surprised if we get a knock on the door,' said Briggs. 'I recommend you don't answer.'

'No?'

'No, this won't last forever.'

'No?'

'No, no one has yet been killed by a ghost.'

'You said you didn't believe in ghosts.'

'I slip into jargon sometimes.'

Below the ceiling the lamp swung from side to side. There was a pause between the noises from upstairs. Owen heard a light switch click. The ceiling lamp added brightness to the room. Briggs grinned and winked. The noises reappeared and boomed. As the lamp swung from side to side above their heads, parts of the room alternated between being bright and dark. Owen heard the lens on the camera click and click. The upstairs noises began again. The ceiling lamp continued to swing, each time the lamp came close to the ceiling. The plastic cord that held the lamp was tight and rigid. The bay window stayed black against the night outside but, as the ceiling lamp swung back and forth, reflections of Owen and Briggs appeared and disappeared. The small explosions paused. Owen heard different noises, knocking but not above the ceiling and not as sharp as when the noises upstairs had sounded like heels stamping. His doorbell rang. A neighbour was knocking on the bay window. The neighbour shouted something but the booms from upstairs meant that he could not be heard. Owen shrugged his shoulders and stared at the bay window. Briggs stood up, walked in front of his camera and tripod and headed towards the bay window.

'Hold on to the tripod,' he said.

Owen kept one hand on the cassette player. His other hand gripped the nearest leg of the tripod. Briggs faced the neighbour that stood outside. He switched on his torch but kept the beam away from the face of the neighbour. Seeing the powerful beam confused the neighbour but he was able to say something and point upwards. The neighbour was paunchy and, because of his raised arm, his polo shirt exposed some pale stomach. Briggs took out his wallet and held his business card in front of the face of the neighbour. Briggs nodded his head. The neighbour frowned. Briggs smiled, pretended what was happening was normal and under control. The neighbour peered past Briggs and towards Owen who was still sitting on the far side of the living room. Owen leaned his head backwards until it touched the door behind him. He closed his eyes and listened to what was booming above his head. Owen had not been infected with Covid but, listening to the threatening booms, he felt sorry for the people that had suffered and died. The chaos we stumble into, thought Owen.

The hand of Briggs touched the shoulder of Owen.

'Just as well I'm here to do the dirty work,' said Briggs.

Owen opened his eyes. The noises continued. The ceiling lamp swung high and hit the ceiling. The bulb inside the lamp cracked open and small pieces of the lightbulb fell down and landed on the floor. A piece of lightbulb landed in the hair of Briggs. He brushed the piece of glass away. When the camera lens clicked the flash added strokes of light that made Owen think of his migraine at the shopping mall.

'I'm not sleeping here tomorrow night,' said Owen.

'We can't give up after one night,' said Briggs.

The painting above the gas fire fell off the wall and joined the other painting on the living room floor. The thermometer dropped close to the feet of Owen. Briggs stood behind his camera. Owen heard the lens click and click.

'Thank Christ for technology,' said Briggs.

'Are these noises going to last all night?' said Owen.

'I reckon not.'

'I can't stand them.'

'You get used to them. A few bangs aren't going to harm us. It's what might come next.'

'You said no one gets hurt.'

'I said no one gets killed. Plenty have been scared shitless, and there've been a few injuries.'

'You're not going to show me your scars?'

'You're lucky. I'm the steady type.'

'The noises aren't as loud.'

'I told you. You're getting used to them. You've done alright. You've held on to the cassette player.'

'You got rid of Joe.'

'The neighbour?'

Owen nodded.

'I only showed him my business card. He didn't get a proper look. I've been told I look like a copper.'

'People say the same to me.'

'Hailey mentioned us both looking like policemen.'

The noises were not as loud as before. The two men with the faces of policemen looked at one another. Their two policemen-faces noted the change in volume but Briggs and Owen said nothing. The spaces between the booms became longer, and the noise from each boom was not as loud as the one before. Briggs looked at his watch. Owen noticed how the watch was large and heavy and had several dials. To Owen it looked like a portable encyclopedia. Owen stared at the bay window and worried about more neighbours appearing and knocking on the window. The damage in the living room was not serious. The gas fire had a slight dint from when the painting had fallen. The pieces of lightbulb could be picked up and hoovered. Tomorrow he would ring PC World and tell them to deliver the new television to his mother. From tomorrow the only person that would walk into the house would be an estate agent. Owen listened to the silence and thought about what selling price the estate agent would recommend.

'Ah, the noises have stopped,' said Briggs.

'It feels so peaceful,' said Owen.

'It's quiet.'

'It's more than that.'

'That's you. Your mind is preparing, getting ready. It's like being in an empty car park at night and walking over to your car before a long journey.'

'You reckon?'

'I've done this kind of thing before. You compare after a while.'

'How often?'

'Enough to think it through.'

'How often?'

'Often. Most of the time nothing happens. I wish you'd gone upstairs.'

'I've disappointed you?'

'You have a bit.'

'Hurt your feelings?'

'Not really.'

'Pity.'

The two men smiled.

'If we smoked, we could have a cigarette,' said Owen.

'You've not got any biscuits left?' said Briggs.

'You ate them all.'

'You had some as well.'

'That's true.'

'We can have a Mars Bar now and a Mars Bar after.'

'You think there'll be an after?'

'I've said, haven't I?'

'I know, scared shitless.'

'Traumatised at worst.'

'Very nice.'

'You're being gloomy. It happens. You'll adjust. That's why I brought the Mars Bars.'

Briggs sat down next to Owen and put the thermometer next to the torch that was near his foot. Briggs took a Mars Bar out of his trouser pocket. He handed the Mars Bar to Owen and waited while Owen unwrapped the Mars Bar and broke it into two almost equal pieces. Owen checked the tape in the cassette player. The men ate the chocolate and the usual goo.

'I haven't had one of these for years,' said Owen.

'I've had a few,' said Briggs. 'I always buy Mars Bars when

I make a visit. Trouble is I always feel guilty eating one when nothing has happened.'

'You should save them for hangovers.'

'That's not such a bad idea.'

Briggs and Owen ate what was left of their Mars Bars.

'I'll be glad when this is over,' said Owen.

'You're just looking forward to the other Mars Bar,' said Briggs.

The two men laughed.

'I'm wishing I had told Hailey I loved her,' said Owen.

'You don't believe in love,' said Briggs. 'Hailey said so. She said you don't tell lies.'

'Right now I wish I had.'

Owen crumpled in his hand the wrapping paper from the Mars Bar. He threw it on the sofa.

'I said everyone loves someone,' said Briggs, 'but she wasn't the one for you.'

'Thanks very much,' said Owen.

'She loved you. I know that. But she hated you as well.'

Owen adjusted his head so that his neck was comfortable against the door into the kitchen. Briggs uncrossed his legs and let them stretch. Owen was aware that, sitting against the living room wall, the shoulders of Briggs and him were almost touching. He remembered standing outside the Lowry Centre and posing for the Japanese looking couple from Fulham.

'Hailey wanted vengeance,' said Briggs.

'She said?' said Owen.

'Not quite.'

'She didn't ask you to kill me then?'

'She loved you.'

'And we don't want you losing your gun licence, do we?'

'I only shoot pigeons. I do it as a favour for the farmers.'

'You get paid for that?'

'I get bottles of wine. One farmer gave me a couple of chickens but they still had their feathers on them. I took them to the tip.'

Owen pictured Hailey and this man together. Yet, if Owen could imagine Hailey talking and listening to Briggs, whatever must have happened inside her brain was beyond Owen. Her having thoughts while listening to this man was the place or point where the imagination of Owen ended.

'I always felt Hailey just wanted to get even with you,' said Briggs.

'I was surprised she didn't leave when I offered,' said Owen.

Briggs said nothing.

'You sensed Hailey wanted vengeance.'

'I did. At first I was pleased because it gave me hope. Later, I found it less attractive. I didn't blame Hailey. She had her reasons.'

'So you thought.'

'We all have our reasons. She didn't say she hated you. She was going to give you a second chance.'

'If I said I loved her.'

'If you'd said.'

'But you knew she wanted vengeance.'

Briggs shrugged his shoulders. He flicked a tiny piece of lampshade from his jeans.

'Well?' said Owen.

'I sensed she was looking forward to you finding out,' said Briggs. 'If it hadn't been for me holding her back, you'd have found out sooner.'

'She wanted a reaction?'

'Hailey certainly wanted that.' Briggs paused and took a breath.

'Well?' said Owen.

'Hailey was never romantic in bed,' said Briggs. 'She just wanted to screw me. I didn't like it in the end.'

'You said the sex was great.'

Briggs waited before speaking, 'I didn't dislike it, that kind of aggression. It was how it felt afterwards.'

'You poor thing,' said Owen.

'You're taking the piss.'

'Muted sarcasm. Somehow I feel entitled.'

Owen thought about grinning but he remained still and quiet.

Briggs said nothing.

Owen remembered the sickly taste of the Mars Bar inside his mouth. He wiped his teeth clean with his tongue. He remembered how Hailey in conversation could sound so earnest.

'Have you noticed how dark it's gone?' said Briggs.

Owen stared around the room. The shape of everything was still visible but the objects were no more than shadows. The bay window was black, as if there were nothing outside. He heard a rapping on the window. Briggs picked up his torch and switched on the beam. The torch made everything on the other side of the window bright, the cul-de-sac and the clouds in the sky appeared. The face at the window was tired and confused and pressed close to the glass. The old woman that owned the face hunched her shoulders. Owen stood up and walked over to the bay window.

'The noises,' said his neighbour.

The woman was shouting but inside the living room her voice sounded faint.

'I know,' said Owen. 'It's terrible.'

Because of the window and in case she was deaf, Owen had shouted. He did not know the name of his neighbour. She was Mrs something but he had forgotten.

'We're worried about you,' said his neighbour.

The woman wore corduroy trousers and a buttoned shirt. Corduroy trousers might be an idea for his mother, thought Owen.

'It'll be just the one night,' said Owen.

The neighbour frowned.

'If you can just bear with me for one night.'

He held up his hand and closed all his fingers except one.

The neighbour shook her head. Her smile indicated distrust.

Owen mouthed the word one, said goodbye and turned away. He thought it the right thing to do because smoke had appeared around his ankles. The smoke was not white but as black as the bay window had been. Briggs saw the smoke and switched off the torch. The neighbour disappeared from view. Black smoke travelled up the legs of Owen. He watched the smoke rise throughout the room. Briggs was still sitting down. The smoke covered his head and shoulders. Everything in the room was hidden by the thick black smoke. Briggs switched on the powerful torch but it looked to Owen like a tiny light in the far distance.

Owen stepped away from the small bay window and walked across the living room. He knew the room which meant that his steps were not awkward. He was, though, hesitant. He felt the edge of the sofa brush against the side of his knee. Under his foot a piece of lightbulb cracked. Owen walked with the sofa against his leg because it would stop him walking into Briggs.

'Switch the damned torch on,' said Owen.

'It is on,' said Briggs.

Owen stopped walking. He reckoned he was a couple of feet from the wall.

'How am I going to put in the cassettes?' said Owen.

Briggs laughed.

'Briggs?' said Owen.

Owen lifted his face to think about how the black smoke felt against his face. It felt like nothing, in the same way mountain mist had been when he had climbed mountains with Hailey. Owen remembered standing on the edge of a mountain and looking down into the thickest mist he had ever seen. The drop to the hidden valley had felt endless. That was how it felt to him in the middle of his living room, as if he were standing in the middle of nowhere.

'Briggs?' said Owen.

Briggs said nothing.

'Briggs, say something.'

Briggs said nothing.

'Briggs, switch on the damned torch.'

The room stayed black. Owen stretched his arm and opened

his hand until his fingers were rigid and straight. He remembered how the cord attached to the ceiling lamp had been.

'Briggs, are you alright?' said Owen.

Briggs said nothing.

'Briggs, I'm terrified too. You could at least say something.'

Owen stepped forward. His stretched arm pushed through the black smoke. Owen thought about that day on the mountain when the white mist had been thick and he had looked down. He had imagined the white mist lasting forever and thinking that he was in an alien world. He felt the same as he reached for the wall. His fingers touched the door that led to the kitchen. The gloss paint on the door felt cold and sharp against his fingers. Owen stepped forward, turned around and pressed his back against the kitchen door. Using his back and the door as a guide, he slid down the door. On the way down to the living room floor the thigh of Owen caught the edge of the cassette player. Owen used his right hand to shift the cassette player to the side. He sat down on the living room floor. The six cassettes were lost in the thick black smoke.

'Briggs,' said Owen.

There was no answer.

'Briggs, please.'

The room was silent. Owen leaned sideways and used his hand to feel the wall at his side. As he leaned, his knee touched the torch. Owen reached across the wall until his fingers touched a corner. The black smoke was still but there was a noise, not a boom or a knock but something continuous like powerful and relentless breathing. A deep and enormous buzz that was close but like the mist reached somewhere distant and unknowable.

Owen dragged his hand back against the flat and empty wall. He sat still and pressed his back firm against the kitchen door.

'God help you, Briggs,' said Owen.

Owen bent forward and found the cassette player. He lifted the machine onto his thighs. Owen was not sure why but having the cassette player and touching it helped him feel he had some protection against the dark and the black smoke and the buzz that was drilling into his ears. He used his hands to trace the surface of the cassette player. His hands groped the old-fashioned and bulky knobs, the plastic tray cover. The cassette player shifted a little and became ice-cold. Owen felt the weight of the cassette player lift from his thighs. The cassette player rose in the air. Owen knew it was happening because his arms and elbows that rested on top of the cassette player were being lifted. The loud breathing that was a deep baritone buzz changed. Owen heard a bang and felt a force under the cassette player. The force lifted the cassette player and pushed his arms away. The noise around Owen sounded like a roar from the black smoke. The cassette player was hurtled into the air. It hit Owen full on the face. His head cracked back against the kitchen door. The black smoke disappeared, and Owen saw a white light. He slumped to the floor.

# TWENTY-SEVEN

Owen opened his eyes and said hello to a headache. The room had been tidied. No pieces of lightbulb were scattered on the living room floor, and the paintings were back on the walls. The black smoke had disappeared. Daylight lit the room, and outside could be seen. The thermometer, camera, notebook, torch and microphone were not where they had been. Briggs sat in the armchair near the bay window. His aluminium case was at the side of the armchair and standing on its side.

'All packed and ready to go,' said Briggs.

'My head is banging,' said Owen.

'You don't look so good. I'm warning you before you look in the mirror. If there wasn't Covid and I knew where the hospital was, I'd have taken you there. And you didn't bleed that much.'

Owen touched his face.

'Sore eh?' said Briggs. 'You might have a couple of scars. The bruises on your face will fade. Don't look so good now, though. I can make you a cup of tea.'

'We ate all the biscuits,' said Owen.

'Actually we didn't but we have now. I was hungry and waiting. You've been out for a while.'

'Where did you get to?'

'I didn't get anywhere. You disappeared. I panicked a bit. I'll need a new battery for my torch.'

'There was black smoke.'

'I remember that.'

'I went over to the window to talk to the woman. I came back from the window, and you weren't there.'

Briggs chuckled. He was being authoritative.

'How long have I been out?' said Owen.

Briggs looked at his phone.

'Nine hours.' Briggs said it as if he was asking a question.

Owen stood up and groaned. The effort made him take a deep breath.

'You're best staying still,' said Briggs. 'I closed my eyes while you were talking at the window. When I opened them you weren't there. I thought you'd gone upstairs. The bangs had stopped. I went and had a look. When I came back downstairs you were sitting against the wall. You were bleeding and out cold. I put you on the sofa, mopped up the blood around your face and had a cup of tea and ate what was left of the biscuits. It's been a long night. A good one, though. There's a glass of water and some paracetamol at the side of the sofa.'

Owen leaned over the edge of the sofa and found the water and painkillers. He took the tablets. His body slumped back against the sofa. Owen let the tablets settle.

Briggs said nothing.

Once or twice he smiled.

Owen stood up. He felt lightheaded but he was able to walk using the edge of the sofa. From there to the bathroom he walked with a hand on the nearest wall. In the bathroom he washed his face, touched the two deep cuts above his eyes, felt his swollen lips and tapped a finger against the bruises. Owen reckoned the cut above his eyes would heal into a scar that would be noticed. He was glad he had not been taken to hospital. As he had the night before, Owen thought about the Covid deaths and the risks nurses and doctors had to take. The scars would be future testimony to his timidity. Owen walked downstairs. He was not as lightheaded as before but he used a wall for support.

Briggs had not moved from the armchair. When Owen entered the room Briggs was writing something in his notebook. Owen sat down on the sofa.

'I feel queasy,' said Owen.

'You'll be hungry,' said Briggs. 'I can make you breakfast.'

Owen shook his head.

'I've still got the Mars Bar,' said Briggs.

Owen smiled.

'I'll make some tea, and we'll split the Mars Bar in two.'

'You ate the last of the biscuits.'

'I'll have the small piece. I can make some toast.'

'We'll split the Mars Bar.'

Owen closed his eyes, and Briggs walked into the kitchen. Owen sat with his eyes closed and waited to heal and for nothing in particular. Briggs carried two mugs of tea and two small dishes into the living room. In each of the dishes there was a piece of Mars Bar. The two slices of Mars Bar had a neat and straight cut.

'Those Mars Bars look the same size to me,' said Owen.

'Yours is definitely bigger,' said Briggs. 'I can make some toast.'

The two men drank their tea and ate the pieces of Mars Bar.

'Better?' said Briggs.

Owen was hungry and would have liked to have eaten some toast. He was reluctant, though, to have Briggs wander around his kitchen. Owen thought about Briggs wandering around upstairs after he had thought Owen had disappeared, Briggs searching through the rooms that he knew because of what had happened between him and Hailey.

'You didn't take any pictures, did you?' said Owen.

'I've taken loads,' said Briggs.

Owen touched his face.

'Not of you, no,' said Briggs.

'The cassette player smashed me in the face,' said Owen.

'You look like you've had a good belt.'

Owen stared at the ceiling because it eased the pain in his head.

'I checked the cassette player,' said Briggs. 'It's still working.'

'I am pleased,' said Owen.

'It wouldn't have been intentional. I don't suspect malevolence.'

'You weren't there.'

'Deliberate hostility is very unusual.'

'The whole thing was unusual.'

'Never happens I would say. You get plenty of drama but not violent attacks.'

'Wrong man, wrong place, wrong time?'

'That's a definition of accidents I don't accept.'

'No, I'm not the wrong man in all this.'

Briggs chuckled in the same authoritative way as he had before.

'You're made up, aren't you?' said Owen.

'We've made progress,' said Briggs.

'I nearly got my head taken off. If I had any sense, I'd be going for brain scans.'

'I can take you to the hospital if you want.'

'Not with Covid. I'll take a chance.'

'Is the headache any better?'

'It is a bit.'

'The painkillers are working. That's good news. Look, let's have some breakfast, get ourselves in a state where we can talk about what we do next.'

'We're not doing anything next.'

'You should eat.'

'I'm leaving this house today, and it's going up for sale.'

Briggs frowned and sighed. Owen was not sure why but he felt responsible.

'I'll make the breakfast,' said Owen.

'You should rest,' said Briggs.

'It's a headache. If I put butter in the tea and milk on the toast, you can take me to the hospital.'

The two men walked into the kitchen. Owen grilled the toast but Briggs insisted on making the tea. They sat at the kitchen table and ate. At the back of the house and away from the sun the daylight was different. Owen appreciated the reduction in heat and glare.

'I've never seen that before,' said Briggs.

Owen touched the bruises on his face. He gulped some tea.

'No, disappearing, slipping out of the present,' said Briggs.

Owen stared into his cup and at the surface of his tea. He was disappointed not to witness a whirlpool.

'It's like I said,' said Briggs, 'time, the present, past, the future. What happens is this.'

'I've got the idea,' said Owen.

'You didn't see anything other than black smoke?'

Owen shook his head. He continued to stare at the surface of his tea.

'Pity,' said Briggs.

Owen put two hands around his cup of tea.

'You can't have everything,' said Briggs.

'When did you figure that out?' said Owen.

Briggs smiled and shrugged his shoulders.

'You've done alright, haven't you,' said Owen.

'I can make some more toast,' said Briggs.

'Have you cooked in this kitchen before?'

'No.'

'No?'

'Honest, I haven't.'

'I bet you've had a few cups of tea, though.'

'That's all in the past.'

'I'm sorry, what past is this? See, I remember what you said before. I know what you think about me disappearing. According to you, I've got in my hand a cup of tea that never goes away.'

'It's not as simple as that.'

'It'd be an awful lot of cups of tea. The cups must get confused, being filled with tea and washed at the same time.'

'I think of it as more ephemeral than that.'

Briggs took a breath and opened his hands.

'Please,' said Owen, 'don't explain.'

'Your face has got a bit more colour,' said Briggs.

'More colour than bruises?'

'In between the bruises. The breakfast has given you a lift.'

'I'm due in work on Monday.'

'Have a quiet weekend. I was wondering.'

'When was this?'

'Just now. I was wondering if you'd give me the house keys. I could try again. You don't have to be here. It's better if you are but I could bring a mate.'

'I don't think so. You haven't done so bad.'

'If nothing happens to my mate and I, you can sell the house with a clear conscience.'

'Well, we all take risks with our conscience, don't we?'

Briggs stood up and took the cups and plates to the sink. He washed the dishes. He talked as he faced the window.

'I was out of order getting in touch with you,' said Briggs. 'I knew that. But you meet someone and you start to have trust.'

'In Hailey?' said Owen.

Briggs stared out of the large window and at the brick wall on the other side of the entry.

'In everything,' said Briggs.

Owen stared at the back of Briggs. The polo shirt looked less tight on the body of Briggs than when he arrived. Owen remembered the navy blue Crombie overcoat that Briggs had worn the first time they had met. Owen imagined Hailey taking the clothes off Briggs and noticing the difference between how he looked dressed and naked. He tried to imagine what Hailey would have thought but, like before, imagining her thinking was beyond Owen.

'You trust fate,' said Briggs.

'Most of the time,' said Owen.

'I had to know what she'd said to you.'

'You felt entitled.'

'No, I knew I wasn't entitled. I just had to know.'

'You know as much as me. I'm entitled to flog this house with a clean conscience. And if whoever buys it gets pestered then they can also sell it with a clean conscience.'

'I think so.'

'So it goes.'

'So it will go.'

Briggs turned around and faced Owen.

'I suppose this is goodbye,' said Briggs.

Owen nodded his head.

'At least we've made our mind up about what to do next.'

'I wouldn't go that far.'

Briggs chuckled, and so did Owen.

'We never go that far,' said Briggs.

# TWENTY-EIGHT

Pops lay on top of the bed and in the middle of the striped mattress. His head rested on his paws. On the floor and next to the bed was a pile of a dozen strips of large cardboard. Will took a strip of cardboard from the top of the pile and folded the cardboard so that it made a box. He added masking tape to the bottom of the cardboard box. The books that had been thrown onto the floor the night Briggs had visited had been returned to the shelves by Owen. This had been done by Owen before Will had arrived. The two men now took books from the shelves and placed them into the cardboard boxes. The bedroom was not large but there was space for Will and Owen to work. Pops had been curious the first time Owen had lifted a full cardboard case onto the bed. Now the dog wanted to doze. Like the bedding that had been stripped from the mattress, a compact chest of drawers and a small chair had been moved out of the bedroom.

Owen sealed another full cardboard case. He ruffled the hair of Pops. Will looked and thought about the cover of a novel by Richard Yates. Will bent down and put the book in a cardboard case.

'We could have put these in alphabetical order,' said Will.

'We'd have been all day,' said Owen.

'I don't mind.'

'I wouldn't have asked Rhys if I'd known he was going to send you along.'

'Rhys has got work to do.'

'Then I should have done it on my own.'

'I don't mind.'

'Maybe you should.'

'Rhys was worried about you.'

Will leaned forward and put out a hand towards the face of Owen. His fingers stopped short of touching the bruises.

'Touch them if you're desperate,' said Owen.

'I must be a frustrated doctor,' said Will.

He touched a couple of bruises and the deep cut above the right eye of Owen.

'I tripped on broken paving,' said Owen. 'I wasn't drunk.'

'Rhys didn't think you were,' said Will.

'My mam did.'

Will smiled, took a final look at the bruises and packed more books.

'You might have a couple of scars,' said Will.

'I'll need thicker eyebrows,' said Owen.

'We can sort that for you.'

Will grinned and let the smile linger.

The two men kept packing the books. Pops twisted his body so he could lay on his back.

'You know you're welcome at our place,' said Will. 'Rhys worries about you.'

'I'm better off at my mam's house,' said Owen.

'You'd have all the third floor to yourself.'

'My mam doesn't charge me any rent. I just pay for food and stuff.'

'We wouldn't charge any rent.'

'I was kidding.'

Will paused and looked at the book that was in his hand.

'You can borrow some books if you want,' said Owen.

'How do you remember all these books?' said Will.

'You don't and when you do you get it wrong.'

'There doesn't seem much point in reading them.'

'They help carry me along, not much more.'

Will stopped packing and stepped forward. He peered through the bedroom window. On the bed Pops lay flat on his back. His four paws pointed at the ceiling. The dog opened his eyes a little and for an instant looked sideways at Will. Owen packed some books, and Pops closed his eyes.

'You won't have any problem selling this house,' said Will. 'Not this close to the sea.'

'You can't see the sea,' said Owen.

'They'll know where it is alright. I wasn't joking. You wouldn't have had to pay us rent.'

'I'd get in the way of you and Rhys.'

'That wouldn't be such a bad thing.'

Owen looked at the bookshelves that were on three of the four walls. Outside the bedroom window there was plenty of sunshine.

'Hailey never minded the books being packed into this room,' said Owen. 'And she wouldn't have bothered about getting another house if her parents hadn't pestered her.'

Owen had put the books back on the shelves the day after Briggs had left the house. The task had helped Owen to not think about his bruises and the lies he would have to tell people. And now, thought Owen, the shelves would be empty again.

'If I'd known Rhys was going to be busy,' said Owen, 'I wouldn't have asked.'

'It gets me out the house,' said Will.

'I appreciate the help.'

Will smiled.

'I'll make you a cup of tea,' said Owen.

'We'll soon be finished,' said Will.

'I fancy a tea break. My mam has made a cake. I've still got the kettle and a couple of cups.'

Will and Owen walked downstairs. Pops woke and jumped off the bed. Owen led the way down the narrow staircase. Because there was not enough space for Pops to overtake the two men, he barked and crowded the heels of Will. Owen made tea and cut cake. Will gave Pops some water and fed the dog a couple of biscuits. Owen opened the kitchen door and let Pops breathe the fresh air in the entry.

In the living room Will sat on the floor and in the corner where Briggs had erected his camera. Owen sat below the bay window.

Pops was outside in the back entry. He was drinking water from the washing up bowl Owen had taken from the sink. The living room had no furniture and the curtains on the window had been removed but there was carpet on the floor. The furniture that had been moved to the house of his mother would be now gathering dust in her attic. Owen was aware of the damage that had been done to the living room, the dents and abrasions. He hoped that the cuts on his face would become scars that would be more visible to him than anyone else. Owen had not been afraid to return to the house. He had company, and there was daylight outside.

'I'll miss this house,' said Will. 'If I lived alone, this house would suit me. What is this cake?'

'Fuck knows,' said Owen. 'Not sure what happened to the currants.'

'There aren't any currants.'

'That's what I mean.'

'Banana.'

'If you say so, Will.'

'Tastes alright to me.'

'Tastes alright to me.'

The two men laughed.

'It would do no harm you staying with Rhys and me,' said Will. 'It would help.'

'Oh, yes,' said Owen.

'Rhys might not drink as much with you there.'

'I doubt that, Will.'

'He's not listening to me.'

'Watch a couple of films that have alcoholics.'

'We watched the one with Nicolas Cage in Las Vegas. I needed a drink after that.'

'The woman in that was alright.'

'I felt sorry for her.'

'She was a dish if I remember right.'

'I don't remember.'

'I'll talk to Rhys. I'll threaten him with his mother.'

Owen turned his head to look over his shoulder and out of the bay window. Moving his head produced no pain and he was pleased that he was headache free. When Holly had rung about them meeting at some point Owen had promised to ring her but thinking about it while he was sitting under the bay window made him nervous.

'It's a symptom,' said Will.

Owen said nothing.

He thought about Holly eating in his kitchen and how she had looked.

'The drinking,' said Will. 'It's a symptom. I worry about what will happen to Rhys when he stops drinking.'

'He'll have to suffer being ordinary like the rest of us, Will,' said Owen.

'I wonder what will happen to Rhys and me.'

'The two of you stand more chance if you get him off the sauce.'

'He drinks a bottle of wine a night.'

'He's consistent then.'

'If we have company, Rhys drinks more.'

Owen said nothing.

'And if we go out.'

'Right.'

'Owen, it's not very flattering.'

'I suppose not.'

'We all think we can make someone happy.'

'Will, have you seen how much alcohol they sell?'

Will pouted. He ate a small piece of banana loaf.

'Rhys knows he's blessed to have you,' said Owen.

'You think so?' said Will.

'He told me so.'

'A long time ago, I bet.'

'The last time I saw him. Rhys says it most times I see him. Why shouldn't he? He's got a handsome and honest water carrier.'

Will sighed.

'And now someone that has a career.'

'I wonder if I should ease off that.'

'You might not have a choice.'

'Rhys is more important to me than a damned job.'

'He won't be when you're getting your pension. Just because I'm not so desperate to spend on things doesn't mean I don't take money seriously.'

'I don't want to lose Rhys.'

'You won't. Just worry about the alcohol. I'll talk to my mam.'

'She's given him looks.'

'I'll get her to go on the attack. My mother can be a force. And I'll have a few words. I might go on the wagon myself. Rhys doesn't like being outdone.'

The smile from Will was appreciative, superior to anything that Owen had ever received from Hailey.

'On one condition,' said Owen. 'You work hard at that job.'

'You can't sacrifice people for ambition,' said Will.

'How are you sacrificing Rhys? We'll talk to him. Remember, Will, the poor are at their best when they behave themselves. The rich are at their best when they graft. I read that. It's upstairs somewhere in a book.'

'Sounds like the beginning of another drunken argument.'

'Not if we're all on the wagon. Will, I'll talk to my mam. Come on, I'll lend you a couple of books.'

Owen touched the scar above his eyebrow. It had become a habit.

'The scars suit you,' said Will.

'You can see them?' said Owen.

'They're only small scars.'

# TWENTY-NINE

'I appreciate this, Owen,' said his mother.

Owen picked up a cucumber and put it in the shopping trolley. He wore a pale blue Covid mask and thin transparent gloves. His mother wore a patterned mask but no gloves. His mother added two small and not so green gem lettuce to the fruit and vegetables that were in the trolley.

'I don't rate coming to Waitrose the best of days,' said his mother.

'I don't mind,' said Owen.

His mother put a packet of stir fry peppers into the shopping trolley.

'I couldn't face walking round Waitrose alone today,' said his mother, 'not the day your dad died.'

'You could have come tomorrow,' said Owen.

'I always do my shopping Friday night.'

'I don't mind, Mam.'

His mother wheeled the trolley around the corner of the shopping aisle.

'I'll have a good talk with Rhys,' said his mother. 'I'll tell him his father would turn in his grave if he knew his son was a drunk.'

'I'll go on the wagon myself,' said Owen.

'Rhys will have to stay on the wagon longer than you.'

'That's what I thought.'

His mother put two filleted haddock steaks in the shopping trolley. She crossed the shopping aisle and added four cans of sardines and two tubs of mackerel pâté.

'You don't miss out on the fish,' said Owen.

'You don't have to eat it,' said his mother. 'You can sneak a beer in the house, Owen. I won't snitch.'

'I've said to Will that I'll go on the wagon. It'll do me no harm.'

Owen wheeled the shopping trolley to the end of the aisle. His mother peered at the shelves but was unimpressed. Even behind the Covid mask her face indicated disapproval. In the next aisle Owen put yoghurts, cheese, eggs, milk, tea and coffee into the trolley. Owen and his mother reached the end of the aisle and the back of the store. Owen watched his mother add packets of ham to everything else.

'For your lunches at work,' said his mother.

Owen would have liked to have an argument against her organising his lunches but his favourite takeaway food shop in Liverpool was closed because of Covid. The numbers working in the offices each day were now few. Owen and his mother turned into the next shopping aisle. His mother added washing up liquid, washing powder and fabric conditioner to the shopping trolley.

'I'm not doing a big shop,' said his mother.

'Oh no?' said Owen.

'I do the big shop at Sainsburys next week.'

'I can help with cash, Mam.'

'You're paying your bit with the food. I don't want you paying for stuff I always have to pay for. I'm not short of a few bob.'

For a moment Owen forgot which shopping aisle they were in. He watched his mother select packets of muesli and porridge. Owen added ginger nuts and shortbread biscuits. He wheeled the trolley around until they arrived at the corner where the alcohol was on display. Owen ignored the wine but looked at the racks of bottled beer and thought about the future. He added a 24 can pack of Diet Coke to the shopping trolley.

'I won't tell if you do,' said his mother.

'No, it'll be a way of life soon,' said Owen. 'I might relapse when I move into a new house but not before then.'

'Maybe Rhys should move in with me and you move in with Will.'

'That would be interesting but I don't think so.'

'Your dad would turn in his grave if the two of you went that way.'

Owen stared at his mother but she turned her head away and grinned until it was almost a giggle. Owen put two sourdough loaves into the shopping trolley. He picked up a packet of scones.

'What are you supposed to be doing with them?' said his mother.

'I like a scone with a cup of tea,' said Owen.

'We're not buying cakes. Don't you like my cakes?'

'Of course, I do.'

'If you like scones so much, I'll make some. Scones are easy. If I can do apple pies, I can do scones.'

'I did like the apple pie.'

'There's nothing as simple as scones.'

'Maybe I should have a go.'

'No, Owen, I don't think so.'

'You don't trust me.'

'I let you open a packet of biscuits. Small steps, Owen. You're doing very well.'

His mother grinned. She pushed the trolley towards the tills. Footprint transfers that indicated the distance people had to maintain between each other were pasted on the floor. Owen and his mother joined the queue for the tills. They waited six feet behind the hefty old woman that was before them in the queue. An attractive young woman in a Waitrose uniform organised the queue for the tills and ensured that the shoppers maintained the social distance. The woman had shiny black hair and a clean pale face. The young woman saw Owen and his mother standing close together.

'He's with me,' said the mother of Owen. 'He's my son.'

The young woman that worked for Waitrose smiled.

'Handsome, isn't he?' said his mother.

'Mam, please,' said Owen.

The young woman smiled.

Owen nodded his head and shrugged his shoulders. Another shopper asked the young woman a question and led her down an aisle. A relieved Owen followed his mother towards the tills.

Owen stared at what was in the shopping trolley and thought about the missing alcohol. The woman on the till was the same age as his mother. Owen pressed a knuckle into the back of his mother and whispered into her ear.

'I won't say anything,' said his mother.

In the car park Owen loaded the shopping bags into the back of his Volvo.

'I appreciate this, Owen,' said his mother.

Owen said nothing.

He closed the boot of the car.

'I was dreading this,' said his mother. 'I knew I'd feel funny the day your dad died.'

Owen walked to the front of the Volvo and climbed in behind the steering wheel. His mother sat down next to him. Owen and his mother put on their seat belts.

'You're not going to tell me you miss Dad,' said Owen.

'I just feel funny the day he died,' said his mother. 'Maybe it makes me think things.'

'Things?'

'The past, all those years.'

Owen said nothing.

He thought about what his mother had said in the store.

'Owen,' said his mother, 'people would take to you if you didn't brood so much. Even Hailey thought you had your kind moments. She said you weren't so awful underneath.'

'What, without my clothes on?' said Owen.

'Don't be difficult, Owen. I appreciate you helping today. It didn't occur to Rhys.'

'My brother has deadlines.'

'Don't you, Owen?'

'I have routines.'

'Is that what you're thinking about all the time?'

Owen stared out of the windscreen and at the rear of the car that was parked in the space ahead. He tilted the rear mirror, looked at his face and touched his bruises and scars. Owen looked at his mother and shook his head.

'If you've got something to say, Owen, say it,' said his mother.

'Right,' said Owen.

'Right?'

'You said Dad would turn in his grave.'

'If he knew Rhys was drinking, so he would.'

'Not the drinking. If, to use your words, Mam, the two of us went that way.'

'It's my age, you get clumsy with words. Owen, don't tell Rhys. I'm sure we've all said worse without realising.'

Owen said nothing.

His mother watched a white four-wheel drive Range Rover leave the car park.

'Mam, are you going to tell me?' said Owen.

His mother said nothing.

Owen listened to her take a deep breath.

'You said Dad would turn in his grave if the two of us,' said Owen.

'We should get this food home and in the fridge,' said his mother.

'I don't want you to lie your way out of this, Mam.'

'I could if I wanted.'

'Did Dad know?'

Owen waited. He put the car key into the side of the steering column. He thought about the food in the boot and his mother and him sitting in the car park until the food rotted.

'About Rhys?' said Owen.

He took his hand off the steering key.

'He guessed?' said Owen.

'Well before Rhys told him,' said his mother.

'Rhys told Dad?'

'Rhys knew his father had guessed.'

'No one told me.'

'Your dad didn't want you to know.'

'He must have known that Rhys would tell me.'

'Oh, he'd worked that out. Your dad didn't want you to know he knew about Rhys. That was all. He thought it best you not being able to say anything. Maybe I should have said something after your dad died. I meant to. Your dad was very protective of Rhys. He always thought it would have been best if you'd been the one that was gay.'

'That would have been good. He could have thrown me out the house. You could have told me Dad knew.'

'I thought about it after your dad died but the longer it went on, Owen, the harder it got.'

'And our Rhys wouldn't want his part in this to be known. So what did Dad think I didn't know?'

'He knew that you knew Rhys was gay. Your dad just didn't want you saying anything in front of him. He thought you'd twist the knife.'

Owen took the key out of the steering column.

'This takes the biscuit,' said Owen.

'I forgot the ginger biscuits,' said his mother.

'You didn't. I put them in.'

'I suppose you feel compromised.'

'I feel insulted, Mam.'

'Can you tell Rhys about this when I'm not there? We don't want a big argument. Once Rhys and you get going.'

'I'm not telling Rhys.'

His mother turned her head and smiled.

'Good, son,' said his mother.

'Not because of you and this family,' said Owen.

His mother chewed her lip and stared through the windscreen.

'If I know Rhys, he won't have told Will,' said Owen.

'Rhys hasn't,' said his mother. 'I know that.'

'There you go. Will has helped me pack the books. I owe him something.'

# THIRTY

'You can always stay here,' said Holly.

Owen sipped from his can of Diet Coke. He ate a mouthful of hot lasagne.

'Are you sure you don't want some wine?' said Holly.

Owen shook his head.

'As long as you don't drink in front of your brother.'

'I said I wouldn't. Sneaking drinks wouldn't be right.'

'I don't see why not.'

'It's fine lasagne. I'm enjoying it.'

The dining room in the semi-detached home was small and square. The table was close to the window. The standard lamp in the opposite corner of the room threw shadows on the closed venetian blinds. Owen hoped the low light would flatter his scars and bruises.

'I don't like the idea of you staying in a hotel,' said Holly.

'I'll be fine,' said Owen. 'I'll calm down in a week and go back to my mam. Let her brood for a change.'

'I'm not sure I like you going back to her that much either.'

Owen grinned and ate more lasagne. Holly drank some red wine. She smiled.

'I haven't said anything about your injuries,' said Holly.

'I thought you hadn't noticed,' said Owen.

'As if.'

'I tripped on a crack in the pavement.'

'As if.'

'You wouldn't believe me if I told you.'

'I was going to mention it after you said something about my outfit.'

'I hadn't realised you'd got dressed up.'

'Thanks very much, Owen.'

'You look very nice.'

Holly wore a grey skirt and a white shirt with a large collar and cuffs. Owen had noticed her nylon covered legs as soon as he had arrived. The shoes had block cork heels.

'Well, if your heart skipped a beat, you're entitled to keep it to yourself,' said Holly.

'Really nice,' said Owen.

'The lasagne?' said Holly.

'No, you, you dope.'

'You've looked better.'

'I was going to leave it until the bruises healed.'

'But you didn't want me to wait and worry. How considerate.'

'I had a row with my mam and I needed to get out of the house.'

'I see. Oh, well.'

'I was looking forward to seeing you.'

'Counting the days?'

'Kind of.'

Holly poured herself some wine and put the cork back in the half full bottle.

'Have you missed me?' said Holly.

Owen smiled and nodded his head. He reckoned words were best avoided.

'Stay the night, Owen,' said Holly.

Owen said nothing.

'I understand you not wanting to feel callous after the death of your wife. But this delay is hanging over us. It's making me nervous thinking about it, me being the first one after you've paid your penance. And now you're on the wagon that makes it worse.'

'Don't be nervous, Holly. I look alright with my clothes off.'

'And me?'

'I won't look.'

'Maybe we should wait for the dark nights.'

Owen and Holly laughed. They ate the rest of the meal and talked about how Covid had affected what they did in their jobs.

As they talked, Owen remembered what Holly had said about his appearance and more than once he touched the bruises on his face. At some point Owen mentioned Will and him packing the books.

The living room was an almost identical shape to the dining room, square and not quite as small. Holly and Owen sat on opposite sofas. Holly finished the wine in her glass. Owen drank a cup of coffee and ate a macaroon.

'I'm on nights next week,' said Holly.

'I don't think much of those macaroons,' said Owen.

'You could have had something else. I've got plenty of biscuits.'

'I fancied something Italian.'

'You're changing the subject.'

Holly stood up and found her smartphone. She stood in front of Owen.

'I want a photo,' said Holly.

'I'm not taking my clothes off,' said Owen.

'It's for my mum.'

'I've still got my bruises.'

'That's the plan, Owen. If she sees the bruises and still likes you, we know we're all right. Come on, Owen, a grin is allowed.'

Holly took the photograph, and afterwards Owen touched his bruises. Holly showed Owen the photograph she had taken. He watched Holly walk across her living room and sit down on the opposite sofa. The skirt, blouse and shoes with the block cork heels that she wore made him think about upstairs and staying the night.

'You do like the outfit,' said Holly.

'Very smart,' said Owen.

'Smart?'

'Very.'

'Thank you, Owen.'

'My mam just goes round in jeans and smocks all the time.'

'I got dressed up for you.'

'I'm nice and clean.'

'So you are, Owen. You're what I expected.'

'Tonight?'

'From the first time I heard your name. I hadn't even seen you. I walked into the house of your brother. I was met by Joe on the crime scene team. I remember what he said word for word. 'The husband is upstairs. His name is Owen Pittman.' As soon as I heard your name, I knew we would be important to each other. I even pictured you and when we met I saw you were what I had imagined, almost. This wasn't love at first sight, Owen. It happened well before that.' Holly paused. 'Are you sure you don't want a drink?'

'I'm okay.'

'I'm okay too. I don't want you to think I'm crazy, Owen. God, that night, visiting a crime scene and then seeing the bloke meant for you.'

'As soon as you heard my name?'

'You do think I'm crazy.'

'Believe me, I don't. I'm the one with the bruised face.'

Holly smiled. She pressed the screen on her phone and looked at the photograph of Owen.

'You can take a photograph of me,' said Holly.

Owen mumbled okay and took a photograph of Holly. He gave her his phone so that she could look. Holly returned the phone to Owen.

'I don't have them so much anymore,' said Holly, 'but when I was young I used to have these dreams. They would be based in the future. Not all my dreams. I would only know I was dreaming the future when the future confirmed it. I couldn't predict the future but when it happened I'd remember the dream. None of what I dreamt meant much. I wasn't dreaming cup final winners.'

'That sounds like bog standard déjà vu,' said Owen.

'No, it was more precise than that. I'd even have conversations about the dreams with Mum and then later it would happen.'

'You're predicting the future for you and me.'

'I know we have a future, that's all. No doubt you will make a lot of it difficult, Owen, but whether you like it or not you are my future.'

Owen said nothing.

Holly removed her block cork heel shoes and wiggled her toes.

Owen waited.

'My feet need a rest,' she said. 'With my conviction about fate and your loyalty we don't have a lot of choice, Owen. I suspect there'll be plenty of stumbles. You'll hesitate and be awkward about making a commitment but I know you're worth a bet more than most.'

'Me or it?'

Holly said nothing and smiled.

'Both?'

'Both, Owen.'

'I'm not staying the night.'

'I didn't expect you to believe me. I must sound crazy.'

'Wait till I tell you about the bruises. Holly, knowing my wife had to die for us to meet is hanging over our heads.'

'And it might never go away but I know what I know. Owen, we will face the future together. We might not even be good for one another but it will happen.'

'I'm not staying the night. Not just yet.'

'Your family will understand, Owen.'

'They like you. Not that I'm bothered about what they think.'

# THIRTY-ONE

Owen locked his Volvo and walked the path towards Swinside Stone Circle. Above Owen were white clouds and intermittent blue sky. Around him were green hills and sunshine. The colours were bright. Owen thought of the colours in a paint catalogue. The path was dry and puddle free. Hailey had liked climbing hills but hated wet British weather. On the bad days Hailey had found something else to do and Owen had been obliged to walk alone. Owen looked from side to side and behind. He was alone. As he walked, Owen thought about what day he would see Holly and what may happen between them. He remembered what she had said about her intuition. Owen thought about what had happened in his home the night Briggs had visited. Somehow it had primed him for a future with Holly and her predictions.

The stone circle appeared on his right. Owen wore trainers instead of walking boots and a thin cardigan over his Marks and Spencer shirt. Since Covid the dress standards in work had been relaxed. Owen looked like someone going to the office rather than a walker. He hoped the sunshine would tan his skin and disguise some of his bruises.

Owen stopped walking when he was level with the middle of the stone circle and close to the gate that led into the field. He took a chewy bar of nuts and raisins out of his pocket. Owen stood behind the wall and ate his chewy bar. From a distance the standing stones looked clean and smooth. In the ground the stones rested at different angles. Owen was curious about whether it was no more than a consequence of effort and struggle and some primitive man saying, 'Bugger this, that'll do.' Whatever the reason the difference in size and angles gave each stone an individual distinction, a history and identity. The ashes of Hailey were God knows where, and apart from the weather and land being dry nothing was different, just a few extra atoms from Hailey, not even a smudge.

Owen let the sun feel warm on his face. He remembered Hailey losing her temper in the home of his brother. He thought about why he had to say what he did in the argument, why he could not have just provided simple flattery. Now he remembered the argument and he was aware of how Will and Rhys were not arguing with him. He was being encouraged to be conciliatory. The dopes meant well, thought Owen. He thought about before he had met Hailey and those nights and occasions when with different women he had used flattery and lies. Owen folded the chewy bar wrapping paper until it was as flat and as small as possible. He put the folded paper in his shirt pocket.

Owen heard a voice.

'At least you're taking it home with you,' said the farmer.

'That's the idea,' said Owen.

The farmer looked much the same. He wore the flat cap that he had worn when they had met previously. If the trousers were different they, like before, also had deep pockets. The farmer walked over to the wall.

'Warm, isn't it?' said the farmer.

'This isn't going to be a regular thing,' said Owen.

The farmer waited. Like before, he took off his flat cap and wiped the sweat away from his head. His Collie dog arrived, stood on his hind legs and put his front paws on the wall. Owen leaned over the stones at the top of the wall and stroked the top of the head of the Collie dog.

'My wife didn't have a proper funeral because of Covid,' said Owen. 'I'm not sure I thought it through the last time I was here.'

'I'm not going to stop a man standing there and having a think,' said the farmer.

Owen nodded his head and smiled.

'You look as if you've been in the wars, mate.'

'I was assaulted with a cassette player.'

'Must have been a reel to reel man that did it.'

'Real something.'

The farmer stood back and turned around and stared at the hills and whatever else was there.

'It's a fine day,' said the farmer.

Owen said nothing.

'I used to pray for days like this when I was married. The rain just brings a load of muck. My wife never could take the rain.'

'I'll go. I just wanted another look. I wasn't going to go over to the stones.'

'Don't worry about that. Spend as much time as you want. First, though, you're having a cup of tea. No buggering off this time.'

The farmer opened the gate. Owen walked through, closed the gate and followed the farmer. The dog wagged his tail and walked at the side of Owen. At the door the farmer and Owen took off their shoes. The kitchen had the usual cooker, refrigerator and sink but there was also a dining table and chairs and a couple of very old armchairs. The farmer gave the dog some water and put some biscuits in another tin bowl. Owen sat on one of the battered armchairs. On the dining table was a used copy of the *Daily Mail*, some clean crockery and a cake covered with transparent plastic wrapping. A clothes maiden hung from the ceiling, and the cord of the maiden almost reached as low as the head of Owen. The farmer covered the newspaper with his flat cap. He boiled a kettle, put tea bags in a teapot and milk into two large mugs. He poured boiling water into the teapot.

'My mum has made me some cake,' said the farmer. 'I'm having a piece.'

Owen smiled.

'If I'm having a piece then you are.'

Owen nodded and smiled.

The farmer found two plates and two forks and cut two large pieces of cake.

'This will keep you awake on the way home,' said the farmer.

Owen took his piece of cake and the large mug of tea. The farmer sat in the other old armchair. Owen and the farmer faced one another.

'The living room is a bit posher than this,' said the farmer. 'I don't put new stuff in the kitchen.'

'Makes sense,' said Owen.

'My father had a coal fire in here. I liked the coal fire but it was a lot of muck. And the one thing I'm not short of is muck.'

'This is strong tea.'

'That's man's tea, that is.'

'Strong but good.'

'My mum used to make tea like that.'

'My mam was always making coffee,' said Owen.

'I could have made you a coffee,' said the farmer.

'No, I like tea and I like it strong. It's a good cup of tea.'

'I'm not sure what the cake is. My mum did say but I forgot. She makes the odd cake for the teashop in the village. They pay her for it.'

'The cake tastes fine.'

'You've no idea?'

Owen used his fork to cut another piece of cake. He ate the piece of cake and wondered what it might be.

'I couldn't say,' said Owen. 'It's confusing when they don't put currants in.'

The farmer laughed, and Owen finished his slice of cake. The Collie dog left his water and biscuits and sat down between the two men. The farmer gave the dog a few crumbs of cake.

'The poor bugger doesn't get much out of life,' said the farmer.

'I don't want to take up your time,' said Owen.

'Quiet day this. Farming is either working all the hours God sends or wondering what you could do next. My wife never did get used to it. One of the things that unsettled her. That and the muck. I did think about giving up the farm.'

Owen said nothing.

He drank more tea.

'I would have done if I'd been convinced it would have made her happy,' said the farmer. 'But once you've learnt to be bitter it becomes a habit. If we'd married and never come anywhere near the farm it might have been different. You get what I'm saying?'

'You can repair anything but the past.'

'I miss the woman. I won't deny that. The weird thing is I don't picture her. She's become a voice in my head. I'm lucky. I have Buster and the sheep for company. You're not a bad dog, are you, Buster?'

The farmer stroked the back of the dog.

'The sheep are what cause the work,' said the farmer, 'but they are company. I don't talk to them but I'm glad of the daft buggers. You're here because you're missing your wife. I know what it's like.'

'I've been thinking about her,' said Owen. 'I thought working hard would sort it but since Covid it gets harder and harder to put in a decent shift.'

'You need to come home from work buggered.'

'It would help.'

'I'm better when the farm gets busy.'

Owen said nothing.

'Haven't seen my wife since she left. I wonder what happened to her. I hope it's turned out alright for the woman. There's half of me that would like to see her suffer but I don't want her to perish. I don't want her life to end in ruins.'

Owen waited.

'If it did, I'd blame myself. You understand what I'm saying?'

'Very much.'

'If I'm honest with myself, I had a feeling walking down the aisle. I saw her grin at her giggling mates and thought this woman won't last the course with me.'

The two men laughed.

'My mum wants me to go on those online dating sites,' said the farmer. 'I had a look but there wasn't much that interested me.

None that would last. So what's the point? You'll be alright. You don't think so now but you'll meet someone.'

Owen said nothing.

'You can have another cup of tea but I know you came to see the stones. I won't keep you. Be there as long as you like.'

'I've enjoyed my cup of tea.'

Owen had enjoyed more than that. He had been pleased to see the old-fashioned kitchen and to sit in an old battered armchair and sip strong tea and eat old-fashioned cake. The farmer may have been hostile to tourists but he had a friendly voice that had authority. His northern accent admitted suffering but promised endurance. So it seemed to Owen. Because he had to, Owen left the farmer and the dog.

# THIRTY-TWO

The sunshine, white clouds and blue sky remained. Owen sat on the dry turf. His back was pressed against the largest stone in the circle. The sun was warm on his face but there was enough of a breeze to make Owen fasten his cardigan. Owen had hoped for a revelation or at least for him to feel an emotion that he had never felt before. He thought about the cake that the mother of the farmer had made, what the flavour might be and how the flavours of the cake compared to what his own mother baked. Owen remembered the conversation with the farmer. He was surprised that he had an image of the wife of the farmer. Owen imagined a woman that looked like Holly but someone without the blonde streaks and perhaps taller and a little more old-fashioned. He pictured this imaginary woman wearing sensible flat shoes. Owen was surprised that this image of a woman he had never met had as much substance as the ones of Hailey that were in his brain. Owen recalled what the farmer had said about his ex-wife being no more than a voice in his ears.

The farmer had said not bringing his wife to live on the farm in the first place might have made a difference. Owen thought about what he had said about not being able to repair the past. The phrase had popped into his head. Owen wondered if he had read it in some novel. The past, of course, thought Owen, did not need to be repaired. The damage the past did to the future was what caused the problems. Owen imagined being younger and visiting the stone circle and either being alone or walking with someone here who was not Hailey. Owen thought about how most hillwalkers annoyed him, the fashions and self-righteous pretensions he witnessed rather than the romanticised self-effacement he had anticipated as a young man. He imagined Hailey walking the hills and with someone that would irritate Owen but someone that would have brought her more fun and helped Hailey and Owen avoid a premature fatality.

The air had turned cold but Owen believed it was nothing more than a breeze. He sniffed the air but could smell no yeast. There was no revelation or surprise, just the mysterious future. Owen remembered the argument at the dinner table of his brother. He thought about when he had said that love did not exist, there were just feelings created by kinship, dependency and intimacy. He remembered Holly talking about intuition, and it seemed to Owen that what people called love at first sight was nothing more than an instinct that this person would be someone with whom they could establish kinship, dependency and intimacy. The rest was an illusion defined by the mysteries that we all were, to ourselves and others. Owen stood up and rubbed his back. He walked across the field to the Volvo. The breeze was not as strong as it had felt by the standing stones but the day was now colder and there were more clouds in the sky. He was glad he had eaten a piece of the cake baked by the mother of the farmer.

The temperature controlled heater warmed up the inside of the Volvo. Owen, though, still had the shivers. Owen switched on the engine and looked in the rear mirror. His intention had been to check the bruises but he forgot about the bruises and his own face when he saw the person sitting in the middle of the back seat. The shivers of Owen turned ice cold. His spine felt as if it was turning to liquid. He stared at the image in the rear mirror. His initial thought was that the man was his father but then he realised that the nose was not long enough and the face was too wide. The expression in the eyes of the man behind him had confused Owen because the look in the eyes of the face in the mirror belonged to his family, his kin. This man, though, was neither Rhys nor his father. This man was too old to be Rhys and younger than when his father had died. This man had grey hair but at least the man had hair and there were fewer wrinkles than Owen associated with grey hair. The man sitting on the back seat smiled and nodded his head.

The man disappeared from view. The spine in the back of Owen stiffened, no longer felt like cold mush. Owen remembered how solid the image had been in the mirror and the concern and sympathy that there had been in those older eyes, more than anything he had seen in the eyes of his father. Owen remembered the face of the man and how it had been shaped differently by age. The bruises on the face had disappeared but over the right eye there was a small scar. That had remained.

Lightning Source UK Ltd.
Milton Keynes UK
UKHW042128220921
391040UK00001B/136

9 781909 086302